To Ben, without whose dedication,
untiring help, and priceless suggestions,
this book would have never seen the light of day.

ISBN: 1460900979
ISBN-13: 9781460900970

RUSTLER'S CANYON

Will VonZastrow

1

Dressed in dusty, sweat-stained range clothes, Dan Hittle lay on his stomach on a grassy knoll overlooking the draw, his cheek resting against the smooth stock of his rifle. A hundred yards below him, two men were hazing a herd of cattle across a small stream, trying to keep the animals from stopping to drink. Taking careful aim at the man on the left, Dan squeezed the trigger. The report from his Winchester echoed out over the hills. The stricken cowboy threw up his arms and pitched out of the saddle to fall face down into the shallow water, a crimson stain seeping from his body. His partner, startled by the gun report, instinctively twisted around in the saddle only to have a second bullet penetrate his neck, sending him sprawling from his horse.

"Bullseye." Dan looked down at the prostate bodies with a satisfied smirk on his face. "Them two boys will be chasin' the devil's herd from now on." He stood up, brushed himself off, and picked up his wide-brimmed hat. "C'mon," he said to two men who had been lying in the grass behind him, "Git your horses, round up them cattle and vamoose before somebody comes lookin' for them two hombres."

"What are you gonna do, Dan?" One of the men asked.

"Don't give it no never mind." Hittle dismissed the man's question. "Just do as I say and meet me back at the rendezvous."

2

School had let out and the children, delighted to have escaped the confines of their stuffy classroom for another day, had scattered like autumn leaves in a brisk afternoon breeze. Amy Cabbett stood behind the small window of her white-washed, one-room school watching the children skipping down the street toward town when she saw a tall, ruggedly handsome cowman ride by. He sat erect in the saddle of his magnificent Bay. Upon spying the pretty young schoolteacher's image distorted by the small glass panes, he touched the brim of his hat, smiled, and bowed in silent respect. Instead of acknowledging his polite greeting, however, she withdrew to the back of the room out of sight of the window, leaving a dark, empty space where her face had been.

Ben Savage squinted at the empty window for a moment before turning his attention back to the task before him. Dressed in comfortable range clothes, he was a tall, powerfully built man, deeply tanned from working his large ranch throughout the year. His piercing blue eyes and broad shoulders commanded attention wherever he went and the easy way in which he carried his sidearm in a low-slung holster as if it were a part of him added to his formidable appearance. Savage, commonly addressed by his brevet rank of major acquired in the Union Army during the Civil War, was a quiet man not given to idle chatter. Yet he mixed easily with his neighbors and the town folk of Riverside who respected him for his fairness in dealing with friend or foe alike. Though feared for his wrath over jobs and activities which he felt were handled to his dissatisfaction, he was known for his fairness toward his the men in his employ as long they gave him their best. Slackers at the Double-T ranch were handed their wages and told to move on.

Being a private man who husbanded his words, it came as no surprise that the small-town rumor mill labored mightily to fill the void of his background with hearsay. It was whispered that Savage had ridden with Quantrell's Raiders, or that he had won the Double-T ranch in a poker game, never mind that Joshua Ransom, the previous owner, had never touched a playing card in his life. Others had it on good authority that Savage had robbed a bank – how else would he have been able to buy the Double-T ranch? – or that he had been a gun for hire. If Savage knew of these rumors, he paid no attention to them and kept his past to himself.

Major Savage was on his way to town to testify in court against a squatter on his land. The farmer and his wife had moved to the area a few months ago and had started working a patch of Double-T land without permission. Within days of their arrival, Savage had ridden out to confront the man telling him to move on in no uncertain terms. Even though the rancher had no quarrels with farmers as a rule, it wasn't in his character to allow anyone to squat on land that was rightfully his. To his extreme irritation the squatter remained defiant. It would, of course, have been easy to forcibly drive the stubborn settler and his wife off the land; but despite his quick temper Savage had no stomach for vigilantism and preferred to fight the nester in court.

Entering the ragtag outskirts of the town of Riverside, he encountered increased traffic. Individuals on foot, families in their farm wagons full of children, their bare legs dangling over lowered tailgates, and men on horseback were all streaming into the center of town. Other children swirled around their mothers' skirts, playing tag, calling to each other in excited, shrill voices. All were in a festive spirit. The circus had arrived the day before and had erected its big tent on the meadow west of town. Its first performance was scheduled for this afternoon. Men, dressed in their Sunday finery, clustered in small groups, smoking and passing the time of day. Their conversations focused on the outcome of the court case pitting the big rancher against the settler and wagers were being made. Savage guessed that prior to taking in the afternoon's entertainment they planned to attend the trial. It was, after all, another special event for a small town where nothing much ever happened.

The houses along the road leading into the center of town changed from tents to makeshift wooden hovels which served as saloons or houses of prostitution. Riding toward the center of town, Savage smelled the acrid odor of burned wood and creosote. Looking to his right he noticed that one of the structures had been torched. The flames had consumed everything except for the clay chimney and a large cast iron stove which stood among the charred rubble like a blackened thumb.

Closer to town, the street was framed by more stately homes surrounded by white picket fences. While some yards were bare, others had been lovingly tended and rewarded their owners with a profusion of flowers and blooming shrubs. These houses gave way to more substantial buildings, most of them constructed of wood with false fronts, but the bank, city hall and the new combined jail and marshal's office building were made of solid red brick. In the middle of town the street widened into a plaza dominated by a white church with a lofty tower containing a single bell.

Major Savage guided his horse over to Paxton's Livery stable, a barn-like building made of weathered boards. The hostler, a portly man with thinning hair, shirttail hanging out his trousers, stood in front of his building. He had a piece of straw in his mouth and his thumbs were hooked in his suspenders.

The hostler acknowledged Savage and took hold of the horse's reins. "Howdy, Major, planning to put up your horse?" He peered at Savage who nodded a greeting.

"Yes." Savage dismounted, reached into his pocket and tossed a coin at Paxton.

The hostler caught the coin and glanced at it, before looking back at the Major.

"Thanks. You planning to spend the night?"

Savage shook his head. "No, I'll have to leave this evening. But I want you to rub General Chamberlain down and feed him some oats."

The hostler was no stranger to the fancy names owners gave their horses. He grabbed the Bay's reins.

"You might be interested to know that the court meetin' will be at Jimmy's." Paxton called after the Major who had turned to go. "They's doing some work inside the church."

Savage waved his hand over his right shoulder to acknowledge the man's remark and walked away.

On his way toward Jimmy's Saloon, Savage decided to drop in on Marshal Ed Boudreaux to discuss a matter that had been weighing on his mind for some time. The marshal's office was identified by a large, hand-carved shingle over the door. A handwritten note was tacked to the door saying: *Back in five minutes.*

Savage walked into the empty office. He sat down in one of the chairs, tipped it against the wall and looked around the office. Aside from the marshal's cluttered desk, the room was furnished with a gun rack holding a couple of shotguns and a dozen or so Winchester repeating rifles. A second roll-top desk occupied the opposite wall, crowding against a large, ornately inscribed safe. The walls were decorated with wanted posters some of which had yellowed with age. Last year's calendar, distributed by the Cattlemen's Association and still depicting the month of July, hung forgotten to the right of the door to the jail. The wooden floor was sprinkled with sawdust. The office had a look of benign neglect, a male world where few women came to visit. Some hapless soul was coughing in one of the jail cells located behind the door in the back of the office.

Savage and the marshal had known each other for the past ten years. Before pinning on his star, Boudreaux had owned a small ranch west of town, butting up against Savage's property. About a year ago, his young wife and baby girl had perished in the flames of their clap-board ranch house. The baby, horribly burned, had hung on to life for two days, crying and moaning softly while Doctor Wood did everything in his power to save the tiny girl. Boudreaux had kept vigil at her bedside, refusing to sleep, overcome by grief at watching his baby die. After her death, he never returned to the ranch. A month later he had sold his spread and accepted the job of marshal offered him by the people of Riverside. He kept his grief to himself and threw himself into the task of enforcing the law.

Savage heard footsteps on the boardwalk and tipped his chair forward. A tall man walked in, closing the door behind him.

"Marshal Boudreaux." Savage said in greeting and stood up.

"Major." The marshal said. The two men shook hands. Boudreaux walked around his desk and leaned his Winchester against the wall behind his chair. As always, Savage was impressed with the lawman's physique and demeanor. Ed Boudreaux was over six feet tall, lean, without an ounce of fat. A cavalry moustache covering his upper lip gave his face a somber, unsmiling look. The brim of his hat was pulled low over his eyes and his pants were tucked into his cavalry boots. The marshal carried his gun on the left side, butt facing forward. Savage knew that his friend was an expert marksman who was not one to shy away from a fight. A former cavalry officer in the Confederate army, Boudreaux was well respected by the townsfolk and he had managed to keep the town peaceful. His appearance and the unflinching stare with which he fixed any adversary were usually sufficient to persuade potential troublemakers to take their trade elsewhere.

"I hope you haven't been waiting long, Ben." The marshal said, and hung his hat on the coat rack next to his desk, "but I had go over to Jimmy's to talk to the Manson Brothers."

"Oh? Trouble?"

"Naw, they were just making a nuisance of themselves in the saloon, blowing off steam and didn't want to give up their weapons. I told them to hand over their guns to the saloon owner for safekeeping or leave. That earned me some dirty looks but they backed down." Boudreaux looked out of the window. "Well, I guess they're leaving."

Savage walked over to the window to stand beside the marshal and followed the lawman's gaze. The two men walking out of the saloon did not look like brothers. The one the Major recognized as Seth was tall, broad-shouldered, of medium height, with a chiseled face topped by a shock of sandy hair. Jonah, his brother, was at least two inches shorter than Seth, slim, with an almost ascetic face. His hair was thinning and he moved in a stoop-shouldered way. The brothers weren't well-known in town. Except for infrequent visits to Riverside, they usually kept to themselves at their ranch.

Savage and Boudreaux watched the two brothers unhitch their mounts from the rack and swing into the saddle. They whooped and urged their horses into a dead run, their mounts hoofs making a staccato sound on the dry dirt road.

"There they go. Good riddance," the marshal said and turned away from the window. He pointed to his desk and sighed with ill-concealed disgust. "Please excuse the mess. I've got more paperwork than I can shake a stick at. Anyway, won't you sit down? What gives me the pleasure of your visit?"

Savage sat down. "Actually, I came to talk to you about something that has been bothering me for some time." He looked at the marshal. "Somebody's rustling my cows."

"Oh?" Boudreaux unbuckled his gun belt and placed it on the desk. "Since when?"

"About eight – nine months ago. A couple of head at first, but it's been getting worse lately."

The marshal's eyebrows shot up. "Nine months ago, and you're only telling me now?" he asked. "Why?"

Savage looked at his friend in frustration. "I thought I could handle the situation myself, what with my problems being sort of outside your jurisdiction. But I'm beginning to think that I'll need all the help I can get."

The marshal stroked his moustache. "Nine months, huh?"

Savage looked at the lawman. "Did you notice any new faces in town? Beside the Mansons?"

"Are you suggesting that the Mansons are behind this?" Boudreaux walked over to the stove to pour himself a cup of coffee. He held up the pot and made a questioning gesture.

Savage shook his head. "No thanks. I don't know about the Mansons. It crossed my mind but I just don't know. I sold them some of my Herefords. All I can say is that those brothers have always acted in a courteous and civil manner towards me. I've never had any trouble with them and if you hadn't just told me of their behavior in the saloon just now… Well, I don't know," he repeated. "Ed, I've got well over a hundred-thousand acres. I don't have enough hands to watch over every one of my cows." He made an annoyed gesture with his hands. "Anyone wanting to rustle my stock can do so with near impunity. Hell, about a week ago, somebody took a shot at me on my own land."

"What?" Boudreaux set down his cup. "Somebody shot at you? Did you see the shooter?"

Savage shook his head. "No. The shot could've come from anywhere. Too many trees and brush to hide behind." He shrugged. "I can only assume that whoever shot at me has something to do with the rustling." Savage looked disgusted. "I don't know what's happening to the valley. It used to be so peaceful around here. Killings, arson. You know that two of my hands were shot the other day and the killers drove off the herd my boys were rounding up, right?"

"Yes, I heard about that." The marshal frowned and picked up his cup.

Savage stretched out his legs in front of him and contemplated the scuffed toes of his boots. "Some of my men are following their tracks. I should be with them instead of spending my time battling some squatter for my land." He sighed in frustration and rubbed his face.

Marshal Boudreaux walked behind his desk and sat down. He gave his friend a thoughtful look. "You don't give me much to go on, Ben. You're the only one who seems to have problems of that kind. None of the other ranchers told me they're losing livestock."

"Hell," Savage retorted in an annoyed tone, "they don't have anything worth stealing."

Boudreaux frowned but decided to let the rancher's claim pass. "I'll keep my eyes and ears open," he said, "and let you know if I run across anything worth looking into."

"Alright." The rancher stood up and put on his hat. "I guess that's fair enough." He looked down at the marshal who leaned back in his seat. "You know what? I think I'll take a detour on my way home and pay the Mansons a quick visit, have a look around. Have you been to out to your ranch since you sold it to the brothers?"

The marshal shook his head.

"My boys tell me that the place looks kind of run down." Savage offered. "They say it looks nothing like when you and Lorena..." He saw the pain in Boudreaux's face and stopped short. "Lord, Ed. I'm sorry. I shouldn't have... I..."

Boudreaux set his jaw. He leaned forward and pulled the stack of paper close to him. "See you at the hearing. Court will be held at Jimmy's bar."

"Yes, thanks, I know. Paxton told me." Savage stepped outside and closed the door behind him.

3

Amy Cabbett stepped outside and locked the door of the schoolhouse. Lifting her skirt slightly, she negotiated the three wooden steps and turned right toward town. It was a pleasant afternoon. As always, she enjoyed her walk home after a long day cooped up inside the small classroom. Moving along the dusty street, Amy responded to the approving looks and greetings from passersby with a nod and a quick smile.

When Amy first arrived a year ago to take up the position of Riverside's teacher, she had created a sensation among the men and consternation among the women who feared that the striking young teacher would raise havoc among the male population of the small western town. Amy was indeed beautiful. Tall and slender, she had auburn hair which framed her face with its generous mouth and sparkling green eyes that radiated an inner warmth but which could turn to ice when rebuffing an unwanted suitor. She was always stylishly dressed in an understated way and moved gracefully in a self-possessed manner. Amy spoke with a pronounced upper class New England inflection in her voice; but since she did not put on airs, this accent had simply become part of her identity.

The women of Riverside need not have worried. The young schoolteacher conducted herself with the utmost decorum, keeping both single and married men at a distance. She soon gained the respect of townsfolk and the citizens of Riverside of both genders vied for her affection.

Walking along the street, Amy heard the staccato sound of rapidly approaching hoof beats. Looking up she spied two horseman racing toward her and quickly stepped aside to make room for them to pass. At the sight of her, one of the riders reined in his mount hard and skidded to a stop. A cloud of dust enveloped the rider and drifted towards the young woman who stepped back with a grimace of disgust, waving a hand in front of her face to disperse the cloud.

Seth Manson jumped out of the saddle and took off his hat. "I'm sorry, Miss Amy for raisin' a cloud. Didn't mean to, honest. My horse don't know no better," he said with an engaging grin.

Amy smiled back. "You are forgiven, Mr. uh…?"

"Manson, Seth Manson at your service," he said and bowed, gallantly sweeping his soiled Stetson in a wide arc low to the ground. "That's my brother Jonah." He pointed to the other rider who had slowed and turned his mount around to ride back to where Amy and Seth were standing.

"Howdy," Jonah said, still slouching in the saddle and touched the brim of his hat.

"Mr. Manson." Amy said in reply.

"The reason I stopped to pay my respects is…" Seth said and turned his hat in his hands. "…is 'cause I was wondering if you'd like to go to the dance with me at the hall…" He pointed a thumb over his shoulder, "Two weeks from Saturday." He gave Amy a beseeching look. "I would be plumb honored if you would."

Amy had no intention to go dancing with the cowboy who stood in front of her, eager for her reply. She smiled at him, shaking her head. "I'm afraid I have to decline your kind invitation, Mr. Manson," she said. "I have a prior engagement which I can't call off," she added to forestall his protest, "but It was kind of you to ask."

"Well, I'm sorry to hear that." Seth gave the young woman a dejected look before he put on his hat and stepped back into the saddle. Looking down at her he grinned and said, "but that don't mean I don't aim to come and ask you again, hear? I don't give up easy." Seth nudged his horse with his spurs. "Come on, brother, let's ride." He whooped and rowelled his horse into a dead run down the street, trailed by Jonah. Bemused, Amy smiled at the thought of the brash young cowboy as she watched him ride away.

A group of pedestrians had gathered on the other side of the street, watching the blond cowboy speak to Amy. Presently Joe Helmsley, the tall, burly blacksmith stepped out of the crowd of onlookers. He walked over to Amy and touched the brim of his hat. "Miss Amy, you alright?" he asked.

Amy smiled at him. "Yes, Mr. Helmsley. I'm fine. Why do you ask?"

Joe Helmsley pointed at the disappearing riders. "Just watch out for them Manson boys, ma'am. I don't rightly know why, but I think they's trouble."

"I do not intend to associate with them," Amy said and smiled at the blacksmith. "But thank you for your concern."

She continued down the street into the center of town, where she joined a cluster of about a dozen women standing irresolutely in front of the saloon where the court would be in session within the next half hour.

"Hello ladies," Amy said. "Are you here to attend the court session?"

"Oh, hello Miss Cabbett," Mrs. Donnelly, the mayor's wife, replied. She was a tall, gaunt woman, who basked in the importance of her husband's position. "We were planning to attend alright, but they changed the venue" – she was proud of the word 'venue', which she had learned from her husband just yesterday – "from the church to the saloon and we ladies don't think it's proper for us to go into that... that place."

Amy studied Jimmy's Saloon. It had been constructed during Riverside's early days and dominated the center of town despite its ramshackle look and peeling paint. Repeated attempts to replace the saloon with a modern brick structure had run afoul of Jimmy, the proprietor, whose business sense told him that the unassuming exterior would attract cowboys, farmers and prospectors who were wary of the high fashion establishments springing up around town.

"The court being held in a saloon isn't going to stop me from attending," Amy said with conviction. She looked around at the other women. "Let's all go in together," she suggested brightly. "There's strength in numbers, as they say."

Most of the women still harbored doubts about the propriety of walking into a bar but, bunching together for protection and with Amy and the mayor's wife in the lead, they marched through the swinging doors acutely conscious of the curious and appraising looks of the men clustered in the street in front of the saloon.

The makeshift courtroom was beginning to fill up. The men waiting inside Jimmy's stepped aside for the women who took their places in the back of the room, much to Amy's displeasure. She would have preferred to view the proceedings up close.

Amy had been curious to know what the inside of the saloon looked like and what she saw disappointed her. Jimmy's Saloon was by far the largest of the town's drinking establishments. The cavernous room with its tin ceiling boasted a primitive bar which consisted of planks placed on saw horses. Cases of whiskey were stacked behind the bar below a large mirror going blind with age. The tables had been pushed up against the far wall along with the highly polished brass spittoons to provide space for the chairs arranged in rows. The entrance was framed by two windows and there was an exit door at the opposite end. The walls were decorated with pictures of various hunting scenes. A buffalo head shared the east wall with a large painting which the proprietor had draped hastily with a moth-eaten horse blanket when he saw the women approach his establishment.

The planked floor was badly scuffed by thousands of spurs having been dragged across it by cowboys looking for a good time. The most eye-catching object in the room was a beer barrel, which crowded against the smoke-blackened tin ceiling. It lay in an ornately carved cradle, a large, lovingly polished brass spigot sticking out of its front.

For the purposes of the trial, a table covered with a green cloth had been placed in front of the rows of chairs and makeshift benches with a high-backed chair for the judge. Another chair, facing forward, served as a witness stand. The two windows provided little light and the saloon owner was in the process of lighting the two chandeliers which hung from the ceiling. His rhetorical announcement, that no liquor would be served during the court session, a standard procedure already known to everyone, was met by satisfied silence of the women present and good-natured groans by the men. "And no spittin' neither," Jimmy admonished them. "They's ladies present."

The saloon filled up slowly with the citizens of Riverside until there was standing room only. The back door swung open. A brief stir of anticipation rippled through the spectators as the judge entered the room. A stout, older man dressed entirely in black, his florid face was framed by luxurious sideburns. Removing his hat, he walked to the front of the room and placed it on the table. He busied himself pulling a gavel and sound block out of his satchel and cast a stern look around the room before taking his seat.

"This court will come to order." The sound of his gavel reverberated like an opening shot around the cavernous room. The judge put the gavel aside, placed both hands flat on the table and waited impatiently for the audience to quiet down. When the scraping of chairs subsided and the last murmur had been killed by his hard, unwavering gaze, he picked up the gavel and pounded it again.

"The court is now in session." He cleared his throat. "Most of you know who I am, but for the record I will introduce myself. I am Circuit Judge William Kauffman. This trial will be conducted in a fair, speedy and open manner." He imperiously leaned back in his chair and folded his arms across his chest. "Before I start the proceedings, there are some administrative matters to be clarified. First. I will not tolerate any weapons in the court room. If anyone in the audience is carrying a weapon of any kind, I want him to dispose of it now. Is that understood?"

"Ain't no guns in *my* establishment, Judge," the saloon owner piped up. He made a sweeping gesture. "Hell, Judge, I don't allow no guns in here *ever*. I know guns n' liquor don't mix. Won't be no drinkin' neither while this court's in session."

"You'll address me as 'your Honor,'" Judge Kauffman admonished him with a stern gaze.

"Yes, Ju... your Honor," the saloonkeeper said and retreated behind the safety of the bar.

"Marshal, are you present?"

Marshal Boudreaux raised his hand and stood up. "Yes your Honor."

"No weapons in the court?"

"No weapons, your Honor. We have a city ordinance that prohibits weapons within city limits. The ordinance is strictly enforced."

Judge Kauffman nodded. "Good, thank you." He waved at the marshal to take his seat. "Second, I insist upon proper decorum in this court. I won't say this twice. There will be absolute silence during the proceedings. The only persons to speak up will be myself and the witnesses under questioning. Any demonstrations in the room and I'll clear the court." He stopped to let his words sink in. "Good. Now then, the issue at hand," he reached down into his satchel and pulled out a notebook and a dog-eared bible with a cracked spine "is a dispute between the owner of the Double-T ranch, uh, Mr. Ben Savage, and John Wilhelm, a farmer by profession. The dispute is over forty-five acres of land which both parties claim to own. It is the purpose of this court to determine the rightful ownership of the land in dispute." The judge looked around the room. "Mr. Savage, are you present?"

Savage stood up. "Yes, your Honor."

"Thank you." Judge Kauffman waved his left hand at him without looking up. "You may sit down."

"Mr. Wilhelm, are you present?"

"Yes, I'm here." John Wilhelm replied, raising his hand.

"Kindly stand up so we can see you," the judge demanded in an exasperated voice. Wilhelm raised himself up from his chair, holding on to his wife's hand for emotional support. He was a young, solidly built man of medium height, dressed in clean overalls and a checkered shirt under his suspenders. He looked down at the floor, visibly embarrassed to be the center of attention. His eyes darted around the room before he sat down again.

"Alright, Mr. Wilhelm, we'll start with you. Approach the bench and place your right hand on the Bible."

John Wilhelm stood up again, still embarrassed by the attention the onlookers paid him as he made his way between the chairs. Reaching the bench, he raised his right hand as directed.

"Do you swear that you'll tell the truth and nothing but the truth, so help you God?" Judge Kauffman intoned.

"I do."

Judge Kauffman pointed to the witness chair. "Be seated and tell me what your complaint is."

Wilhelm sat down and shifted uncomfortably in his chair. "I bought the land fair and square, see?" He pulled out an official-looking parchment, unfolded it and handed it to the judge. "It says right there..."

"Thank you, I can read, Mr. Wilhelm." The judge gave the farmer a caustic look before turning his attention to the document. Rebuked, Wilhelm shrank back into his seat and looked down at his hands.

"Now let's see what we have here." The judge scanned the document in his hand.

"Hmm," he said, "this is odd." He looked up. "Mr. Savage, where are you?"

Savage stood up. "Right here, your Honor."

"Do you have the deed to your land?"

"Yes, your honor, I have it right here." Savage reached into his breast pocket.

"Well," Judge Kauffman sounded irritated, and waived his hand in the air, "then be so good as to bring it to me."

Savage felt the heat rise in his face at being addressed in this manner but maintained his composure as he made his way to the front of the saloon. Amy watched the rancher as he stopped in front of the table behind which Judge Kauffman presided. Despite her natural reservations towards the cowman, she had to admit that Major Savage looked the way a man should look, tall, bronzed, with a lean face and wide shoulders. He moved in a self-assured, coordinated way and was the only clean-shaven face in a sea of walrus mustaches. *He has nice eyes*, she thought to herself even as she felt her sympathy for the unfortunate settler rise. Despite having been told how well regarded the big rancher was throughout the valley, she was adamant that it did not give him the right to bully poor, hardworking farmers like the Wilhelms. She was familiar with stories of big cattle ranchers running farmers off their land and her heart went out to the settler and his pretty, young wife.

Judge Kauffman, brows knit in concentration, studied the deed which Major Savage had handed him. He compared it with the document which Farmer Wilhelm had given him and placed them both on the table in front of him, straightening them with the palm of his hand.

"Thank you Mr. Savage. You may return to your seat. Uh... you too, Mr. Wilhelm. I think I have enough evidence to render a verdict." The farmer showed his relief at being dismissed and stood up and hurried to the back of the saloon to rejoin his wife while Savage returned to his seat.

Judge Kauffman cleared his throat. "Now then. Having studied both of these documents it is clear that Mr. Savage is the rightful owner..." A murmur went up from the crowd and the judge held up an imperious hand, demanding silence "is the rightful owner of the land in dispute, having bought it and additional acreage upon his arrival in Paradise Valley. The land purchase was properly recorded by the Atchison Land Office, signed and sealed with the Great

Seal of the Territory. Now then," the judge held up the deed belonging to John Wilhelm. "This document, recorded by the Lawrence Land Office, is also a properly signed deed. There is only one problem with your document, Mr. Wilhelm. The Lawrence Land Office has no jurisdiction over this county. Not only are you claiming ownership of a parcel of land which is rightfully and lawfully owned by Mr. Savage, but your deed is also invalid in this county."

John Wilhelm came out of his seat as if stung by a tarantula. "I own this land! I paid good money for it," he shouted, shaking his fist at the judge. "You can't take it away from me. You... you're in cahoots with that big rancher."

The audience gasped audibly and stirred, awed by the audacity of the farmer. "Silence. Silence in the court!" Judge Kauffman thundered. His face was red and he pounded his gavel furiously, glaring at the farmer. "You are in contempt of court, mister. If you don't desist immediately, I'll have you thrown in jail."

Gertrude Wilhelm, tears streaming down her face, took her husband's arm and tried to calm him. White-faced, his eyes filled with anguish, Wilhelm collapsed in his chair, head drooping, his hands between his knees, a picture of hopelessness and dejection. Amy eyes felt moist and at this moment she detested Ben Savage and the judge with all her heart, jurisdiction or no jurisdiction. She shook her head in fiercely dismissive annoyance at the mayor's wife's whispered suggestion that the ruling had been fair. The rancher had thousands of acres of land and yet he was willing to destroy the livelihood of the young farmer and his wife by denying them the land they had begun to cultivate. Amy lifted her head in defiance and decided that she would let the big rancher know how she felt as soon as the opportunity presented itself.

Judge Kauffman pounded his gavel again. "In light of the fact that there is no additional legal business to be conducted at this time, the court is adjourned."

Stairs scraped noisily, and the crowd, chattering excitedly, pushed toward the exit. The judge gathered up his Bible and gavel, and dropped them into the satchel. Both Savage and John Wilhelm walked up to the judge's table to pick up their deeds. While his wife looked on, horrified, John Wilhelm tore his deed into little pieces and dropped the scraps on the floor. Without looking at the rancher, he walked back to his weeping wife, took her by the arm and steered her out of the bar, leaving Savage to scowl at his back.

"The judge done left. The bar's open," the saloonkeeper shouted over the din of voices. The men whooped and crowded around the crude bar, clamoring for a drink. The women gathered their skirts and fled outside; but not before they had telegraphed their husbands with their eyes, warning them not to come home drunk.

Ben Savage stood on the walk in front of the tavern and pocketed his deed. There had been no doubt in his mind that the verdict would be in his favor.

As he walked to the livery stable to collect his horse, he saw the young school teacher glaring at him from across the street. He touched the brim of his hat, but she deliberately turned her back to him and walked away.

4

"Look! There they are, the thievin' sons-a-bitches." Josh, the Double-T's rangy foreman pointed a finger. He was a tall, raw-boned man, his upper lip covered by a shaggy moustache. He and two other range hands were in a prone position, concealed in the tall grass, looking down into the draw where two men were pushing a herd of bawling cattle in a northerly direction. Josh and the others had been hunting for the missing herd for the better part of two days, trailing them over difficult terrain, not sparing their horses or themselves. Rain had twice washed out the tracks of the herd and it had taken them almost half a day to pick up sign again. They were hungry, tired, sweaty and mad as hell.

"Jesus, Jim. Look at that." Josh pointed again. "There's them ponies our boys rode when they was bushwhacked." Jim watched the cords of his boss's neck stand out, his hand fingering the butt of his colt. He craned his neck over his right shoulder and looked at his companions. "What say we give those murdering bastards a taste of their own medicine?"

"Couldn't think of anything I'd rather do." Jim made a grinding sound in his throat and aimed his Winchester at one of the men below.

Lying in the tall grass, Josh made an effort to contain his rage. As much as killing the outlaws would give him a feeling of sweet revenge, he had to admit to himself that taking them alive was the sensible thing to do. "Boys, changed my mind. Let's take the bastards alive if we can," Josh said his eyes glued to the outlaws. "I wanna find out who these miscreants work for."

"Aw hell, Boss." Jim felt cheated and his disgust was mirrored in his eyes. "Look what they did to Tom and Rube. The bastards didn't even bother to bury 'em. This is payback time, for Chrissake. We gotta..."

Josh shook his head.

"Maybe they work for theirselves." Jim added.

The foreman shook his head more vigorously. "Naw. Two rustlers would never be able to handle all them cows by themselves for too long. Look how much trouble they's having keepin' the herd moving. There's got to be some kind of gang or something."

There was a moment of silence as the two cowboys eyes were riveted on each other. Eventually Jim's stare broke. He sighed and looked down at the ground with an annoyed expression on his face. "Fine," he said, clearly still favoring out and out revenge but ceding to the foreman's logic. "In that case, why don't me an' Andrew here," Jim pointed to the other cowboy, "mount up and try to head them off if they try to make a run for it. Just gimme a couple of minutes before y'all start anything." Without waiting for an answer, he motioned to Andrew to follow him. The two crawled backwards, out of sight before standing up and walking down to where they had tied their horses to a tree. They disappeared behind a rise in the ground as the foreman silently counted to ten and then trained his rifle on the rustler trailing along behind his partner. "Alright, you murdering' bastards," he yelled and jumped to his feet, his voice trembling with barely controlled rage. "Reach for the sky."

The two rustlers pulled up short, startled. But instead of obeying Josh's command, they yanked their ponies around and raced back in the direction where they had come from. Josh raised the rifle to his shoulder and squeezed off a shot at the rustler closest to him. The bullet hit the man in the shoulder and knocked him off his horse. As he fell, his boot caught in the stirrup. The spooked horse thundered along the draw, dragging his helpless rider behind him; his body obscured in a cloud of dust. The foreman yanked the gun to his shoulder again and fired at the other thief who was bent over the saddle, savagely spurring his pony on.

"Goddammit," Josh swore. He was an excellent marksman, but either because of the distance or perhaps due to his anger and the rush of adrenaline, his bullet failed to meet its mark.

Just then, Jim and Andrew burst out from behind a dense stand of trees to Josh's left and into the fleeing man's path. The rustler veered away and spurred his horse for the cover of a thicket. But Jim, reining in his horse, managed to snap off a round before the rustler could reach cover. Blood spurting from its neck, the rustler's mount squealed and reared up, throwing its rider. The outlaw scrambled to his feet. Panicked, he drew his six-gun and dove behind a clump of bushes, frantically emptying the weapon at his pursuers. Although the hastily fired shots went wild, Jim and Andrew wheeled their ponies around and made a dash for the safety of the trees.

Josh mounted up and galloped over to join them. "Looks like we got him cornered." He gazed at the spot where the outlaw was holed up and furrowed his brow in concentration. "Tell you what we'll do. I'll circle around in back of him while you keep him occupied. Without his horse, the bastard don't have no chance in hell against three mounted men. You just make sure you keep him distracted."

Jim and Andrew nodded and turned their attention back to the cornered outlaw. Josh prodded his horse into a lope. Keeping under cover, he rode west for nearly a quarter of a mile, his ears tuned to the sporadic gunfire behind him. Coming to the bank of a small stream, he turned his pony south, crossed the water, and then east, using the irregular landscape and vegetation to mask his progress.

As he approached the thicket, Josh heard several rapid reports of a revolver being fanned to his immediate left, followed by rifle shots further away. He dismounted quickly and wrapped the reins of his horse around a branch of a lone aspen. Walking in a crouch, his pistol drawn, Josh moved stealthily toward the area where the shots had come from. There, another report, much closer now. Josh dropped down on the ground and inched forward on his belly, leading with his gun in his right hand. He was aware of the dangerous position he found himself in and, under different circumstances, might have never even considered such a tenuous plan. The rustler was pinned down, desperate, and would fight savagely for every inch of his life. But the memory of Tom and Rube, killed in cold blood, combined with the heat of the chase drove him to act, danger or no danger. He took off his hat and carefully raised his head above a mound of dirt which hid him from view. About twenty feet away, the stocky, bareheaded rustler lay on his stomach, facing away from Josh, peering intently at the other side of the open space.

Josh raised his gun. "Drop that gun and put up your hands!" he shouted. But instead of complying, the rustler turned and exploded toward Josh from his prone position like a coiled snake. Both men fired simultaneously. The rustler's shot went wild but Josh's bullet found its mark. The wounded man screamed, dropped his gun, and slumped to the ground with his hands clutching his stomach. Holstering his revolver, Josh ran over to the downed man and kicked his gun away before bending over him. A bullet zinged past his head and buried itself in the trunk of a tree behind him.

Josh threw himself on the ground. "Jesus! Jim! Andy! Stop shooting!" he yelled. "Do you hear me? For God's sake, you nearly drilled me! Come on over here. I gutshot the bastard."

Josh was bending over his victim who held his stomach with blood-smeared hands when Jim and Andrew rode up, the other outlaw's horse in tow. "Who're you working for, mister?" he demanded.

Lying on his back, eyes closed, the wounded man did not respond. He rolled his head back and forth and moaned in agony.

"Dammit. Who're you working for?" Josh asked again. He grabbed the wounded man's hands and pressed them harder into the wound in an attempt to staunch the bleeding. A shudder ran through the rustler's body and his head stopped moving. Josh pressed harder on the man's wound as Jim stepped off his horse and felt the downed man's neck for a pulse. "You're wastin' your time Josh," he said. "The man's dead."

"Dammit to hell," Josh swore. He stood up and looked down at the dead rustler, wiping his bloody hands on his chaps. "What happened to the other varmint I shot?"

"He didn't make it neither, Josh," Andy said.

"Oh, for chrissake! I wish we would've been able to catch at least one of 'em alive." The foreman waved his hands in disgust. The two cowboys watched their foreman in silence as he squinted down at the still body lying in the long grass. After a minute he sighed. "Let's put those two stiffs on them extra horses and tie 'em down. Maybe somebody will know who they are."

5

Savage was on his way out of town, satisfied with Judge Kauffman's verdict. The court session had gone better than expected and he was glad to have the matter settled. He had ridden well past the school house at the edge of town when he caught up with the Wilhelm's wagon. Drawing abreast, he leaned forward across his horse's neck and said, "Mr. Wilhelm, I would like a word with you."

"I'm through talking to you." The farmer's voice was hoarse. He glowered at his adversary. Savage saw that Wilhelm had been crying.

"All I want to tell you is that I'll give you three months to clear off my land. I won't be driving my herd to the railhead until that time. That should be more than enough time for you to settle your affairs and clear out."

The farmer shot him a furious look and pulled viciously on the reins forcing his team to stop. "I said I'm through talking to you," he said, his face twisted with hopeless rage. He lunged forward and came up with a rifle which he pointed at Savage with an unsteady aim. Savage sat back coolly on his Bay and regarded the farmer through narrow eyes. His hand swept back the rim of his coat to reveal the sidearm holstered at his hip. Although he did not reach for the weapon, his demeanor was such that the farmer's resolve immediately began to falter.

"John, don't!" his wife cried in alarm, clutching her husband's arm. "John, for heaven's sake, put that gun away! Please!" she shrieked in panic and tugged at his arm. "Shooting him isn't going to solve our problem. It'll only make things worse. Please! The land ain't worth it. What's going happen to me if you get yourself killed?"

Savage sat on his horse, his eyes on the farmer, waiting. His hand was relaxed but still rested menacingly near his revolver. He felt sympathy for the farmer and his young wife, but his face remained impassive.

Wilhelm hesitated, then scowled and dropped the rifle back down on the floorboard. Wordlessly he slapped the reins and the horses leaned into their harnesses, pulling the wagon forward. Savage urged his horse to a walk and kept abreast of the wagon. "Remember," he said, "three months."

When Savage reached the fork in the road at the edge of town, he guided his Bay to the left which would take him past the Manson ranch on his way home. The afternoon air was clear and uncommonly warm for this late in the year. The ride past the Manson's place would add a day to his journey, but he was curious about the brothers and wanted to see what they had done with the spread which had belonged to Ed Boudreaux. More importantly, despite what he had told the marshal, there was a part of him that still had questions about the brothers.

About an hour's ride out from town, the terrain became hillier. Savage's horse made its way through clusters of Longhorns which he identified by their distinctive brand as belonging to the Mansons. The small herd of Herefords which he had sold the brothers last year were nowhere to be seen.

As he was skirting a stand of trees, the report of a rifle and slap of a bullet cutting into the ground in front of him brought Savage up short. Instinctively bending low over the saddle, he pulled hard on the reins and yanked his Bay around toward the meager protection of some trees. Two more shots followed in rapid succession. Savage reached the trees and jumped out of the saddle while another round sang overhead. He yanked his Winchester rifle out of its boot and stood behind his mount for protection. His heart was pumping and his breath was coming hard. Looking back to where he thought the shot had originated from, he spied two men partially hidden behind a small overgrown mound about two hundred yards away. They appeared to be arguing with each other. Savage laid his rifle across his horse's saddle, took aim and squeezed off a round. He could not tell whether the bullet had found its mark but his attackers scrambled behind the mound and out of his view. Savage cursed and looked around him. The copse of trees hardly offered much protection for either himself or his Bay. Still keeping low, he hastily staked his horse and retreated behind a dead tree stump which partially hid him from his assailants.

There was a stillness in the air which made Savage uneasy. Were the shooters trying to work their way around him? Had they left? He craned his neck to scan his surroundings. *This is going to be a long day*, he thought, in a grim mood. He reloaded his rifle and laid his six shooter on the trunk in front of him. He suddenly felt thirsty, but the canteen was hanging from the cantle of his saddle and his horse was clearly in the line of fire. Quenching his thirst would have to wait. Savage sighed and settled in for an extended stay.

Seth and his brother Jonah, lying on their stomachs, peered out from behind the thicket, looking at the man holed up in the stand of trees a below them.

"Jesus Christ, Seth, what did you shoot at him for?" Jonah asked his brother. "He didn't do anything to us."

"Hell, I don't like no folks snooping around our property," Seth said. "Makes me nervous."

"We got nothing to hide, for Chrissake." Jonah squinted at the man below. "Jesus, you know what? I recognize the horse. That's General Chamberlain. Belongs to Ben Savage, for godsake. You were shooting at *Savage*!" He glared at his brother. "He's got a lot of men riding for him. What if he sends them down here to tear up the place?" Jonah threw up his hands. "Now what do we do?"

"Shit," Seth said with feeling. "I just aimed to scare him." He scratched his head. "If we ride down there he'll drill us for sure. That Major is a mean shot and he's gonna be madder'n a wet hen. Think of something, Jonah."

"Christ! You always go off half-cocked and then you want me to up and fix it. You started it, you finish it." Jonah glowered at his brother. "There's gonna be hell to pay."

"Come on, you gotta think of something, Jonah. You're the smart one." Seth pleaded with his brother.

Jonah stared down into the valley, thinking. "We could ride off and leave him. But what if he's already identified us bein' on our land and all? Naw, we had best take off our guns and ride down there and talk."

"Are you out of your mind?" Seth protested. "If you think I'm gonna stand up and let myself be killed by the Major, you're crazy."

"Alright, I'll go by myself then if you ain't got the sand to rectify the situation you got us in." He slapped the barrel of Seth's gun aside. "And put down the gun." Jonah stood up and unbuckled his gun belt. He grabbed the reins of his horse and walked it to the edge of the thicket. "Hey Major!" he yelled. "Can you hear me? This is Jonah Manson. Sorry we shot at you." He listened but there was no response. "Will you let me come down there and talk to you? I'm not armed." He carefully peered out over the mound and waited for a reply.

There was a pause. "There's at least two of you," Savage shouted back from below. "I want all of you to come down here, slowly, and keep your hands away from your bodies."

"Alright, just give us a minute," Jonah shouted back. He looked at his brother. "You coming?"

Seth pouted. He hesitated before laying down his rifle. "Alright, I'll come along. I just don't fancy facing the Major. He must be chewin' nails." He stood up and removed his gun belt.

"Okay, Major, we're coming down. We're not armed." Jonah yelled. "You ready?"

"Come on down," came the reply. "Remember, keep your hands where I can see them."

Jonah waved to his brother. "Come on, let's go," he said. They mounted their horses and slowly rode out from behind the thicket, keeping their hands well away from their bodies. Savage stepped out from behind his horse and walked up to the edge of the trees, keeping his rifle trained on the approaching horsemen.

"We ain't armed, Mr. Savage," Seth called out nervously and reined in his mount. He mustered a tight smile and gestured towards Savage's weapon. "No need you keepin' that gun aimed at us."

Savage lowered his rifle. "Come closer," he demanded, "and no funny stuff, hear?"

The brothers nodded and resumed their way. Savage backed up to his Bay and swung into the saddle to meet the brothers who stopped a horse's length away, looking guilty.

Savage was clearly mad. "What the hell did you shoot at me for?" he rasped. "Do you fire at anyone who comes on your land?"

"Was me done the shootin, Major," Seth said, looking sheepish. "We didn't know it was you until Jonah spied your Bay. I'm truly sorry for causin' you grief." He paused and cleared his throat. "We heard that there's been some rustlin' going on and we... we was just defendin' our property, ain't that right, Jonah?" He looked back at his brother who nodded in silent assent.

"What brings you here, Major?" Jonah asked, drawing abreast with his brother. "Anything we can do for you?"

Savage slid his rifle into the boot. "Is there any law against visiting your neighbor? I've had some trouble with rustling and wanted to talk to all the ranchers out here."

The brothers exchanged quick, nervous glances. "You won't like what you see, Major," Jonah said. "We haven't done a lot of work on the property since the marshal sold it to us, but you're sure welcome to visit."

"Okay then," Savage said, still annoyed. "Pick up your weapons and let's ride."

6

The Wilhelms stood, their backs to their tent contemplating Trudy's vegetable garden. John had surrounded it with a high chicken-wire fence to ward off rabbits and other animals who considered his wife's vegetables and flowers a special kind of delicacy.

"All this work for nothing," Trudy said, her eyes brimming with tears. "At least that horrid man gave us another couple of months before he kicks us out."

"I could kill that goddamn judge," her husband replied and clenched his fists, "and that Major, too." He rubbed a weary hand across his face. "You coming inside? Getting chilly out here."

"In a minute." Trudy said. "I just want to finish a couple of things before it gets dark."

"Alright. I think you're wasting your time, but you do what you think is right. Just don't stay out here too long." John ducked inside the tent and pulled off his boots. He had just poured himself a drink when he heard Trudy call his name. The urgency in her voice caused him to rush to the door of the tent and thrust his head outside.

"John, there's a rider out here. He's just sitting there, staring at me." She said in a tremulous voice.

"I'll be right out, Trudy." John called back. He retreated into the tent, grabbed his Henry rifle, levered a round into the chamber and hurried outside.

The hard-eyed, heavily armed horseman spied John as he approached and stopped his horse in front of the farmer. His gaze shifted from Wilhelm's wife to John, traveled down his body and came to rest at his stockinged feet.

John studied the rider's red, angry-looking knife scar which ran down the right side of his face. It began near his eyebrow, divided his cheek in two and ended near his mouth. The disfigured cheek gave a man a cruelly diabolic appearance.

"Anything I can do for you?" John asked.

The horseman's cold eyes assessed the farmer and his gun before he answered. "Lookin' for some stray cows. You seen any hereabouts?"

John looked up at the rider looming over him. "Mister. This is cow country. There's always cows around this place."

The horseman nodded and shifted his gaze back to the young woman, who stood rooted in her garden, watching the two men. "Got yourself a right purty wife, sodbuster."

John Wilhelm's ruddy face flushed crimson. He raised his rifle, pointing at the intruder. "I'll thank you to turn your horse around and vamoose before I ventilate your gut," he said in a hoarse whisper.

The horseman, leaning on the pommel of his saddle, contemplated the farmer with a contemptuous smile on his face. Only when the farmer made a threatening gesture with his rifle, did he straighten up, leer at Trudy and tip his hat to her. He turned his horse around. "Be seein' you," he said over his shoulder and rode off without looking back.

7

Winter was beginning to set in. The trees had shed their leaves and stood as spidery skeletons against the sky. Ice had formed along the banks of the creek and a dusting of early snow covered the range. Bundled up against the cutting wind, Savage leaned out of the saddle. His eyes were glued to the ground, tracking sign telling him that three men on horseback were driving cattle north, away from the Double-T Ranch. Savage and two of his hands had left at daybreak to round up any livestock they could find within a half day's ride and drive them back to the fenced-in pastures close to the ranch. They had expected to find the herd bunched up in a rocky ravine that shielded the animals from the icy wind and which provided plenty of grass and water. But the cattle had vanished.

"Damn," Savage swore under his breath. His foreman had killed a couple of cow thieves not too long ago and he had hoped that that would be the end of it. Now his cattle were being rustled again. *Must be a sizeable gang* he ruminated.

One of the cowboys by the name of Alex rode over to Savage and looked at the tracks. "What do you make of it, Boss?"

Savage looked up. "What, the tracks?"

"Injuns, maybe?"

The cowman shook his head impatiently. It bothered him that others were so inept when it came to reading sign. "Look at the tracks. Here." He bent over the saddle again and pointed at the ground in barely concealed exasperation.

"See those hoof prints? These horses were shod. Indians don't shoe their ponies. Besides, Indians will just run off a couple of cows more or less for immediate consumption. What I can tell from these tracks is that three white men are rustling fifty to sixty head of my cows."

"I wonder where they's driving them cows to? Ain't nothing north of here but mountains," Alex wondered. "That don't make no sense."

"I expect that the rustlers have found a convenient hiding place for the stock somewhere in the foothills," Savage said. He pushed back his hat and looked up at the gathering storm clouds promising snow.

"I don't know them mountains too well," Alex allowed. "I wonder where that might be."

"I intend to find out." Savage said, still staring at the distance. "Do you have anything to eat in your saddle bags?"

"Got some beef jerky. Why?"

"Let me have it. I might be gone for a bit." Savage looked at the cowboy and held out his hand, palm up.

Alex dug into his saddle bag and handed him a small packet of beef jerky wrapped in a cloth. "That's all I got," he apologized. "I wished I had more. You want us to go with you? It's you against three of them."

Savage shook his head. "No, I don't intend to fight them. I just want to find out where those bastards are stashing my cattle." He put the beef jerky in his saddle bag. "When you get back to the ranch, tell Josh that I may not be back for a day or two, though I don't think that the rustlers have gotten very far. Cows don't travel fast, especially not over this terrain." He kneed his horse forward and rode north.

Alex watched him with some misgivings until his boss disappeared among the Ponderosa pine which dotted the bottom of the ravine. *Some tough hombre, that Major*, he thought to himself, going up against a bunch of rustlers by hisself. It was some time after the Major disappeared over a rise before Alex turned away. Well, best to get the few strays they had rounded up home and tell Josh that somebody was stealing the Major's cows again.

The tracks were easy to follow and Savage made good time. The early afternoon sky was gray. The Major, still on level ground, was approaching the foothills whose contours melded into the snow-covered mountains looming up behind them. It was cold and the sea of grass undulated languidly in stiff waves under the icy wind. The frigid air hurt his lungs. A hush of silence permeated the air around him as if Mother Nature had put a finger to her lips shushing all of creation into silence. It added to Savage's feeling of isolation. He half regretted having turned down Alex's offer to tag along. A hint of snow was in the air and it gave him cause to worry that it would cover the tracks before he had an idea where the cows were being driven. He was convinced that the rustlers were stashing away the stolen cows in some hidden valley, out of sight of the prying eyes of the law or the cowboys riding for him. *Well*, he thought grimly, *that was about to change*. He would find the hiding place and put an end to this lawlessness if it took him a whole week. He spurred his horse to a canter to make up for time before it go too dark to follow the trail.

Just before sundown the terrain became more rugged. Large and small boulders grew out of the tall prairie grass. Riding on, Savage came upon a narrow band of water tumbling noisily into a deep glacier pool. The water was surrounded by a small stand of trees whose bare limbs stood dark against the cloud-laden sky. Smelling burned wood, he dismounted quickly and tied up his horse. Gun in hand, he cautiously followed the smell until he came upon the remnants of a campfire. He stealthily withdrew into the shadows of the trees and peered around him to ascertain that he was not being watched. When he was sure that he was alone, he holstered his gun, walked away from the cover of the trees, and squatted down to feel the ashes. They were no longer warm. Cigarette butts littered the ground. He scrutinized his surroundings. Soon it would be too dark to see the tracks. It was time to find a place to bed down. Remounting, Savage headed north again looking for a defendable spot to camp for the night when he spied what appeared to be a cave of sorts. Riding closer, the cave turned out to be a small space, open to the sky, surrounded on three sides by tall boulders. It was a perfect spot to spend the night protected from the cutting wind. He would even be able to build a fire since the opening faced south. Unless the rustlers backtracked, the glow of the fire would go undetected. Savage dismounted, hobbled his mount, collected firewood, and spread out his bedroll. *All the comforts of home*, he thought grimly. He ate some of the jerky Alex had given him and drank his fill of water. Minutes later, yawning hugely, he curled up in his bedroll, closed his eyes, and was soon asleep.

He awoke before dawn. His whole body was stiff and he stretched to limber up before crawling out of his bedroll. Soon he had a roaring fire going. He warmed his hands on the leaping flames before putting on the small pot to boil water for his coffee. Waiting for daylight, he ate the biscuits, which his cook had handed him the day before. They were hard and he dunked them in his steaming coffee before biting into them. Savage did not relish the idea of leaving the cozy cave and dancing fire; but when daylight came, he buckled on his chaps and gun belt, scattered the ashes and walked outside to saddle his horse.

The wind had abated during the night and the snow had held off so Savage continued on his way as soon as he was able to make out the tracks. It was a cold morning and he rolled his shoulders inside his mackinaw to keep warm. The tract of land he was riding through was still and bleak. The tracks told him that the uneven, rocky terrain was giving the rustlers trouble keeping the herd together, which meant that their progress would be slow. The ground was not yet frozen solid which made it easier for him to follow the sign made by the cattle and the three horses.

Savage dismounted from time to time to inspect the droppings to see whether they were still warm. The sun rose higher in the sky, driving away some of the chill in the air. General Chamberlain, his belly full of grass stepped out smartly, closing the distance between the hunter and the hunted.

The sun stood at its zenith when Savage came upon a deserted farm. He dismounted, took cover inside a stand of pines, and scanned the terrain. The dilapidated buildings showed no sign of life. The absence of cattle told him that the rustlers were pushing the herd further north. He pulled the Henry out of his boot and cradled it in his arm before leaving his hiding place. He was alert to the sounds around him as he approached the farmhouse, his eyes peeled for any sign of possible danger. The trampled earth was proof that during the night the rustlers had penned the cattle in the corral, behind a ramshackle structure which had once served as a tool shed.

Savage cautiously pushed the door of the small farmhouse open with the muzzle of his rifle. The house was empty. Constructed of sturdy logs, the long-abandoned building had held up well except for the roof, which showed daylight in several places. The rooms were empty except for one lonely chair that smelled of rotting wood and the droppings of birds whose empty nests in the rafters, a testimony to warmer days. The rustlers had built a fire in the oven. The glimmering ashes emitted the acrid smell of burned wood, meaning that they had left only a relatively short while ago. When he cautiously peeked out the door at the rear of the house, he saw the fresh carcass of a slaughtered cow. The rustlers had eaten the best parts and had left the rest for the wolves and coyotes to find. Savage unsheathed his knife and cut off several pieces of meat and took them inside. He rekindled the fire and cooked the meat. When it was done to his satisfaction, he ate half of it and wrapped the rest in oil cloth and put it in his saddle bags together with his remaining food. No telling how long he would be out here.

The fire warmed the room and Savage began to feel drowsy. He stretched his tall frame, yawned and got up from the rickety chair. *Time to get going* he thought and stepped outside. He swung into the saddle and kicked General Chamberlain into a steady pace, following the tracks leading away from the farm. Looking around him, he marveled at the cunning of the rustlers. A man could hide hundreds of cows here where nobody would ever find them.

A few hours later, Savage no longer had to dismount to check the droppings. He could smell them from the saddle, which told him that he was closing in on the herd. Sure enough, within minutes he could hear the faint bawling of the cows, protesting at being driven further into the steepening landscape which was strewn with man-sized boulders.

With the dexterity of a seasoned marksman, Savage drew his Colt and rotated the cylinder to check the load before placing the gun back in its holster. He levered a cartridge into the chamber of his rifle and rode on with care, using the rocks and stands of trees as cover.

Skirting a copse of firs, he had his first glimpse of the herd. The cows were dispersed among the rocks and trees and two rustlers were hard at work rounding up strays and reuniting them with the rest of the herd. Oblivious to the rancher's presence, they dashed about on their ponies trying to keep the reluctant animals together.

But where was the third man? Savage sought cover behind a large boulder and dismounted. Creeping to the edge of his cover, he scanned his immediate surroundings. There was no sign of the missing rustler. Frustrated, Savage stood up and put his foot in the stirrup, preparing to mount his Bay, when he felt a hot sting on the left side of his neck followed by the report of a rifle. The impact of the bullet was enough to cause him to tumble to the ground, blood seeping from a wound on his neck. A second shot ricocheted off the boulder and hit the pommel of his saddle, causing General Chamberlain to rear and bolt.

"Damn!" Savage cursed. He pressed his left hand against the wound to staunch the flow of blood while his right hand went for his gun. Adrenalin flowing, he scrambled for cover further behind the boulder.

Startled by the gunfire, the other two rustlers drew their guns, wheeled, and spurred their horses toward the scene of the shooting. Savage fumbled with his Colt. He felt disoriented. Blood was trickling past his fingers down into the collar of his shirt. Trying to focus on his attackers, he pulled the trigger in rapid succession but he knew that his shots were wide of their mark. Cowering behind the boulder, he stuffed his kerchief between the wound and the collar of his shirt. With an unsteady hand he shucked the empty shells from his gun and reloaded.

Savage had no illusions about the desperate nature of his situation. His horse was gone. The rustlers would come at him from both sides while the man who had shot at him would keep him pinned down. Help, if any, was days away. Lying behind the rock, Savage felt the coldness of the ground penetrate his clothing in contrast to the warm wetness oozing from his neck. His vision dimmed and silence enveloped him as he let his head slump forward, coming to rest on the ground.

The sudden report of a rifle opening up behind him caused Savage to jerk up his head. There was a scream and the gunman who had wounded him rose up from behind a boulder before crumpling to the ground. The rifle boomed again in rapid succession. Straining to see, Savage craned his neck and saw the remaining rustlers race off, disappearing behind a jumble of rocks. Savage tried to keep his head raised but it was too great an effort. He had never been so tired in his life. His vision blurred and he closed his eyes as his head sank back to the ground.

8

Alex had watched his boss ride off alone with a sense of misgiving. The Major was a tough hombre and could take care of himself but three against one were not good odds. Alex knew better than try to argue with Ben Savage, though. Giving his boss's retreating back a final look, he turned his horse and rode up to help Chad round up the few strays which the rustlers had missed. "Let's get them critters home, pronto," Alex said. "I need to talk to Josh about the Major riding after them rustlers all by his lonesome."

Even though they pushed the cattle hard, it was dark before they reached the ranch. While Chad drove the cows into the holding pen, Alex cantered over to the bunkhouse and dismounted. He stepped onto the small porch and, using his fist, pounded on door of the foreman's living quarters. A few moments later the door opened and Josh, dressed in his underwear stuck his head outside. "Jesus, don't you know how to knock?" He mustered the cowboy. "Kinda' late getting' back, ain't you, Alex? What's the idea wakin' me up in the middle of the night?" he growled.

Alex cleared his throat. "Sorry, Josh, but me, Chad and the Major rode up to the North Meadow to collect the cows but most of 'em was missing, driven off by three men according to the tracks we found. The Major thinks that the rustlers was driving about fifty to sixty cows and he lit out after them."

"Alone?" the foreman was incredulous. "You let him ride off by hisself?"

The question stung Alex. "I offered to go along," he responded heatedly, "but the boss said no. You don't argue with the boss. He says no, he means no. C'mon Josh, you know that better'n anybody else."

"Damn. We gotta go after him. No time to waste," the foreman rasped. "You and Chad get yourself some fresh horses. I'll rustle up some grub."

An hour later, Josh, Alex and Chad were riding north. It was bitterly cold again and the vapor of their breath mingled with that of the horses, rising above their heads before dissipating in the night air. The three men were tired and they rode in silence, each busy with his own thoughts. Josh felt that his boss had used bad judgment riding off alone in pursuit of the rustlers. The possibility that Savage might be killed filled him with dread. The rustlers meant business and had already killed two of his men. It was bad enough to have their cattle stolen but killing innocent men was an unconscionable act that, he promised himself, they would not get away with.

They rode steadily for six hours, pushing their mounts hard with only a ten-minute break to let the horses rest. Each of them maintained the silence, their ears trained for any sound, anxious to catch up with the Major until the lack of sleep took a toll on the men and their mounts. Josh reluctantly decided that they needed to make camp to rest a few hours and catch up on their sleep.

Four hours later, the men were in the saddle again. They passed the abandoned farm, surprising a small pack of gray wolves dining on the carcass of a cow. The land was getting hillier and the afternoon sun cut some of the chill from the air. Josh pulled the scarf off his head and was about to stuff it into his saddle bag when he heard what sounded like a gunshot. He reined in his horse, stood up in his stirrups and put a hand to his ear. "Did you hear that?" he asked Alex.

"Yeah, I heard it," Alex said, his voice high with excitement. "There. There's another one."

Chad nodded in agreement. His face was hard. "Just ahead."

A rifle boomed, and then again.

"The boss must be in trouble," Josh said his voice thick with an acute sense of foreboding and put the spurs to his horse. "Let's move, boys." Throwing caution aside, the three men whipped their mounts into a dead run. Dodging rocks and boulders, they raced in the direction where the shots had come from. Alex, who rode neck to neck with the foreman, was the first to spy General Chamberlain. The Bay stood head down near a small spring cropping grass. He reined in his horse and approached the Bay slowly, leaning forward in his saddle to pick up its reins. Savage's Henry rifle was still in its boot.

"Josh, there's blood on the saddle," he called.

"Let's spread out." The foreman's voice was tense. The three men jumped off their horses and fanned out among the rocks. They craned their necks looking for the rustlers. There was no movement except for the milling cattle. "Where the hell are they?" Josh hissed, frustrated.

"Hey Josh," Alex called to him. "Look." He pointed. "Ain't that the Major layin' there?"

"Jesus,' Josh said softly. He slid out of the saddle and ran to where the prostrate figure was lying. His heart sank. It was Savage and he was bleeding. Josh dropped to the ground and examined the wound, causing his boss to moan. "Alex! Chad!" he yelled. "He's alive. Somebody get me them bandages out of my saddle bag, pronto, and watch out for the rustlers."

"If you're looking for them rustlers, they lit out, exceptin' for the one whose lights I blew out," a deep voice said behind him. Josh whirled, Colt in hand, and stared into the black face of a huge man whose muscles were straining the fabric of his faded army tunic. He cradled a Winchester in his arms. "You can put up that gun, Mister. I'm on your side," the man added.

Josh nodded. He holstered his gun and turned his attention back to his boss. Alex dropped down beside the foreman and handed him the bandages. "Looks like he's coming to, Boss," he said excitedly. Savage stirred and opened his eyes. He looked from Josh to Alex and put a hand to the side of his neck.

"Don't touch that wound," Josh said more sharply than he intended. He carefully removed the blood-soaked handkerchief and examined the cowman's neck.

"You're lucky, Boss. It's just a gash, but you've lost some blood. Let me bandage it and then we'd best get you home quickly." He expertly bound the wound with the bandage which had Alex handed to him. "Good, that ought to do it." He inspected his handy work. "How does it feel?"

"Not bad, thanks," the rancher said, still feeling faint.

"Good, Boss. Can you stand up?" Josh asked.

Savage nodded and allowed himself to be helped up and on his feet. He stood head down, feet planted wide to gain his equilibrium. His wound throbbed. He took two tentative steps forward and his knees began to buckle. Grabbing onto his foreman's arm to steady himself, his gaze fell on the black soldier and started in surprise. "Sergeant Major Jefferson?" He blinked rapidly to clear his vision. "What are you doing here?"

Josh pointed to the soldier. "This man saved your life, Major. He shot one of the bastards and chased the others away."

"I suppose I ought to thank you." Savage touched his wound and winced.

The black Sergeant shook his head. "Don't bother. You kinda saved my ass at Shiloh. When I seen you go down, I figured I owed you one. Now I guess we're even." He mustered Savage with a cold stare and turned to go.

"Did you come looking for me, Sergeant-Major?"

"Now why would I be lookin' for you of all people, Major?" the Sergeant replied in a sarcastic voice, turning back to face Savage. "If I'd known I'd run into you, I would've headed in the opposite direction."

Savage regarded the soldier. "Mind telling me what you are doing on my land?"

"Just passin' through. No law against that, is there?" he replied in a gruff voice. He walked over to his horse and stepped into the stirrup.

"Where are you headed, Sergeant-Major?" Savage persisted. He knew that his cattle needed to be driven back but that there were too many for Alex and Chad to handle alone, especially with the ever present danger of rustlers on the trail.

The old soldier settled in his saddle and looked down at Savage. "Not that it's any of your business, Major, but I guess I'll tell you anyhow. I ain't goin' nowhere in particular. Only got discharged a couple of weeks ago. Still tryin' to get my bearings bein' a civilian." He stroked his horse's neck. "I kinda enjoy my freedom. Don't have to answer to nobody. No more yessirs and nosirs, standing at attention or salutin' some shave-tail lootenant who's still wet behind the ears. Thirty years as a buffalo soldier was long enough for me."

Savage narrowed his eyes. "Well, Sergeant Major. That was quite a speech. Downright poetic. I didn't know you had it in you."

"Why don't you go to hell, Major?" Jefferson replied evenly.

Savage's cowboys held their breaths, expecting their short-fused boss to vent his wrath on the disrespectful interloper. The two former soldiers glowered at each other. Savage was the first to draw a deep breath. "Let me get something straight, Mr. Jefferson. You're on my land and I could have my boys run you off. But you did me a great service by saving my life and I'm in your debt. So, how about burying the hatchet for now. If you'll help my boys trail my cows back to the ranch, I'll stake you to grub and a warm bunk. You can leave anytime you want to. How about it?"

The tall black soldier looked at Savage for what seemed to be an eternity. Then he shrugged. "Alright. I been herdin' a bunch of brainless recruits all my life. Herdin' a bunch of dumb critters can't be much different." He paused and shook out his reins, "But don't expect me to stick around."

"Fine with me," Savage dismissed him. He was beginning to feel light-headed again.

The foreman saw the vacant look in his boss's eyes. "Let's go, Major," he said and motioned to Alex. "Unbuckle the dead hombre's gun belt and give it to Mr. Jefferson. He earned it. Also, before you bury him," he pointed at the dead rustler, "check his pockets to see if he has anything on him to identify him." He turned back to Savage. "Let's get you up on your horse, Boss and get you home."

Savage nodded. It would be a long and hard ride back to the ranch. A sense of extreme fatigue permeated his body and he had an overwhelming desire to lie back down and go to sleep. He knew that if he succumbed to this desire, however, he would certainly die. He felt the eyes of his men on him, and he knew that despite their loyalty to him they would also be watching for any a sign of weakness. Besides, he was not about to give Jefferson the satisfaction of seeing him to succumb to a relatively minor wound. Savage inhaled sharply. Supported by Josh and Alex, he approached his Bay in a halting way. He grabbed hold of the cantle, pulled himself up and swung his right leg over the saddle. The foreman watched him closely as he handed Savage the reins.

"Are you ready?"

Savage nodded and sat up straight. "Let's go home," he said.

9

"Jeez, that was a close one, Cal. That old colored soldier almost got us," the rustler named Roy said, as they reined in their blowing horses. "I hadn't figured they was on to us and showing up so soon. Who in hell was that black man anyway?"

Cal did not reply. He shot Roy a dark look and savagely dug his spurs into his tired horse's flanks, sending it flying across the uneven ground. Roy spurred his horse to keep up. He looked at his partner. Cal was a hard-looking man with mean eyes peering out from under bushy eyebrows. Easily given to violence, he was someone you didn't want to have as an enemy. He regarded the angry red scar on Cal's right cheek, giving his companion a cruel look. "Too bad about Rusty," Roy ventured. "Did you see how that colored man plugged him? That was some shooting. I kinda liked Rusty. He was good company." *Unlike you*, Roy thought.

"I don't give a shit about Rusty. He wasn't no good driving cattle. If it wasn't for him we might of got a lot further into the mountains." He scowled at Ray. "I do give a shit about that colored man. I'd sure like to get my sights on the son-of-a-bitch and I will. Mark my words." Cal balled his fist. "I'll know where to find him, too."

They rode without speaking for a while. Roy shivered. "Damn this weather. Looks like we're in for another cold night on the ground. I sure liked that old farmhouse. That cow tasted good, too." He shivered again. "Damn this country. Gimme Texas anytime."

"We ain't gonna sleep on no ground tonight," Cal said with conviction.

"We ain't?"

"Nope. I know a nice little place not too far from here. We should be there by suppertime. Have us something good to eat, a warm bed and good company."

"Yeah? What kind of place would that be?" Roy asked.

"You'll see," Cal said.

They rode on in silence. The sun hovered low over the western mountains, bathing their snow-covered tops in an orange light. It would be dark soon. Roy shivered and tried to picture the cozy place Cal had talked about. He didn't like this part of the country. Sure, it offered lots of good grazing and the cattle were fat and lazy, not like those pesky longhorns back in Texas. Up here the livestock was easy to handle. That was the good part. The lousy part was the climate. Roy thought back to the Texas Hill Country and the weather there. Sure, they had their Blue Northers when the temperature dropped by forty degrees in a few hours, but then it turned warm again. Here you had your blizzards with snow up to your eyeballs for weeks. Roy instinctively huddled deeper into his mackintosh. You froze your tail off every day. And then this rustling business. Roy had never been averse to appropriating a few cows that belonged to somebody else, but this large-scale rustling? Hard work and downright dangerous. He had come close to getting killed today. And for what? He had yet to be paid. He and his compadres couldn't ride into town for fear of arousing the curiosity of the townsfolk and the marshal, and he hadn't seen a woman in weeks. All he wanted to do was to sit in a warm saloon, maybe with a girl on his lap and drink his whiskey and a beer chaser. Maybe he'd play a little poker and, if it was that kind of establishment, take the girl upstairs for a poke. The men he was riding with were a rough bunch and he wasn't even sure that their boss – whoever he was - knew what he was doing. Too much going on all the time. If he could draw his pay, he would be on his way back to Texas. Might even move to the right side of the law for a spell and join them Texas Rangers for a change. "You sure you know where you're headed?" Roy asked and urged his pony closer to Cal. "Where's that place you mentioned?"

Cal was exasperated. "Hell yes, I know where I'm going, Roy. I'd find that place if hell froze over."

"How far?" Roy insisted.

"I *told* you, goddammit! We ought to be there in time for supper."

"I could sure use some grub," Roy grumbled. Both men fell silent again. Cal surveyed the countryside and changed course twice, heading due south. Finally he said, "I think we're getting close. I bet it's just over the rise there."

He spurred his pony ahead and topped the rise. "Yep," he said triumphantly. "There it is. Didn't I tell you I'd find it?"

Roy's eyes followed Cal's pointing finger. It was getting dark and the windows of the small tent sent out a warm, inviting glow. The two riders put their horses in motion again.

"Sodbusters, right?" Roy said, contempt lacing his voice. "They friends of yours?"

"Let's just say I've met them. The punkin' roller and his pretty wife, too. We'll wait here until it gets dark," Cal said and stepped off his horse to relieve himself.

Roy gave the inviting tent a longing look. "It'd better be dark soon before I freeze to death," he complained, but received no response from Cal who had remounted.

When darkness finally set in, Cal and Roy approached the tent on horseback. They skirted what was left of Trudy's vegetable garden and dismounted.

"Let's hobble our horses here for now. I don't want the sodbuster to see us. I hope he don't have no dog," Cal said in a half whisper.

Roy was confused. "Why don't you want him to see us?"

"Keep your voice down, dammit." Cal's mouth curved up in a malicious smile. "It's supposed to be a surprise," he said.

John Wilhelm opened the flap of the tent and peaked in. "Trudy. Supper ready yet?" he asked. He put down the rake he was repairing, rubbing his cold, dirty hands on his overalls.

"In a minute, John. Why don't you go and wash up." Trudy stood at the stove, attending to the heavy iron skillet and two steaming pots. The inside of the tent was warm and the food smelled delicious. John took two glasses off the shelf and placed a bottle half filled with whiskey on the table. "I'll be right back," he said and stepped outside to go to the privy standing twenty yards off to the side of the tent.

Cal pushed Roy down as the light from the open flap spilled across the yard. "Duck!" he hissed. Both men crouched down.

"You sure you know these people?" Roy whispered.

"I know them, alright," Cal whispered back. "I told you I want to surprise them." They watched the farmer disappear inside the privy. When he came out a few minutes later, he strode over to the pump, swung the squealing handle and washed his hands and face. Shaking the droplets off his hands, he reached blindly for the towel hanging on a peg near the pump, dried himself and disappeared inside the tent, closing the flap behind him.

The rustlers stood up and dusted off their knees. "Let's take them chaps off." Cal smirked, "We don't want to intrude on our hosts in our working clothes."

Back inside, John poured himself a drink before he sat down at the table. His wife smiled at him and he beamed back at her as she put down the food in front of her husband. "Sure smells good, Trudy," he said. Even though they had been married for two years now, John still couldn't get over his shock when Trudy had agreed to become his wife. She was uncommonly pretty, worked hard and stood by his side during good and bad times. And there had been plenty of bad times. She never quarreled or complained. Looking at her pretty face, John felt a sea of love surge through him that caused his heart to skip a beat. The tent was warm and John Wilhelm felt a sense of well-being. Even though the Major had ordered them off his land, he had, unasked, given them until Spring to move on, allowing them enough time to make plans for the future.

He waited until Trudy had filled her plate and had taken a seat. They folded their hands and said a brief prayer of thanks. John had just picked up his fork and knife when he heard quick footsteps on the hard ground outside. The tent flap was thrust aside and two unshaven, dirty, and rough-looking men crowded into the room. One of them drew his gun and pointed it at the farmer and his wife.

"John!" Trudy cried out in alarm. John sat, frozen, his fork halfway between his plate and his mouth.

"Well, howdy, sodbuster, remember me?" said Cal with a leer that caused the jagged scar on his face to turn an angry red. "You chased me off your land a-ways back, remember?"

John swallowed and dropped his fork and knife on the table. "What do you want from us?"

"What do we want?" Cal shook his head as if in sorrow. "What do we want? Now, that's a fine howdy-do. What kind of hospitality is that?" He pretended to be offended. "That ain't being very neighborly. Ain't you gonna invite us to sit and have dinner with you and the missus? Where's your manners?"

"Where's yours?" John responded angrily. "Coming in here uninvited, waving a gun in our faces, scaring my wife?"

Cal smirked and holstered his gun. "You gonna give me and my partner something to eat or not?" He sniffed the air. "The food sure smells good, ain't that right?" he asked Roy, who nodded in agreement.

"Trudy, set another couple of plates. I guess there's enough food for all of us." John stood up and took a step toward the uninvited guests. He held out his hand. "My name is John Wilhelm, what's yours?"

Cal ignored the farmer's gesture and, hand on his hips gave John's wife an appraising look. "Trudy, is it? Now if that ain't a purty name for a purty lady, don't you think, Roy? The name's Cal, at your service, ma'am." He executed an exaggerated bow. "Now, Trudy, you just set one extry plate. Your hubby ain't gonna be eatin' with us." He walked up to the farmer. "Turn around and put your hands behind your back. I'm gonna hogtie you so's I don't have to watch every move you make." When the farmer did not comply instantly, Cal pulled his gun and laid it hard alongside John's head, causing him to stagger against the table.

"John!" His wife screamed at the sight of blood running down her husband's face.

"Shut your face, bitch, or I'm gonna kill your man right in front of your eyes," Cal hissed. He holstered his gun and nudged the dazed farmer. "Alright, sodbuster, hands behind your back." John obeyed and the rustler tied his hands with a string of rawhide. "Now sit." The outlaw pushed him roughly down on the floor and kneeled down to tie his legs.

Roy was eyeing the farmer's wife and he liked what he saw. "Hey, Cal, why don't we just plug the sodbuster and get it over with. Get him outa the way?" he asked.

"Na," Cal replied. "What's your hurry? We got all night." He stood up and snatched the whiskey bottle off the table, taking a long swig before he relinquished it to his partner. Belching loudly, he sat down in John's chair. "Let's eat."

Trudy, tears staining her cheeks filled the intruders' plates with meat, beans and potatoes and went to cower next to her husband.

Cal, his back to the farmer, looked over his shoulder and scowled. "What are you doing, settin' on the floor? You come here and sit down at the table and be sociable."

When Trudy refused to move, Cal spun half out of his chair and pulled his gun. "You come and sit with me right now or I'll blow a big hole in that husband of yours." He thumbed back the hammer.

Trudy cried out in alarm. She scrambled off the floor and took her seat at the table.

Cal leered at her. "Now that's better. You do as I say and we'll get along fine." He holstered his gun and returned his attention to his plate. "M-M-M-M! Good food. You sure know how to cook. Trudy. She knows how to cook, right Roy?"

Roy, with his mouth full, nodded. The food was good and he was happy. Sitting in a warm, tidy tent, eating hot food, having his second drink and watching the farmer's uncommonly attractive young wife, he felt a sexual desire for the woman build up within him that swept away any doubts he might have had about the rough treatment of these people who had done him no harm. He wondered what Trudy would look like without her clothes on. It had been a long time since had had seen a real-live naked woman, except for paintings of bare-assed ladies in saloons. The outlines of her legs that showed underneath her long skirt as she moved aroused him. Roy was not long on conscience and here he was faced with the opportunity of a lifetime. He meant to take full advantage of the situation.

John sat on the floor where the rustler had pushed him down. The rawhide was cutting off the circulation in his hands and his head felt as if someone was pounding him with a hammer. He knew that the outlaws meant to kill him and he was prepared to die. But he was half insane with misery, dread and rage knowing what would happen to his wife. He was completely helpless. Even if he could loosen the ties that bound his hands – and he knew he could not - the intruders would shoot him down before he would be able to get to them. There was no chance that anyone would happen by. Their luck had played out. John felt tears running down his cheek and he lowered his head to hide his face from the intruders and his wife.

The two men at the table paid no attention to him. They noisily shoveled down their food, washing it down with the whiskey straight from the bottle.

"Hey Trudy, how about some more of that meat?" Cal said and held up his plate. While Trudy busied herself at the stove, he twisted around in his chair to look at the trussed-up man sitting on the floor. "Where'd you get the beef?" Doing a little rustling on the side, huh sodbuster? Well, I wouldn't blame you none." He said expansively and belched again. "A man's gotta go and take what he wants. Ain't that right, Trudy?" He turned back to Trudy and smirked. Trudy walked up next to him, holding the iron skillet in which the meat sizzled.

"Shore smells good, don't it Roy?" He put his arm around the stony-faced woman's waist and pulled her close. Before he released her, his hand traveled down her leg.

"Look at that skillet," Cal chortled and dug into his steak. He was enjoying himself hugely. "That what you use to bang over the sodbuster's head if he don't obey?" He held up the empty whiskey bottle. "Got any more of this stuff?"

"Go look for it yourself!" Trudy screamed at Cal.

"Now, now, no need to get testy, you sweet thing. Roy," he motioned to his partner. "go see if there's another bottle."

When the men had eaten their fill, they pushed their plates away to make room for their elbows. Cal rubbed his stomach, "They say the way to a man's heart is through his stomach." He grinned and nodded his head. "I gotta tell you, Trudy, I really like you and I'll prove it to you."

"Hey, Cal." Roy loved to eat, but now that he was full, his thoughts were on the farmer's wife. He fidgeted in his chair. "What are we waiting for. We're wastin' time. Let's go and do it. Now."

"Now, you hold on, Roy." Cal leaned back in his chair. "We got plenty of time, don't we honey? What I'd like to have right now would be a real good seegar." Cal turned in his chair to face John. "You got any seegars?"

John shook his head. "I don't smoke but I've got some money stashed away. Take it and go away," he wheezed. The pain in his head was getting worse.

"Money? You got money? How much are we talking about?"

"A hundred dollars."

"A hunnerd dollars, huh?" Cal's eyes lit up and held out his hand. "You on the level? Lemme see it."

"Trudy, go and get the money," John wheezed. His head was throbbing viciously. He had no feeling in his hands. Without a word, his wife walked over to the corner cabinet, reached up and brought down a nondescript wooden box and put it down in front of the outlaw. Cal opened the box, took out a small sack filled with coins and tossed the box aside. He weighed the coins in his hand before he stuck the money into his vest pocket.

Roy was excited. A hundred dollars was a lot of money. "Hey Cal. Ain't you gonna count the money?"

Dan shook his head. "Not now. Plenty of time for that. I'll count it in the morning."

Roy cocked his head. "You gonna split it with me?"

"Sure, Roy, sure. You'll get your share." He grinned at Trudy. "Hey darlin', come over here and sit on my lap." Cal patted his knee invitingly. When Trudy did not move, he pulled his gun and fired a shot into the ground, missing John's leg by inches, making him flinch. Trudy stifled a scream.

"Next time I ain't gonna miss, you hear me?" Cal re-holstered his gun. "I said, come here and sit on my lap."

Trudy fought back her tears and did as she was told. She was in a panic but would do anything to keep her husband alive. Their situation was hopeless. She was convinced that after those men were through with her, they would kill them both.

She did not want to die. Trudy knew that the intruders possessed not a shred of humanity and would destroy anything or anyone that got in their way. The thought that she would never bear children drove tears into her eyes. And there was John on the floor. Her good, proud and strong husband, trussed up like a wild animal. She could tell that he was in pain and that he felt wracked with guilt for not being able to protect her, for having let her down. She wanted to rush to him, to tell him that she loved him and that all this was not his fault. What evil had they done that God would let them suffer like this?

"Hello? Where you been, Trudy? You didn't hear a word I said." Cal bounced her lightly on his knee. "I said I'll take you away from all this. You're much too pretty to be hooked up with that sodbuster, I'm gonna come into a lot of money when we make our big move and I'll take you to San Francisco. You ever been to San Francisco?"

Trudy shook her head.

"Well, Trudy, it's a right lively place and you'll love it," Cal said expansively. "You'll wonder why you was ever married to a coot like John. Look at him. He ain't no good to you. A loser. Better just forget him." He reached up and pulled the pins from her hair causing it to cascade around her face. "Now, that's more like it. Makes you look like a young girl, right Roy?"

Roy thought so, too. He fidgeted in his chair. "Hey Cal, when are you gonna stop gabbing and get on with it. Jeez, I'm getting all fired up. It's gettin' late and I want to have some fun like you promised."

"Alright." Cal sighed and pushed Trudy off his lap. He picked up the second whiskey bottle and held it against the light to check its contents. It was almost empty. He tipped the bottle, drank the rest of the liquid and belched loudly before pitching the bottle into the corner of the tent.

"I gotta go to take a pee and get myself ready." Cal stood up and hitched up his pants. "Roy, you watch the sodbuster. I don't trust him."

Roy pulled his gun. "Why don't I shoot him now so's he'll be out of the way."

Cal whirled on him. "Don't even think about it. I want him to sit there and watch when Trudy and me having fun right there next to him on that bed."

"And me," Roy said.

"Yeah, sure and you. We're gonna show the sodbuster how its done, how you please a woman. So watch him till I get back."

"Yeah I'll watch him alright," Roy said and put his gun on the table in front of him. John saw that the man was disappointed and half wished that the outlaw had shot him.

Cal ducked through the tent opening and let the flap close behind him.

Trudy watched him leave the tent. A look of determination came into her eyes. "There's a little piece of meat left if you want it," she told the outlaw. Roy, who had never turned down an offer of food in his life, nodded happily and handed her his plate. Trudy put the meat and a potato on the plate and set it down in front of him. Roy had his back to the stove, watching John. He picked up the fork and knife and cut the meat. As John watched, riveted, Trudy stood behind the outlaw and raised the heavy skillet over her head in a high ark and, with every ounce of strength she could muster, brought it down on top of Roy's head with skull-crushing force. The skillet connected with a sickening thud. Roy pitched forward onto the table, breaking the plate beneath him. His lifeless body slid off the chair and slumped to the hard-packed dirt floor.

"Trudy, cut me loose before the other one gets back. Hurry!" John croaked. At that moment, they heard Cal's footsteps approaching the tent. In one swift motion Trudy grabbed Roy's gun off the table and cocked it. The flap opened, a smirking Cal stepped inside and said, "Know what? I forgot..."

The Wilhelms would never learn what Cal had forgotten. Gripping Roy's gun in both hands, Trudy fired. The forty-five caliber bullet smashed into the outlaw's chest, causing him to stagger backwards. Reflexively, Cal groped for his Colt. Trudy cocked the gun and fired again and Cal was punched backwards out of the tent, his leer transfixed into a deathly grimace. The young woman stood rooted, the smoking gun in her hand looking at the soles of the outlaw's boots sticking through the flap. Then, in a purely mechanical motion, she dropped the gun on the table, sat down, covered her face with her hands and began to sob.

"Trudy, cut me loose. Trudy, please, honey, everything's alright now. You've got to cut me loose, you hear me? Trudy?" John tried to crawl over to his wife but his arms and legs had gone to sleep. "Trudy," he begged, "Trudy?"

After what seemed an eternity to John, his wife looked up. She picked a knife off the table, kneeled down and cut the strings tying his hands and legs.

"Could you rub my arms, Trudy? I can't feel them." His wife gave him a wan smile and rubbed his arms until they began to tingle. He flexed his hands and reached out to Trudy. She fell into his arms, sobbing. Her whole body shook as she burrowed her face into the hollow of his neck, her tears wetting the collar of his shirt.

"There, there." John stroked her as he mumbled encouragements into her ear. "It's alright, sweetheart. Everything's fine now. You did it. You saved our lives, my strong, brave little wife. Everything will be fine."

They sat on the floor and John held her until her sobs subsided. Finally, he disengaged himself gently from her embrace, picked her up and put her down on the bed. He covered her with a blanket. The flap to the outside was open, partially blocked by Cal's body. A blast of cold air blew into the tent. John relieved the dead man of his gun belt and reached into his vest pocket to retrieve the money that Cal had taken from Trudy. Dragging the body away from the tent by the arms he dumped it by the side of the vegetable patch before returning to the tent. Inside, he kneeled and put his finger against the neck of the outlaw who was sprawled on the ground. There was no pulse. The man named Roy was dead. John unbuckled the man's gun belt, put his shoulder under his body and carried the corpse outside, where he dumped him next to his partner. Hurrying back inside, John lowered and secured the flap, picked up Roy's gun, shucked the empty shells and fed new cartridges into the cylinder. He placed the Henry on the table and blew out the light. Faint moonlight illuminated the inside of the tent.

"John, where are you?" Judy asked in a small, tremulous voice. He could barely make out the outline of the bed.

"Right here, my sweet." John said.

"Aren't you coming to bed?"

"No, sweetheart." He shook his head for emphasis. "I ain't gonna make the same mistake twice. I'll just stay up and watch the door."

"What are we going to do?" Trudy wailed.

John shifted in his seat. "Come tomorrow morning, we pack up and head over to the Double-T ranch. I aim to ask the owner for a job."

Trudy sat up in bed. "That horrid man? He'll never hire you."

"Shush, Trudy, it's worth a try. He's short of help and we need to find us a place for the winter. I don't know what else to do. Now go back to sleep."

While John kept watch, Trudy slept fitfully through the night. Once she cried out in her sleep and he comforted her until she was quiet again.

The following morning John, using a pick-ax and a shovel dug a shallow grave in the frozen ground, dropped the bodies inside and covered them with dirt. He left no marker on the graves. Afterwards he and Trudy packed their belongings in their wagon, folded up the tent and set out for Savage's ranch.

10

Marshal Boudreaux looked out the window of his office and saw Savage, accompanied by a huge black man dressed in an old army uniform, dismount from his horse. He watched the Major speak to the man and point down the street. The soldier responded with a curt nod and rode off.

The marshal got up from behind his desk and opened the door. He held out his hand. "Ben, I didn't know you were in town. Sit down, take a load off your feet."

"Thanks," Savage said and pulled up a chair.

Boudreaux sat down on the corner of his desk, his right leg dangling. "So, what brings you to town?"

The rancher slumped back into his chair and stretched out his legs in front of him. "I had to take care of some business. And I wanted to talk to you."

Boudreaux leaned forward and peered at his friend. "Who's that big, angry-looking man you were just talking to?"

"His name's Rufus Jefferson. He used to be my Sergeant-Major." Savage briefly filled the marshal in on what had taken place. "He saved my life and I owe him one." He touched the scar on his neck. "When I prepared to ride into town, he decided to tag along, not that I particularly wanted him to."

"Why not? I didn't think you had anything against black folks."

Savage sighed and shifted his body into a more comfortable position. "I don't, but..." He waved his hands in a dismissive gesture.

"But what?' the marshal said. "Now you got me interested. Tell me what's going on between you and that soldier."

Savage sighed again. "Well, like I mentioned, he was one of my sergeants during the war. His name is Jefferson. He dislikes me, to put it mildly. During one phase of our Virginia campaign I sent him and six men on a reconnaissance mission. Jefferson didn't like the mission. He felt that they were riding into a trap and insisted I reconsider, claiming that it was a suicide mission. Hell, I knew that they didn't stand a snowball's chance in hell but I had direct orders from my commanding general. I demanded that he obey my orders. And well," Savage broke off and gestured at the marshal, "you can guess what happened. Jefferson was severely wounded and only barely made it back. He was the only one who made it back alive. He's never forgiven me for the deaths of those six young men." Savage shrugged. "And I hate to admit it, but he was right. It's something I'll have to live with for the rest of my life." Savage paused, lost in thought. "He's a good man. They don't come much better."

"So why don't you hire him?"

Savage emitted a derisive laugh. "Sergeant Jefferson? I doubt that he'd be willing to work for me. I managed to get him to agree to stick around for a couple of weeks. I expect that's about as good as I'll get."

"Talking about hiring people." Boudreaux pushed himself off the edge of his desk and walked over to the stove to pour himself a cup of coffee. "I hear that John Wilhelm, that farmer who was squatting on your land is working for you, too. Is that right?"

Savage was surprised. "Where'd you hear that?"

"Come on, Ben," the marshal admonished him. "This is a small town and news travels fast." He held up the coffee pot. "Want some?"

"Sure." Savage stood up and accepted a cup from Boudreaux. "Yeah, to tell you the truth, I was more than happy to hire on Trudy Wilhelm to take care of my house and do the cooking before Cookie poisoned us all," Savage said. "Since her husband came along as part of the bargain, I put him to work also, as a blacksmith. He's actually a good man. We don't talk much but we get along."

"So you replaced your cook?"

Savage rolled his eyes. "The man is really a horse wrangler, but he hired on as a cook. Figured he could make more money that way." He shook his head. "He's back to wrangling horses." He blew on the scalding liquid, took a sip and leaned forward to put his cup on the marshal's desk. "Ed, the reason for my dropping in to see you was to ask you if you found out anything new about the Mansons. I rode by their place on my way back from the trial but didn't find anything that would lead me to believe that they're stealing my cows." He told the marshal how he had been shot at by the Manson Brothers and how the brothers had shown him the ranch and put him up for the night. "The boys are clean as appearances are concerned," Savage said. "Except for the Herefords I sold them, their herd consists mostly of Longhorns. "He paused and looked at Boudreaux. "But there's still something that doesn't sit right with me regarding those two."

"I did a little checking myself," Boudreaux said.

"And?"

"And came up with nothing."

"Oh well," Savage sighed, resigned. He leaned forward again and picked up his cup. "The reason I keep coming back to the Mansons is that my rustling started around the time they acquired your ranch. This is getting to be a real problem and I've got to get to the bottom of it, and soon. You haven't seen any strangers in town recently, have you?"

"No." The marshal shook his head.

"Well," Savage slapped his hands on his thighs and stood up. "I'd best get moving. I told Sergeant Jefferson I'd meet him at Jimmy's." He put on his hat. "I'd appreciate it if you kept your eyes peeled. Let me know if you come up with anything, alright?"

"I'll do that," Ed said and waited until Savage had closed the door behind him before he returned to his paper work.

11

Class was in recess. Amy stood in the door watching her students play on the lawn in front of the school house when the Manson brothers rode by. At the sight of the young schoolteacher, Seth's chiseled face creased into a huge grin. He touched the brim of his hat and waved. Amy waved back and turned to walk inside. Seth angled his horse toward the schoolhouse but Jonah grabbed the reins of his horse and pulled him back onto the street.

"I jess' wanna say hello to Miss Amy," Seth groused. "It won't take a minute."

"C'mon, not now, Seth." Jonah said. "Can't you see she's busy? He kneed his horse forward and Seth reluctantly fell in with him." Don't go wasting your time on her," Jonah said. "We got things to do, remember?"

Riding abreast with his brother, Seth squinted at him. "What do you mean by me wastin' my time?"

"C'mon Seth. You and her are living on different planets. She's out of your league, bein' educated and all. She's being polite, thinking you're a nice young cowpoke but that's all."

"You're jess' bein' jealous, brother," Seth replied hotly. "I know she likes me. Don't she smile every time she sees me? Ain't that proof enough for you?"

Jonah rolled his eyes. "Alright, have it your way. Just don't come crying to me if she turns you down again."

Seth was miffed. "Don't you worry about it. She won't," Seth said, turning once more for a glance back at the now empty schoolyard.

They rode along Main Street, dodging large freight wagons, other horsemen, and the occasional cart.

"Jesus, where did all these people come from?" Seth groused. This country is getting' plumb overpopulated." He reined in his horse, causing his brother to stop also. "Look, there's Jimmy's. Let's stop for a drink, what do you say, little brother?"

"Okay, let's," Jonah agreed, "I sure could use a drink." They steered their horses over to the hitching rail and dismounted. "Just don't get plastered, hear?" he said, looping the reins loosely around the post. "And don't start any trouble."

Alright, alright, I hear you," Seth replied, exasperated and stepped out of the saddle.

Jimmy's Saloon was dim and the brothers stopped inside the door to adjust their eyes to the dark, cavernous room.

"Well, if it ain't the Manson Brothers," Jimmy said in greeting as they handed over their weapons. He eyed them with suspicion. "You ain't feelin' your oats and are of a mind to cause trouble again, now are you?"

"Come on, Jimmy," Seth laughed. "You ever see us cause a ruckus?"

The bar owner glared at them. "Just don't get any funny ideas, you hear?"

Seth waved his hand impatiently. "Cut the jabber, man. All we want is a drink."

While Jimmy set up a bottle and two glasses, Seth let his eyes wander around the bar room. The place was empty except for Sergeant Jefferson dressed in his faded army clothes. Seth started and pointed at the black man who was keeping to himself, quietly nursing a drink.

"Jesus, what in hell is *that*?" he said in shocked disbelief.

The bar owner busied himself with cleaning glasses with a towel of dubious color. "If you're referring to the man back there, he come into town with the Major."

Seth's face flushed an angry red. He downed his drink, coughed, and pushed the empty glass toward the barkeeper. "I don't give a damn who he come into town with, Jimmy. He's a nigger. Since when do you allow niggers in yore place?"

The bar owner eyes were chilly and he leaned across the bar, his face close to Seth's. "Let me get something straight, boy. His money is as good as yours and I make the decision who gets served my place and who don't, savvy? You don't like it, pay up and leave."

Seth glowered at Jimmy. He picked up the bottle and splashed whisky into his empty glass. "Well, I aim to do something about that."

Jonah laid a restraining hand on his brother. "Seth, leave it be, alright?" he urged his brother. "We don't want trouble."

Seth shook off his brother's hand. "Trouble, hell. It ain't no trouble." He picked up his drink and swaggered over to the soldier, heedless of the bar owner's warning. "You run away from the army, boy?" he asked with an insolent smile on his face.

Jefferson ignored the cowboy towering over him.

"Hey boy, I'm speakin' to you." Seth leaned forward to fix the black man with his gaze. Cat got your tongue?"

Rufus sighed. He leaned back in his chair and looked at Seth. "Do yourself a favor, sonny and go away before you get your nose busted."

Seth's jaw tightened. "No nigger talks to me that way," he hissed.

Rufus' eyes turned cold. "Well, this one just did," he said. "Don't push it, cowboy. Skedaddle if you know what's good for you."

In one swift motion, Seth picked up the soldier's glass and threw its contents in his face. But before he had a chance to bring his arm back down, Rufus came out of his chair like a coiled rattler; and, putting the weight of his whole body behind his big fist he drove it into Seth's stomach, causing the cowboy to double over with a grunt of pain. Jonah slammed his glass on the bar and took a run at Rufus who swatted him aside, causing Jonah to trip over a chair and fall, toppling over a table in the process. Grimacing with pain, Seth straightened up and took a swing at his opponent. Rufus deflected Seth's fist and jabbed a hard right and left to his face knocking him on the floor.

"You son-of-a-bitch," Jonah yelled. A Derringer appeared in his hand as if by magic. Before he could pull the trigger, Rufus, in one swift motion, kicked the gun out of his hand.

"That's enough," Jimmy thundered. He trained his shotgun on the brothers. "I've had it with you good for nothin' tramps always causin' trouble. Git on your feet, the both of you. I'm turning you over to the marshal. Now! Git on your feet, I said before I do something I might regret later."

Eyeing Jimmy's shotgun warily, the brothers struggled to their feet. Seth slumped into a chair, doubled over in pain. "You Mister," the bar owner addressed Jefferson. "I'd be obliged if you checked to see if they got any other weapons in their pockets."

"Be glad to." Jefferson patted the brothers down and shook his head. "They're clean," he said.

"Alright, then. I'll thank you to help me take 'em across the street to the marshal's office."

"I can't leave you alone for a minute, without you getting into a fight," Savage said. He and Jefferson were sitting in the marshal's office, waiting for Boudreaux to lock up his prisoners.

The old soldier shot him a disgusted look. "Don't start with me, Major. Nobody throws liquor in my face and gets away with it. Besides," he pointed at the Derringer lying on the marshal's desk, "they was armed and I wasn't."

Savage's reply was cut short by the marshal who walked through the door separating the jail from his office. He hung up the keys and sat down behind his desk.

"How long are you going to hold the Mansons?" Savage asked.

The marshal shrugged and swept the Derringer into the center drawer of his desk.

"I can't hold them longer than tomorrow afternoon at the latest." He slapped his desk with his flat hand. "Those two brothers are beginning to get my goat."

Savage shook his head. "I don't know, but I can't help but wonder about those two. They sure seem to be in town a lot for someone trying to run a ranch." He stood up and stretched. "The rustling started shortly after they moved into the valley."

"Look, Ben, I know what you're getting at and you may be right." Boudreaux gestured with both hands. "But if that is the basis of your suspicion then what about Luther Eaton, the fellow who bought the Jordan place around the same time? He keeps to himself and folks around here are suspicious of him." Boudreaux shook his head. "No, I think the rustlers are a bunch of outsiders who are keeping to themselves so as not to arouse suspicion. Besides, you said you checked the brothers' spread yourself."

Savage frowned at the marshal and reached for his rifle. "I need to get to the bottom of this. Not only am I losing livestock, I'm devoting time and effort to this rustling matter. Time which I don't have." He put on his hat and turned to the old soldier who had been quietly following their conversation. "Are you coming back to the ranch?"

Jefferson heaved his body out of the chair and reached for his hat. "Might as well. Nobody in this town would put me up anyway." Looking grim, he nodded to Boudreaux who was watching him. "Wouldn't want to give the marshal here no grief."

The marshal extended his hand. "Not a problem, Mr. Jefferson. You did this town a service today. Come back and see us if fancy strikes you. I'll personally find you a place to stay."

Savage was waiting for the old Sergeant, his hand on the door knob. "Alright then, Sergeant, let's go," he urged. "We've got a long ride ahead of us."

12

Sitting in his office, Marshal Boudreaux was frustrated. He had been neglecting his administrative duties and the new deputy which the city fathers had promised him had yet to come on board. In addition to his peace-keeping duties, the town had saddled him with collecting taxes and had even tried to task him with enforcing the town's sanitation ordnance. But that was where he drew the line. He was not about to inspect the privies in everybody's backyard.

Boudreaux got up from behind his cluttered desk to pour himself a cup of coffee. He tried to swallow his annoyance and his thoughts drifted back to his friend's problems. There had to be a way to catch the rustlers red handed. The city fathers should shake a leg and give him the full-time deputy who he had requested weeks ago so he could devote his time to enforce the law instead of pushing paper work.

The marshal sat back down behind his desk. In hindsight it seemed that selling his spread to the Mansons had been a bad idea. Not that he shared the Major's suspicion, but he could have saved himself a lot of trouble policing up after them. But then again, the Mansons probably would have bought Dwight Jordan's ranch, which had been for sale at the same time and which had eventually sold to Luther Eaton.

As it was, Seth Manson had given the appearance of being a nice, clean-cut, upstanding young man and Boudreaux had been eager to sell out to the young man. His ranch held too many memories, memories which still haunted him day and night.

Boudreaux was brought back to the present by a soft bump against the door to his office. He glanced up to see the waitress, who had served him at the Majestic on several occasions push the door open with her back, carrying a large tray. She swung around to face the marshal and smiled shyly. Boudreaux found himself beaming back at her as he jumped to his feet to help her with the door.

"Hello, Marshal. Here's the food you ordered for the two prisoners." She looked around for a place to put down the tray. Boudreaux quickly pushed aside the mountain of paper on his desk to make room for her. The tray was weighted down by two sturdy plates heaped with potatoes, a large piece of meat, beans and two slices of bread. The third plate was of a far more elaborate design. It also held a large steak, potatoes, and some vegetables. On a second, smaller, equally fine plate, Ed saw several slices of bread covered with jam.

The woman pointed at the fancy plate. "This dish is for you, compliments of Mr. Abercrombie. The others are for the prisoners." She inclined her head toward the door leading to the jail cells. "Should I…?"

"No, no," Boudreaux said hastily. "I'll take it in myself. That jail is no place for a lady. You wouldn't want to go in there."

"Oh," The woman said uncertainly and gave the marshal a questioning look. He stopped, the prisoners' plates in his hands.

"Yes? Something on your mind?"

"Uh, Mr. Abercrombie wants me to wait until you… you and the prisoners have finished eating and bring the dishes back to the restaurant?" The inflection of her voice framed her statement as a question.

"Of course, Miss," he found himself smiling again. "Uh, I don't even know your name. That would be fine." He raised the plates at her. "I'll just take these in to the prisoners. Be right back."

"My name is Anne Parker." She addressed the marshal's back as he pushed through the door to the jail. There was a clatter of dishes as the food was passed through the slots installed for that purpose. After a short but heated exchange between one of the prisoners and the Marshal Boudreaux reappeared and locked the door behind him.

"I'll be glad to be rid of those two," he said and pointed his thumb over his shoulder. He smiled. "Won't you have a seat, Miss Parker?" he pulled up a chair and the young woman sat down demurely, straightening her skirt with the palms of her hands. Boudreaux noticed that she looked older in daylight than she had in the artificially illuminated dining room. He noted the tiny crows feet at the corners of her eyes, the straight nose, and soft lips, and the mass of luxurious blond hair which she had loosely tied in the back with a ribbon. Her dress was simple but surprisingly stylish for a waitress. *She must be about thirty,* he thought.

Anne, finding herself the subject of the marshal's scrutiny, lowered her eyes and blushed. "You should eat your food, or it will get cold," she said to break the silence.

Boudreaux started. "Oh, yes," he said, looking down at the food. He picked up a fork. "Have you eaten, Miss Parker?" he asked.

"I've eaten, thank you," she said.

"Well, I can't eat by myself." Boudreaux picked up the plate with the bread and held it out to the woman who regarded him uncertainly. "Here, please have some bread. No, no, I insist," he said when she made a move to refuse. "If you don't eat, I won't either." He thought that Anne Parker was an uncommonly attractive woman and realized with surprise that he enjoyed her company. He watched with satisfaction when she took the offered bread and dug happily into his steak.

The food tasted good. After Boudreaux had finished, he excused himself and walked back into the jail to retrieve the empty plates from the prisoners. When Anne took them from him, their hands touched and he felt an electric shock race through his body. Blushing brightly, the young woman stacked the dishes on the tray and picked it up but Boudreaux took it away from her and placed it back on his desk.

"Could I offer you some coffee?" he asked eagerly and gave Anne a beseeching smile.

She returned his smile and shook her head. She picked up her tray with the empty dishes again. "Perhaps some other time? I have to run, or I'll get in trouble with Mr. Abercrombie."

Ed hurried to open the door for her.

"Thanks for offering me coffee," she said. "I enjoyed my visit."

"Please come again, Miss Parker," Ed called after her.

13

Winter had arrived in earnest. The snow crept down the distant mountains, invaded the foothills, and a blizzard lasting several days dumped five feet of new snow on the ground. Life on the ranch slowed to a crawl. Several of Savage's cowhands had asked for their wages and drifted south to escape the cold. The rest of his men spent long hours distributing hay that they dragged onto the range on sleds, or, bundled up against the extreme cold, moving cattle away from the wind trying to keep them from succumbing to the icy weather. They skinned the cows that died, assuming they found them before they had frozen stiff. Savage was worried that his supply of hay might not last through the winter. His holdings were so extensive that he was unable to keep track of a large part of the fifteen thousand head of cattle which were scattered over an area of a hundred thousand acres. The survival of his livestock would depend on periodic thaws, known as Chinooks, to allow the animals to forage for food on their own.

Shortly after the New Year, Savage received a letter from an English investor, the Earl of Litchworth, indicating that the nobleman's conglomerate was interested in acquiring the Double-T ranch. Savage had heard that wealthy titled Englishmen were busy buying up American ranchlands in large quantities, but he loved his ranch and saw no reason for selling out. Looking at the letter, though, did prompt him to conduct some business in town. Josh had the ranch operations well in hand and, probably due to the cold weather the rustlers, whoever they were, were lying low. While in town Savage planned to mail a response to the Englishman declining his offer. He would also do some banking and stock up on various items such as clothing and ammunition.

The latest Chinook had long abandoned the valley and the thermometer dropped to zero. Savage spent seven lonely, miserable hours in the saddle, bundled up in his sheepskin greatcoat and fur-lined boots. He wore a cap to keep his ears from freezing. His and his Bay's breaths erupted in clouds of steam which drifted along behind them in the clear, icy air. The only sounds were the creaking of leather and the crunching of snow under the horse's hoofs. Here and there, patches of grass formed small brown islands which the Chinook had coaxed out from the otherwise uniformly white blanket of snow. Seeing these patches gave Savage hope that the cattle would find enough forage to sustain themselves until the next snowfall, but right now his mind was on a warm line shack with its iron stove radiating waves of heat.

It was getting dark when Savage approached his destination. Breaking out of the woods for an instant he found himself thinking that he must have strayed off the trail. There was no line shack. He urged his Bay forward, looking about him. What he saw made him rein in his horse. The only thing that remained of the shack were a few blackened timbers and the brick chimney which had withstood the conflagration. It stood silently as a slender silhouette pointing at the darkening sky. Confused and angry, Savage dismounted and poked around the wreckage for a clue of what might have caused the fire. His boot connected with a solid object and he bent down to investigate. What he found was a soot-covered lantern perforated by a bullet. *Arson*, he thought. His mind went back to the blackened building he had ridden past the day of the trial and further to his friend Boudreaux's ranch. The shack had been torched deliberately. The flush of anger rising up within him, however, was no match for the rapidly plummeting temperature. No use trying to spend the night here.

Savage was no stranger to freezing temperatures. He had braved the cold while serving in the army and even more so during his many years of ranching. But tonight the icy temperature was penetrating his many of layers of clothing, seeping deep into his bones. Shrugging deeper into his sheepskin coat he urged his Bay forward, wondering whether he and his horse would be able to survive until they reached their destination. They were alone in the vast white wilderness. The only sound was the labored breathing of General Chamberlain plodding toward town and the warmth of the stable.

Savage finally arrived in Riverside during the early morning hours. He woke the hostler to put up his Bay in the livery stable and, carrying his saddle bags, hurried to the warmth of the hotel. The night clerk, flustered by the unexpected arrival of the hotel's most esteemed customer woke up the proprietor who, despite the early hour, greeted Savage effusively. "You are a brave man, Mr. Savage, riding all the way to town in this weather."

"Damned foolish. Not brave," Savage responded, his teeth chattering. He set down his bags and opened his coat, grateful for the warm, well-illuminated lobby. "Mr. Abercrombie, I'm looking forward to my warm room and a stiff drink. I'm sure you'll be able to arrange that."

Savage allowed himself the luxury of sleeping in the next morning. After a hearty lunch in the hotel dining room, he bundled up against the cold and stepped out into the street which was as bustling with traffic despite the icy temperature. Savage stopped off at the bank, then walked across the street to post his letter to the Earl of Litchworth and came away with a bundle of mail addressed to him.

The marshal was out of the office when Savage stepped in but he introduced himself to Phil Garrett, Boudreaux's new deputy. Phil was a solidly built, wiry man in his mid thirties. His gaze was level and his demeanor exuded a quiet confidence which Savage had noticed in many a lawman whom he had known. The deputy assured him that he and the marshal regarded the rancher's rustling issue to be among their top priorities.

"Give my regards to your boss," Savage said and turned toward the front door. "I'll be in my hotel room for the rest of the day. Ask him if he would like to meet me for dinner, say around seven?"

"I'll pass it on," Garrett promised.

The marshal had followed his friend's invitation for dinner, which lasted well into the night. During the dinner, Amy Cabbett had walked past their table, acknowledging Marshal Boudreaux's greeting with a smile while pointedly ignoring Savage.

Boudreaux had been quick to pick up on the young woman's snub. "What was that all about?" he asked.

Savage had shrugged his shoulders. "I have no idea, Ed. I wish I knew."

The following morning, Savage was astride his horse again. The way out of town led past Mrs. Koslowsky's boarding house in which Amy Cabbett had taken up residence. It was a clapboard structure, painted white with blue shutters encircled by an oversized porch, giving it a pleasant, inviting look. Savage reined in his horse and gazed at the house. The memory of Miss Cabbett snubbing him at dinner last night angered him. He was also angry with himself for not putting the young woman out of his mind. Being a man of action he knew the only way to bring this matter to a head was to face her directly. He suspected that the young woman had not yet left for school. Savage kneed his Bay forward, dismounted in front of Mrs. Koslowsky's house and tied the reins of the horse to the fence. Stepping through the gate a strode up to the house, he mounted the porch and, using the knocker, gave the door a smart rap. Moments later, as the door opened Savage found himself confronted by Amy whose eyes turned cold when she recognized her visitor.

Savage took off his hat. "Good morning, Miss Cabbett. I would like to speak to you. May I come in?"

Amy was tempted to shut the door in the rancher's face but proper behavior dictated that she step aside and motion Savage to come in out of the cold. She closed the door behind him and leaned against it, hands behind her back. "What would you like to talk to me about?" she asked coldly. She did not offer him a seat.

Savage took off his hat. He decided to get straight to the point. "I believe I have a right to know why you dislike me so," he said. "I have wracked my brain to try and remember where or how I could have offended you, but I can't think of a single incident. Please enlighten me as to what I did to incur your displeasure." He looked at her forbidding face. "It's very important to me," he added.

Amy's voice was flat. "You didn't do anything to me personally, Mr. Savage, but I don't like the high-handed manner in which you treat the less fortunate in the Valley."

Savage was confused. "Less fortunate? I don't understand. Who...?"

The young woman held up her hand to stop him, indignation plain on her face. Her voice was tight. "I was at the hearing where the judge abetted you in pushing that poor farmer of the land which was rightfully his."

"Are you talking about John Wilhelm, Miss Cabbett?" asked, his voice incredulous. "Since you attended the court session you surely heard that Wilhelm settled on land which is rightfully mine."

"That's just it, Mr. Savage. This man made an honest mistake. You have so much land, thousands and thousands of acres and you destroy a family's livelihood by chasing them off."

"Just a minute, Miss Cabbett. You have it all wrong." Savage responded, keeping his rising anger in check. "I don't expect you to know much about ranching, but Mr. Wilhelm decided to settle smack in the middle of the one piece of land which I need to drive my cattle through."

Amy's green eyes flashed with anger. "I don't care. You destroyed this man's livelihood."

"Livelihood," Savage scoffed. "The Wilhelms wouldn't have lasted through the winter. Not too long ago they came to me for help and I gave both of them a job. Trudy Wilhelm keeps house for me and Wilhelm himself is working as my blacksmith."

"Well, it's the least you could do for these poor people," Amy sniffed.

Savage shook his head in wonder. "You certainly know how to carry a grudge, Miss Cabbett."

"There is also something else that bothers me." Amy said and moved away from the door.

"What is that?" Savage said, following her with his eyes.

"Your past."

"My past? I'm afraid I don't understand."

Amy hesitated. "Depending on who you talk to, you are either a bandit, a killer or a card shark."

"I am?" Savage asked, askance. "What makes you say that?"

"That's what the mothers of my pupils told me."

Savage threw his head back and roared with laughter. "The Valley rumor mill in action. How delightful. I hate to disappoint you and also your informants, but I'm afraid my past isn't nearly as colorful and adventurous as that."

"I choose to believe that there must be some truth to these rumors," Amy said, her eyes flashing.

Savage stood silently for a moment. "You believe what you want, Miss Cabbett," he said. He stared at the beautiful young woman whose heart was hardened against him. He hesitated for a second. Then, recognizing that there was no way for him to scale the barbed-wire fence that she had erected around her, he put on his hat, turned and walked outside. It seemed to him to be a symbolic act, severing all connections between him and the lovely girl with her cold eyes and a heart of stone. *Well, so be it*, he thought. It was time to get back to the pressing business at hand.

Amy stared at the door which Savage had closed behind him with a mildly shocked look on her face. She had wanted the rancher to defend himself, even reveal his identity to her, but instead he had simply walked out.

Well, good riddance, she thought, turned and walked back to her room.

14

Ed Boudreaux sat in his office, making annotations to a document in front of him when Deputy Garrett walked into the office, accompanied by a blast of cold air. He slammed the door shut and stamped his feet to shake off the new snow clinging to his boots. His breath had formed tiny icicles on his moustache and he walked briskly over to the stove which was radiating enough warmth to heat a dance hall.

Boudreaux, irritated at the interruption, glanced up at his deputy. "You're back early, Phil," he said. "Anything new?"

Garrett nodded. He stood with his back to the marshal, pulled off his gauntlets and vigorously rubbed his hands over the stove. "Came in to tell you that five hard-looking cases just rode into town." He looked over his shoulder at Boudreaux. "They got their ponies tied up in front of Jimmy's."

"Armed?"

"Yep, to their teeth. One of 'em looks like a pistolero: two guns, strapped down, fast-draw holsters."

"Oh hell," Boudreaux said with feeling. "Maybe you'd better keep an eye on them."

"That's what I was planning on doin'," Garrett said and stopped rubbing his hands. He stepped away from the stove and pulled on his gloves. "Just thought I'd let you know."

"Good," Boudreaux said, his mind still on his paperwork. Let me just finish this. I'll join you in about five minutes."

"I'd like that. Might need all the help I can get. Five against one don't seem such great odds to me." The deputy walked over to the gun rack and rested his hand on the Browning lever action repeating shotgun. "Mind if I borrow this new-fangled scatter gun? Looks like a lot of firepower to me."

"Sure, take it," Ed replied without looking up from his desk. "It's loaded. But don't start anything before I get there, hear?"

"I won't," Garrett said, "I ain't crazy. See you in a bit." He opened the door and stepped out into the icy street.

Ed watched his deputy walk towards Jimmy's Saloon. The continuous cold and snow had swept nearly all traffic from the street. The deputy stopped in front of the saloon and Boudreaux saw him pin his star on the outside of his coat where it would be visible. He checked the load in his revolver, re-holstered it, and disappeared through the saloon entrance. *Good man to have on your side*, Ed thought.

The marshal made an entry on a document and closed the folder in front of him. He stood up and opened the top drawer of the filing cabinet, dropped the folder inside, locked the drawer and put the key into his vest pocket. He strapped on his gun, slipped into his heavy overcoat, and put on his hat before stepping out into the snow-covered street. He stood aside and greeted the blacksmith's wife whose face was red from the cold as she swept past him, drawn to the warmth of the general store.

When the marshal pushed through the door of the saloon, he saw five rough-looking men lounging at a table near the back door, their coats draped over the backs of their chairs, talking, laughing, playing cards and drinking. They ignored Garrett who had taken up position at the far end of the bar, near the entrance, the shotgun cradled in the crook of his arm. Jimmy stood behind the bar, polishing a whisky glass for the fifth time while keeping an eye on the strangers. When Boudreaux walked in, the men glanced up briefly from their cards, mustered the lawman and returned their attention to the game.

Boudreaux walked over to the bar. "Jimmy, you know there is a city ordinance about carrying guns within town limits. Didn't you tell those folks to check their weapons?"

The saloonkeeper shrugged and gave the marshal a resigned look. "What do you think? Sure I told 'em, Marshal. I told them that I didn't allow no guns in my establishment. But they didn't pay no attention to me and I didn't press the point. I took one look at all the artillery they're totin' and I'm not pushin' it. That's your and Phil's job." He put the polished glass down in front of the marshal. "Drink?" he asked.

"No thanks." Boudreaux's attention was drawn to the saloon entrance. Three men, dressed in farm clothes crowded noisily through the door and moved up to the bar.

"Cold enough for you, Jimmy?" one of the farmers said and vigorously rubbed his hands together for warmth. He stopped short when he saw the marshal and his deputy leaning against the bar. He made a questioning motion to the proprietor who inclined his head toward the card players. The farmers turned and eyed the hard-looking armed strangers at the table. They looked back at the lawmen and Jimmy's grim face, whispered among themselves, and one-by-one sidled out of the saloon, back into the safety of the street.

When the door closed behind the farmers Marshal Boudreaux stepped away from the bar and approached the table. "Which one of you is in charge here?"

One of the men sighed at the interruption and folded his cards. He looked up at Boudreaux who was towering over them. "I guess that would be me, why?"

"I'd like to know your business in town."

The man stretched and yawned. "Just riding through. Might stay a couple of days, though. I kinda' like this town."

"Hey Harvey, you playin' or what?" one of the card players asked him.

"Can't you see I'm talking to the marshal, Dan?" Harvey said. "Where's your manners?"

"Funny, I ain't never been accused of having no manners," Dan Hittle replied and guffawed.

"Where are you headed?" Marshal Boudreaux pressed Harvey, ignoring Hittle's remarks.

"Oh' out thataway." Harvey waved his hand in a westerly direction. "Not that it's any of your business."

"Everything in this town is my business," Boudreaux said coldly. He pointed a finger at the man's gun belt. "There's a rule against carrying guns in this town. You gents don't like to play by the rules, do you?"

The man named Harvey eyed Boudreaux with cold eyes. "I didn't know there was a law against guns in town"

"There's a sign on either end of Main Street that says so clearly."

"Didn't see it."

"You rode right by it."

The gunman gestured dismissively and picked up his cards.

"Maybe you can't read," Boudreaux suggested.

Harvey dropped his cards face down on the table and pushed back his chair. He stood up slowly. His face was hard. "Are you trying to pick a fight, mister?"

The marshal met his gaze. "I'm telling you and your people here to leave town. If you have no business to conduct here, you have no business being here. So pay up and get moving."

The gunman's face reddened. "We ain't goin' nowhere," he said in a flat voice. "Marshal, you'd better crawl back into that office of yours before you get hurt. I can't abide lawmen. They ain't nothing but trouble and I don't cotton to trouble. So do yourself a favor. Get your ass out of here and take that depity of yours with you before I blow a window in your skull."

Boudreaux's face darkened. He stepped back and rested his hand on the butt of his gun. There was ice in his voice. "Unbuckle your gun belt and drop it on the floor. The same goes for the rest of you."

Harvey snorted contemptuously. "Boys, it looks like we're gonna have to teach the marshal a lesson in manners. What do you say?"

The men at the table took their time folding their cards and stood up slowly. They walked away from the table and fanned out to face the marshal and his deputy. The remaining few patrons scrambled for the exit and Jimmy, his face tense, withdrew further behind the bar.

Boudreaux realized that he walked into a trap. His mind had been on his paperwork and he had neglected to proceed with his usual diligence and careful planning. It was obvious that Harvey and his gang did not respect his authority as a lawman and would shoot him and his deputy down without further thought. The odds were not in Boudreaux's and his deputy's favor. While Phil might cover some of the men facing them with his shotgun, it would be up to Boudreaux alone to disarm Harvey. The marshal was a good shot, but he was no match for a professional gunslinger who would not give up his weapons without a fight.

Still, Boudreaux stood, his hand hovering near the butt of his Colt. The trick, if he was to survive, was to watch his opponent's eyes because they would betray his intentions. The silence in the saloon was deadly and the seconds ticked by in agonizing slowness.

Boudreaux detected a flicker in Harvey's eyes and went for his gun but his opponent drew with a speed that defied credulity. He had already leveled his Colt at the marshal when an explosion erupted to Boudreaux's left, nearly drowning out the sharp crack of the gunman's weapon. The echo of their reports mingled with the tinkling of breaking glass. Boudreaux felt a stinging sensation on his temple as the buckshot from a shotgun rocked the gunman backward, cutting him almost in half. Harvey's body slammed across the table behind him and slid to the ground, splattering blood against the wall. His unseeing eyes were frozen in surprise and his lifeless hand, still holding the gun, dropped into his lap. The acrid smell of burned gunpowder filled the saloon. Boudreaux slowly turned to his left, his gun still only half out of his holster to see Jimmy standing behind the bar, brandishing a smoking shotgun.

"Don't even try it. The first man goes for his gun gets it!" Deputy Garrett's voice rang out sharply. He had his shotgun trained on the other men who stood, slack-mouthed, hands on the butts of their guns, staring in confused dread at the dead gunmen. "Harvey?" Hittle said. He was in shock and looked at his companions. "Can you believe it? What...?" his voice trailed off.

"Take your hands away from your guns. Unbuckle your belts and drop 'em on the floor." Garrett directed. Boudreaux watched the saloonkeeper reload his shotgun. The men complied slowly, muttering, looking in dark confusion at the marshal and his deputy. Jimmy, his finger still on the trigger, walked among them, picked up their weapons, and dropped them on the bar.

"Thanks, Jimmy," Boudreaux said let his half-drawn gun slide back into the holster, "for saving my life."

"Don't mention it, Marshal. Glad to do it," the saloonkeeper replied and walked behind the bar. Boudreaux bent over the bloody remains of the dead gunman and pried the gun out of his hand.

"Let's march them over to the jail, Phil," he said and turned to the saloonkeeper. "Sorry about your window and the other breakage. Have it fixed and the council will pay for it. And thanks for your support." The surge of adrenalin that had served him moments ago was now fading and he had to fight to keep his voice steady.

"Glad to help. The place needs a whitewash anyway, so no harm done. You think they'll pay for it? The window, I mean. What do you think, Marshal?"

"They'd better." Boudreaux's voice was grim. He felt disembodied and dizzy. His voice sounded far away.

Phil stared at his boss. "Boss, your head's bleeding. Are you alright?"

"Bleeding? Me? Where?" He raised his arms and inspected his body. "I don't..."

"Your left temple. Bullet must've grazed it." Garrett took a step toward his boss to inspect the wound.

The marshal touched the side of his head and his fingers came away smeared with blood. He shook his head in wonder. "Funny, it doesn't hurt."

The saloonkeeper snatched up a rag, hurried around the bar and pressed it into the marshal's hand. "Use this to wipe off the blood. It's clean."

"Thanks." Boudreaux pressed the rag to his temple. As the shock began to wear off, the pain of the wound began to kick in. At least he was beginning to think clearly again. "Phil, let's lock up these birds. We'll pick up their guns later."

"Get somebody to tell the undertaker to come on over and pick up the stiff," Jimmy said and kicked the sole of the dead man's boot for emphasis before walking back behind the bar.

Outside, people hearing the shots had streamed out of their offices and shops and stood huddled in the snow, staring wide-eyed at the marshal's bloody head and the four sullen men being herded to jail. "What happened, Marshal?" the blacksmith's wife, trumpeted shrilly, clasping her purchases to her ample bosom.

The marshal cut her off with a shake of his head. "Not now, Ma'am. I'm sure you'll be able to read all about it in tomorrow's paper. I need to get these men off the street and lock them up." He fixed his gaze on the other bystanders crowding around him. "Somebody do me a favor and ask the undertaker to pick up a body in Jimmy's Saloon."

The blacksmith's wife huffed, clearly offended at being given short shrift by the marshal; but she stepped aside to let him and his prisoners pass.

Once the prisoners were securely behind bars, Boudreaux sought his chair behind his desk. His confrontation with the gunman came flooding back to him. His stomach lurched and he began to shake. Boudreaux had been near death before in his life, but he had never looked his enemy in the eye at such close range. He pulled the rag away from his head and examined it. The blood had stopped flowing and was beginning to form a crust. He felt a headache coming on.

His deputy took the bloody cloth from Boudreaux and washed it out in the basin, turning the water pink before handing it back to his boss. "Hold this against your temple while I get a bandage, or would you like me to fetch the doc?"

Boudreaux shook his head. His headache was getting worse. He pressed the wet cloth to his temple. "No, but I think I could use a drink, Phil."

Garrett reached into the right-hand drawer of Boudreaux's desk and brought out a bottle and a glass. He poured and gave the glass to his boss, whose hand trembled as he tossed the whisky down. The liquid warmed his insides and he hoped that it would work its way up and kill his headache. "Thanks," he said.

Garrett's nodded. He took the rag away from Boudreaux. "You're lucky to be alive, Boss," he said, his back to the marshal as he washed out the bloody cloth. "That man Harvey had cleared leather while you was still reaching for your gun." He shook his head in wonder. "I ain't never seen anybody be that quick. Lucky for you, Jimmy had managed to pull out his shotgun on the sly. Even after he blasted him, the gunslinger still almost killed, you." He handed the clean rag back to his boss. "Another drink?" Garrett held up the bottle to Boudreaux and cocked his head questioningly.

"No more, thanks." The marshal replied, shaking his head. It hurt.

Using his palm, Phil punched the cork back into the neck of the bottle and put it away. The rag Boudreaux held to his head felt cool and the drumming in his head was beginning to subside.

"Well, I'd better do something about that wound of yours," the deputy said. "You sure you don't want me to fetch Doc Wood?"

"No. No need to bother the doc. He's busy enough as it is." Boudreaux replied. Feeling lightheaded, he leaned back in his chair and closed his eyes. Both men started as the door burst open and Anne Parker walked in, an agitated look on her face. She cried out when she saw the bloody rag in Boudreaux's hand and rushed to his side. "You're hurt!" she gasped trying to catch her breath. "I heard about the shooting and I came right over as soon as I could get away. Oh, you poor, poor man." Anne whirled to face the deputy. "Have you got any hot water and a band...Oh good, thank you," she said when Garrett thrust the bandage into her hand.

"Hot water coming up."

Anne probed the wound with gentle hands. "It doesn't look so bad," she said with obvious relief. When Garrett handed her the basin with hot water, she carefully washed the crusted blood away. It hurt and Ed made every effort not to wince. He was feeling lightheaded again, though this time not from his wound. Anne's cool hands against his forehead as she applied the bandage gave him a feeling of pleasure he had not experienced in a long time. He closed his eyes and luxuriated in her soft touch. She was leaning over him, adjusting the bandage and he smelled her fragrance. Not since the death of his wife had a woman stood so close to him. He was stunned and taken aback for feeling the urge to put his arms around her and draw her to him.

"There." Anne stepped back and took a critical look at her handiwork. "You look like a Hindu, Marshal," she joked. Her smile lodged itself in his heart. "I think you'll be fine for now, but I think that you should still have your wound looked at by Doc Wood." Her glance drifted from Boudreaux to the clock on the wall. She started and gasped. "Heavens, I've got to run. I'm supposed to help out in the kitchen. Mr. Abercrombie will kill me if he finds out I'm gone."

"No, Miss Parker." Boudreaux smiled and reached for her hand. She blushed but made no move to withdraw it. "You tell Mr. Abercrombie that a fate worse than death will befall him if he as much as harms a hair on your head. Thank you. I'm so glad that you came by. It brightened an otherwise unpleasant day. And Miss Parker?"

"Yes, Marshal?"

He squeezed her hand and touched the bandage. "Thanks for this."

"You're most welcome, and please be careful." Her eyes were moist and she fled from the room.

Boudreaux released the prisoners early the next morning to avoid having to feed them breakfast. They looked at the marshal's bandaged head and buckled on their gun belts.

Dan Hittle shot the marshal a malevolent look. "You had no right to lock us up, Marshal," he said to the nods of the other three men.

"You broke the laws of this town." Even though Boudreaux had taken the precaution to remove the cartridges from their guns, he regarded the men, hand on the butt of his revolver, half expecting them to cause trouble. Instead, they pulled on their coats and picked up their hats, which the deputy had dumped in a pile next to the jail cells the day before.

"Marshal, I swear we won't forget this," Hittle persisted.

"Since you won't be setting foot in this town again, I don't see where it makes any difference." Boudreaux's eyes were riveted on Dan who lowered his eyes.

"You don't know how lucky you was, just gettin' creased," one of the other men spoke up, pointing at the marshal's bandage. "Harvey was the best. If it hadn't been for that cowardly saloonkeeper, you would be layin' in a pine box instead of him."

Boudreaux's smile was thin. "Your man Harvey is dead and I'm very much alive. Now claim your horses and ride out of town. Don't forget to pay the hostler and don't come back."

"You ain't seen the last of us," Hittle swore and herded the others out the door.

15

A few days later Dan Hittle was perched on the rickety chair in the abandoned farmhouse once briefly occupied by Savage during his nearly fatal search for the rustlers. The carcass of the slaughtered cow in back of the house had long been picked clean by wolves roaming the countryside in search of food. Hittle was talking to Cherokee Charley, his closest friend. They had been riding together for going on two years. Charley was of small stature. A greasy bandana held his long black hair together. His eyes were black and hard. Dressed in western clothes, and worn boots, Charley carried his gun low on his right hip. A bandolier holding thirty-six caliber bullets was suspended from his right shoulder and came together under his left armpit. A large knife was strapped to the back of his left shoulder. Hittle, tall and wiry, his watery blue eyes empty, devoid of feeling, had a ferret-like visage with pock-marked, swarthy skin pulled tightly over the planes of his face. He was still steaming over the treatment received at the hand of the cowardly town marshal, had sought refuge with his gang in the farm after their release from the Paradise Valley jail. They were a rough-looking bunch, dirty, restless, suspicious and tired of doing nothing.

"Why don't we just go and grab us a bunch of cows? What in hell are we waitin' on, Dan?" one of the men asked disgustedly and spat on the floor. "We been settin' on our asses ever since we got here. I wanna make some money and move on. What the hell is the problem?"

Dan rolled his eyes and sighed. "Can't you get it through your thick skull? Jeez, I been tellin' you that this ain't the right time."

"Tell me again," the man demanded.

"It's too early in the year." Annoyance was showing in Dan's face. "The grass in the canyon likely ain't recovered and there's still too much snow, it being up in the hills and all. Even if we get aholt of the cows, how are we gonna keep em alive? You wanna tell me that? Hell, I bet, even them watering holes and lakes up there's still froze." Dan stood up and hitched up his gun belt. "Besides we're still waitin' on them other guys what's coming up from Texas." He waved his hands in a gesture of frustration. "Having said that, I'm tired of settin' around here myself, twiddling my thumbs. This place ain't exactly paradise. So, maybe we should take the chance after all, round us up some more cows and start drivin' 'em north. Maybe the weather will change in our favor." He turned and addressed his friend. "What do you say Charley? You ready to move?"

Cherokee Charley had a perpetually sullen look on his face. "I been ready to move ever since we holed up here," he said. "The weather is gettin' warmer and them ranchers is probably busy hiring on a bunch of cowpokes which will make our job a lot harder."

Dan nodded his agreement. "Yeah, I..."

"Ain't our mysterious employer gonna join us?" George, one of the other men broke in. "Who're we working for anyhow?"

Dan waved him off. "Never mind, George. All you need to know is that whoever he is, he's prepared to pay well. I figger our employer will join us when we make our final push."

"What in hell do we need him for?" Cherokee Charley groused. "We got us enough hands to steal a bunch of critters and high-tail it outta here."

Dan sighed. "Don't believe for a minute that thought hadn't crossed my mind, Charley, but the man payin' us knows where to sell them cows, no questions asked. We do need him, at least until we got our money, understand?"

"Are we gonna' wait on him?"

"Yeah, but not here, at the canyon." He stood up and stretched. "We'll start driving the cattle up tomorrow."

"Tomorrow?"

"Tomorrow," Dan said.

16

"Major, I hate to tell you this, but they's at it again." Josh, dressed in chaps and hat in hand was talking to Savage on the porch of the ranch house. The red sun, arcing downward in the western sky cast long angular shadows across the compound. It was one of the freakishly warm days heralding the coming of spring. The evening was still except for the lowing of cattle in the nearby holding pen and the occasional nickering of horses tied to the rail at the bunkhouse. The smell of fried meat drifted over from the open kitchen window and mingled with the more earthy odors of the ranch. One of Savage's cowboys sat on a chair tipped against the wall of the bunkhouse, practicing the harmonica.

"Dammit, not again." Savage swore "How many?" he asked.

The foreman scratched his head, "Can't tell for sure, Major, but I figure about sixty to seventy head, maybe more. They's headed north. Easy to track. The ground's still soft and them tracks show that there was four riders driving the cows."

"Did you put any of our boys on their trail?"

The foreman shook his head. "I was planning on it and the boys was eager to go after 'em, but there's a big storm brewing" Josh tossed his head at the black clouds beginning to form over the mountains, crowding out the late afternoon sun, "The rustlers have got at least a day's head start on us and by this evening the rain will have washed the tracks out. I didn't wanna put none of the boys into that kind of a situation. Just wouldn't have made no sense."

"I guess you're right." Savage said. "Damn, here we go again. We still don't have enough hands to guard the livestock. I'd be willing to hire more but..." His shoulders shrugged in frustration.

"That reminds me Major," Josh dug into his shirt pocket and pulled out a piece of dirty, wrinkled paper. "Got me a letter from some of the boys what left to go home last fall. They say they want to come back and work for us again. I figured we could use 'em and left word for 'em to ride on up." Josh gave his boss an uncertain look. "Maybe I should've asked you first?"

Savage was pacing back and forth on the porch. He stopped and looked at his foreman. "Jesus, Josh, you're my second in command. Hell, I expect you to make those kinds of decisions. It'll be great to have those boys back."

Savage looked at the sky. While they had been talking, the clouds had begun to roll in, blocking out what had remained of the sun. "I guess you were right about the rain," he said as the first heavy drops began to fall.

"Gonna be a big one, looks like." The foreman turned to go.

Savage was disgusted. "Dammit. We need to come up with a plan how we're going to put a stop to this rustling business once and for all."

It rained heavily without letup for two days. The hard dirt between the main house and the out buildings had been tamped down by thousands of hooves over the years and now turned into a sea of mud, with rivulets of water crisscrossing the soggy ground. Man and beast exposed to the weather were miserable. The cowboys guarding the cattle withdrew into their ponchos and tried to find dry ground under trees wherever possible. The weather reminded Savage of the many times during the war when he had been astride his horse, shivering uncontrollably in freezing weather that seemed to last forever. The other extreme had been the rain and humidity, which penetrated every part of his body, sapping his strength and dulling his sense of fighting spirit. He wondered how he had ever survived the elements which had been just as debilitating as a gaping wound. Now, sitting in his dry, comfortable office in front of a warming fire, he contemplated his foreman who was sprawling in his chair across from him.

Savage looked grim. This rustling business was getting to be a serious problem. He had a ranch to run. Instead, he and his men were spending their time chasing a bunch of thieves. He bent down to open a desk drawer and resurfaced holding a bottle by its neck. "Drink?"

"Don't mind if I do." Josh grinned, leaning forward eagerly. Savage's foreman was not one to turn down an offer for a drink any time of the day.

"Frankly, Josh, I'm at my wit's end," Savage said. He poured drinks and returned the bottle to his desk. "You got any ideas?"

The foreman tossed down the whisky and set the glass down on his boss's desk. "Major, I know that you'n Rufus Jefferson don't get along so good but the other day he talked to me about an idea how to deal with them rustlers. You might wanna' listen to him."

"Where's Jefferson now?"

"Out chasin' cows with the other boys. I expect he'll be back tonight."

"Alright," Savage said and stood up, signaling an end to the discussion. "I want to see you and him in my office as soon as he gets back. We need to come up with a new strategy."

It was late when Josh ushered Jefferson into the office. Savage stood in front of the blazing fire and bent down to toss another piece of wood into the flames. He bade the men to sit down, walked over to his desk, pulled out a bottle of whisky and filled three glasses. The men tossed down their drinks.

"Sergeant Jefferson, Josh tells me that you have a plan how to catch the rustlers?" Savage looked at him expectantly.

Jefferson's clothes steamed and emitted an odor of wet wool. "I might." He set down his empty glass and watched as Savage refilled it. "Can't say it's a foolproof plan, but it might work."

"Any plan is better than none," Savage replied impatiently. "We've got to do something. What have you got to offer?"

"Major, I got me an old army map showing the terrain north of here," Jefferson said. "You mind?" Without waiting for an answer, he pushed the items on his Savage's desk aside and unfolded the map. The three men clustered together and studied it in silence.

"Here's the Double-T ranch." Jefferson pointed to a spot he had marked with a red X. "Here's where the rustlers hid the cattle last time." He pointed to a spot west of the ranch.

"I think the rustlers would be more than stupid using that same hiding place again." Savage mused.

"Not likely unless they are really stupid," Jefferson agreed.

"Josh, what do you think?"

The foreman ran his hand lightly over the map, causing the dry paper to crackle. "Naw, they ain't that dumb. Them rustlers know that we're onto their hideout. Besides, there's a lot of other places north of here they can hide out in." He shot a longing look at his empty whiskey glass, but his boss was too engrossed in the map to pay attention.

"So what's your plan then?" Savage asked.

"I think the rustlers are herding your cattle up to this canyon." Savage's eyes followed Jefferson's outstretched finger. "It's only about fifteen miles east of their old hideout. It's a small box canyon, but there's plenty of grass and water. I came across it before I ran into you."

"Any indication that someone had used it in the past?" Savage asked.

Jefferson shook his head. "No, but you could hide a pretty big herd in there for a couple of months. That's what I would do if I was rustling cattle in the valley."

Savage contemplated the map. "That leaves the question whether the rustlers know about the canyon. I sure didn't. It's still on my land, isn't it?"

"You ain't tryin' to hide your cows, Major," the old Sergeant said and bent over the map. "I figger whoever is responsible for the rustling has been scouting that whole area up here," Jefferson pointed to a spot on the map, "lookin' for a safe place to hold their loot. Ain't no question but they know that terrain better than we do. Looks like the rustlers cut out small bunches of cows at a time, so's not to seem too obvious and stash 'em away in the canyon until they have enough of a herd to make it worth their while."

Savage leaned over the map, brow furrowed, studying it in silence, thinking about what Jefferson had said. The only sound in the room was the ticking of the grandfather clock. "Makes sense," he said after a while and straightened up. "Josh, I need someone to hightail it up there to check it out, somebody who knows the terrain."

"That would be me," Jefferson cut in.

"You?" Savage eyed him suspiciously.

Jefferson 's eyes were locked on Savage. "Yeah, me. It's a challenge, I guess. Maybe I want to earn my keep. Maybe I want to see if my theory is correct. Maybe I just want to be alone by myself for a while. I don't see where it makes any difference. I just know I spent some time studying this map and I know I can find the place again."

"Finding the place is one thing. What we do when we find it is another."

Rufus busied himself folding the old map. He hesitated and cleared his throat. "Well, that brings me to my plan. Major, you remember the summer of sixty-three in Virginia when we were looking to find where the Rebs was holed up? When we found out, we didn't go after them one by one but waited till they joined the other contingents. And then we swept in and got 'em all in one fell swoop? I figger that we're in a similar position now, only that we ain't after the confederates. But we might use a similar strategy." He stopped to gauge Savage's reaction.

Savage frowned at the old soldier. "Yes, I remember that particular operation." He opened the drawer of his desk and put the whisky bottle away.

Jefferson returned the map to its leather case and closed it. "If I'm right and the rustlers are stashing your cattle in that canyon, we ought to pull a faint by sending a bunch of our men to look for the missing cows in the canyon where we found them the first time."

"Why would you do a dern fool thing like that?' Josh protested. "If we know..."

Savage cut off the foreman with a wave of his hand. "Let him finish, Josh." He nodded to Jefferson. "Go on, I'm listening."

"Since we'll come up empty," Rufus continued, ignoring the interruption, "we'll search west of there, making them think we ain't on to them. In the meantime we'll set up some kind of surveillance system to track their operation. We know they can't trail a herd of any size south of here. Too obvious. Same thing going due west. They can't push any livestock east because the Double-T compound is smack dab in the middle of the trail. North is the only way they can go." He looked at Savage. "You with me so far?"

Savage nodded.

"This canyon being a box canyon, there is only one way in – and out, which means that the rustlers won't need a whole bunch of hands to guard the herd. It's like a giant cattle pen. I would recommend that we let 'em... uh, that we don't interfere with their activities and let 'em figure that we don't know what they're up to. If they see us looking in the wrong places, they might get careless. My thinking behind all this is that you might catch 'em all at once instead of chasing 'em all over the place. You don't have enough hands to do that."

The foreman had been sitting quietly, head down, looking at his boots, listening to Rufus' plan. He wasn't sure whether he liked what he heard. Hell, he *knew* he didn't like Rufus' plan. Josh would have preferred to meet the rustlers head-on. It seemed like a dumb idea to let a bunch of thieves drive off the Major's cattle, even if it was part of some grand plan. Rustling was rustling. His job as foreman was to see to the welfare of the Major's stock. Rufus Jefferson was turning the rules upside down. Catch the rustlers once and for all, hang 'em high and get this matter over with so they could go back to ranching. Josh looked up and saw that his boss was watching him, sensing his foreman's reservations.

"Josh, you look skeptical."

The foreman leaned forward and rested his elbows on his thighs. He rolled the empty whiskey glass between his hands. "I'm not sure, boss. Seems a lot of work to me to catch a bunch of lowdown thieves. I just don't rightly cotton to the idea letting 'em steal our cows and holding 'em. Especially if we know where they got 'em stashed. I guess I don't think like a soldier, so I can't say. You're the boss and I'll do whatever you think is right."

Savage sat down behind his desk. "Look, I know how you feel. I don't like some damn thieves, any thieves, to be in possession of my cattle even for a minute. But – and here comes the big but – if we hit them every time they steal some of my cows, I don't think we'll ever be able to catch the brains behind this operation. We need to outsmart them and Mr. Jefferson's plan makes a lot of sense to me."

Jefferson met the rancher back in his office at first dawn. The old army map was spread out in front of them and Savage looked over the old soldier's shoulder following his finger tracing the route he would take to the rustler's canyon.

"The only way for the rustlers to drive the cattle to the canyon is along this valley," Jefferson was saying, moving his finger across the map. "I aim to take this route, up here." His finger traced a different line on the map. "I don't expect to run across any of the outlaws up there. Too high, too many rocks, not enough grass. They have to stay down in the valley with the cattle."

"Sounds good." Savage said. "How long do you think it'll take you?"

"About two days to get up there." Jefferson slapped the map case for emphasis. "I don't know how long I'll be gone. It all depends how long it takes to scout out the canyon. I'll take my old tent and some grub."

Savage stood up. "I'm going with you. I want to see first-hand where they are stashing my cattle. Wait here until I get my gear together."

Jefferson's face hardened. "This was my idea, dammit and I don't need you to come along. Ain't you got better things to do, Major, like running your ranch?"

Savage shot him a malevolent look. "This is my cattle we're looking for, you understand? I can't run this ranch properly until the rustling problem is solved. I'm coming with you. If you don't want to come along, I'll go by myself."

The two formidable men glowered at each other. Finally Jefferson shrugged. "Have it your way, Major. It's your call. Let's not waste anymore time."

Savage and Jefferson rode out after breakfast, trailing a packhorse loaded with supplies. The rain had stopped the night before. The ground was still wet but it was a pleasant, late spring day which did not require an overcoat. They traveled due east at a leisurely pace and made camp after sunset in a hollow surrounded by spruce and aspen with a fresh growth of leaves. A cool wind had sprung up which came in short gusts, rustling the tall grass around them. It tugged at the campfire flames and blew the thin smoke in their faces, making their eyes burn. The two men spent the time in silence, washing their food down with several cups of steaming coffee. The horses cropped grass nearby and they could hear the swish of their tails. Occasionally one of the horses would raise its head and shake its mane before seeking the fresh grass again. Feeling sated, Jefferson left Savage sitting by the fire and retired to his sleeping bag. Savage stayed behind and savored the cool night air. The fire had burned down and an ascending silver moon hung suspended over the black silhouettes of evergreens standing shoulder to shoulder at the end of the meadow. It promised to be a peaceful night.

Jefferson was still angry. He had looked forward to traveling alone, especially having spent the past week listening to the shallow prattle of the other cowhands, their rude jokes, boasts and innuendos. Just last week, a young hand who had recently hired on with the Double-T spread had looked at Jefferson's army tunic with the faded chevrons and announced that black soldiers were cowards. No black man should hold a command position because "niggers" didn't know how to fight. "Ain't that right, Boy?" he had addressed Jefferson and started to smirk when Rufus' fist drove into his mouth, knocking him out of his chair. The kid had spat blood for the rest of the evening and took his leave the next day mumbling dark threats. It was good to lie under the stars alone with one's thoughts - where nobody cared what color your skin was - before drifting off to sleep.

During the night the wind came whispering over the western mountain range, gathering strength crossing the plain and roared through the valley, uprooting trees along the way. An avalanche of air mixed with driving rain cascaded over and around the ranch buildings, trying in vain to sweep them off their foundations. An hour later Savage and Jefferson, camping twenty miles east of the ranch, awakened with a start when a large white bark tree crashed to the ground dangerously close to where they had spread their bedrolls. Buffeted by the gale and drenched by the rain they cursed and fought the wind for their sleeping bags. Jefferson hurried to untie the horses and with the Major's assistance led them to a small depression nearby, which gave them and the animals a modicum of protection from the storm.

The storm moved on as quickly as it had arrived. After an early breakfast, the two men, exhausted from lack of sleep, saddled up the horses, scattered the fire and mounted up. They consulted the old army map and angled north and, after several hours' ride, reached the foothills. The ground became steeper and rockier and they chose their trail with care. Ahead of them they saw a sheer, severely eroded cliff wall, rising a hundred feet out of the ground. The path leading up to it was strewn with boulders of varying sizes which had broken loose from the wall over the centuries. Wildflowers grew among the rocks in a riot of colors. A golden eagle floated high above the wall and small animals, too quick to be identified, flitted from rock to rock, spooking the horses. The two men rode west, parallel to the wall until the faint trail led up over the cliff. Dipping down into a draw on the other side, they came upon a narrow river, which over thousands of years had cut into the massive rock, forming a deep gorge. Savage and Jefferson rode along the rushing water until they found a natural bridge which arched high over the small stream. They stopped on the other side of the creek, dismounted and consulted the map again. The mouth of the canyon was only a few miles away.

The shadows had already begun to lengthen when the two men finally approached their destination. With mounting anticipation, they urged their horses forward. From a distance, the rim of the canyon was marked by huge boulders which were stacked on top of each other in random fashion as if thrown together by a race of giants now long extinct. Keeping a safe distance, they rode along the outer edge of the canyon towards its entrance before deciding on a spot to set up camp. They hobbled their mounts, unburdened the pack horse, and walked to the edge of the canyon, taking care to keep close to cover. Savage, with Jefferson right behind him, crawled between the rocks until he found a protected spot which offered a wide view of the terrain below. What he saw caused him to draw his breath in sharply. He felt a sense of outrage tempered by a strange satisfaction that Jefferson's hunch had been correct. Below them the canyon stretched about a mile in length and measured half a mile across. A swift-flowing stream fed the small lake nestled in the middle of the canyon, and the rays of the setting sun turned the water into a pool of molten gold. In the center of the grassy plain, still showing patches of snow, he saw one hundred and seventy five to two hundred head of his own cattle. *The rustlers had been busy*, he thought with mounting fury.

Savage studied the herd through his binoculars. They were too far away to make out the brands, but the cows were Herefords which the Double-T ranch specialized in. His gaze swept the canyon and focused in on a small structure just below his position, a sod-covered dugout. Smoke from its makeshift chimney spiraled lazily upward and dissipated in the fresh alpine air.

Except for the smoke there were no signs of human activity. Two horses, a dun, and a paint were grazing inside a crudely fashioned corral next to the dugout. It stood to reason that the men guarding the cattle were inside the dugout. They would have to come out sooner than later.

"We don't both of us have to set here and watch for them varmints to show themselves," Jefferson said. "Why don't you keep watch and I'll mosey on back to set up camp."

Savage nodded and settled in for a wait. The last rays of the sun warmed his back. He yawned and closed his eyes. When he opened them what appeared to be a few seconds later, it was dark. Damn, he hadn't meant to doze off. Grumbling to himself, he made his way back to camp in the faint light of the moon, ate the food that Jefferson handed him. Over his coffee Savage told the old soldier that he had seen enough and would head back home in the morning. They agreed that Jefferson would stay behind to keep an eye on the rustlers.

"You sure you can find your way back, Major?" Jefferson asked with a malicious grin.

Savage sighed and poured the dregs of his coffee on the ground. He looked at Jefferson. "Look, Sergeant-Major, I know you hate my guts and I can't blame you. I never meant to send you and your squad into harm's way but I had my orders. You've been in the service long enough to know what that means. You may believe me when I say that the deaths of those men will stay with me for the rest of my life, even after all these years. What I would like to know is to whether you intend to carry this grudge to the grave or see fit to bury the hatchet." He extended his hand.

Jefferson was silent for a long time. Savage was about to retract his hand when the old soldier reached out and seized it in a powerful grip. "Consider the hatchet buried," he said in a gruff voice. They wordlessly shook hands. While Jefferson remained at the fire, Savage unrolled his sleeping bag. He yawned, lay down and fell asleep.

The rancher had left before sunup and Jefferson was back at his observation point under the rocks early the following morning. Nothing had changed below. There was still no sight of any humans. The dun was cropping grass contentedly inside the corral but the paint was gone. Smoke curled up from the chimney of the dugout. Jefferson took care that his binoculars did not reflect the sun and counted the cattle spread across the bottom of the canyon. His tally was one-hundred-and-eighty-five head, give or take a few. The canyon would easily be able to hold ten times that number of cows. Sudden movement near the draw that led to the canyon entrance caught his eye. Focusing his binoculars Jefferson saw that it was a rider on the missing paint, heading towards the dugout. The man dismounted, led the horse into the corral, took off the saddle and carried it inside the dugout, closing the door behind him. A few minutes later, another man stepped out, put on his hat and saddled the dun. He climbed onto his horse, kneed it forward and rode off in the direction of the canyon mouth. Jefferson put aside his binoculars, rummaged in his pocket for a piece of hard tack and settled in for the day.

17

When Savage returned from his surveillance trip he found a young cowpoke waiting for him. He brought word from Bert Sanders, the second largest cattle owner in the valley, that seventy head of Herefords Savage had sold to him had been rustled. "They stole them Herefords but left our Longhorns be," the messenger said. "The old man is fit to be tied and he and his boys want to have a powwow with you, the sooner the better. He wants to know whether that would be agreeable with you."

Savage nodded. "Tell him I want to talk to him too. I'll expect him and his boys on Friday. That's two days from now and should give him plenty of time to make his way up here. Also, tell him that the marshal will be joining us. I have been keeping him up to date on the matter." Savage turned to go. He stopped and turned back. "Get yourself some grub before you head back."

Marshal Boudreaux arrived at the Double-T ranch before sundown on Thursday. As he dismounted he was greeted by his friend. The men shook hands.

"Come inside, Ed, you must be tired."

"Nothing that a shot of your finest whisky won't fix, Ben," Boudreaux said and slapped the road dust off his clothes.

"How was your trip?" Savage asked the marshal as he led him into his office. "I hope I didn't tear you away from anything important."

Boudreaux gratefully tossed down the drink which Savage handed him and set the glass down on the desk. "The trip was fine. Truth be told, I was glad to get away from my daily chores for a while. Coming up here is almost like a vacation – provided you feed me well."

Savage laughed, "I'll see what Trudy can rustle up. Incidentally, you got my message that Bert Sanders and his sons will join us tomorrow, right? Seems they lost all the Herefords which I sold him a while back."

"I heard." Boudreaux leaned back in his armchair and stretched his legs out in front of him. "Sanders isn't the only victim. Day before yesterday, Jonah Manson rode into town all upset to complain to me that their Herefords were stolen also."

Savage raised his eyebrows. "Really? I don't know what to make of the Manson brothers," he said. "I guess if they're getting rustled too, but…" He shrugged his shoulders.

"But what, Ben?" Boudreaux persisted.

"Just a feeling," Savage replied.

"By the way, didn't you also sell some of your cattle to Luther Eaton?"

Savage gave the marshal a quizzical look. "Yes. Why? Did he lose his cattle too?"

Boudreaux shook his head. "No, that's just it. When Phil Garrett asked him about it, Eaton got all flustered and defensive and accused Phil of trying to hang something on him. Luther told him that he and his hands would shoot anyone who came on his land. Said this warning applied to me and my deputy, too. Looks to me that he may have something to hide."

"Eaton? I never did like that fellow. He's a grumpy SOB and impolite but I didn't think he would be stealing my cattle. He's a neighbor, for God's sake."

The marshal shrugged. "So are the Mansons. That doesn't necessarily prove anything. Mind you, we have no evidence that he actually is involved." He gestured at Savage, "Anyway, have you got any plans as to how to put an end to this rustling business?"

Savage nodded and refilled the marshal's glass. "To be fair, it was Sergeant Jefferson who came up with one. I need to talk it over with you and Sanders and see what you think."

"Why don't you tell me now, Ben? We can fill Old Man Sanders in later."

Savage leaned forward in his chair, arms on his thighs and briefly outlined the strategy that Rufus Jefferson had devised. "Jefferson's hunch was on the button. He and I rode up to the canyon together and, sure enough, that's where the rustlers are stashing the stolen cows. Jefferson is still up there, keeping an eye on their activities."

"So you're going to wait until they've rustled all your stock?" Boudreaux asked his friend half in jest.

"Hardly. They can handle only so many head. No sense in rustling more than they can sell."

"So where do I come in?"

"I know that this entire operation is outside your jurisdiction but I would just like you to continue to keep your eyes and ears open, you know, for any unusual activity. Strangers in town, rumors of any kind, that sort of thing. And I'd like you to keep an eye on Luther Eaton. I'm beginning to distrust that son-of-a-bitch after what you told me."

"Ben, we don't know whether Eaton is behind all this," Boudreaux cautioned his friend, "but I'll check him out a bit more."

Savage frowned at the marshal. "Just don't get yourself killed, Ed. Eaton is an ornery cuss and might make good his threat to shoot."

Boudreaux waived his friend's concern aside. "Don't worry about me. I know how to take care of myself. Eaton doesn't scare me."

"Well, anyway, it doesn't hurt to take precautions." Savage got up to toss another log on the fire, watching the sparks dance up the chimney. "I'm hoping that by putting on some kind of pressure, the rustlers will figure to cut the risk and run. With the rustled stock, of course. When that time comes, Jefferson believes that the whole nest of vipers will congregate in the canyon and that's when we close the barn door." Savage paused and contemplated his visitor. "And I agree with him. Does that make sense to you?"

Boudreaux grinned at Savage, "So you two blue bellies have been playing soldier again."

"Yes, Johnny Reb." Savage responded and gave his friend a mock salute. "Jefferson is one cantankerous bastard but I have to admit that I have great respect for the man. He was antagonistic toward me and yet he put in a lot of time to figure out how to help me solve the biggest problem I have."

"Dinner, Major." Trudy Wilhelm stuck her head through the door. "Better eat it before it gets cold."

"In a minute, Trudy." Savage stood up and turned back to Boudreaux. "I know you have your plate full back in town, Ed and I hate to ask you to shoulder this burden, which is really my problem."

"Goes with the territory." Boudreaux stood up to join Savage. "I have little doubt that my problems in town and your rustling problems are interrelated. I can't get shed of my problems without helping you solve yours." He preceded Savage into the dining room. "I'm sure we can get Bert Sanders in on that scheme. He's boiling mad about losing his best cows and I for one wouldn't want a guy like Bert for an enemy."

18

At five minutes after ten the following morning, Old Man Sanders, followed by two of his cowboys rode into the Double-T compound where he was greeted by Savage. Savage respected Sanders as he had literally carved his spread out of the wilderness. In the late forties when the southern ranges became overstocked, Bert, then a young man of twenty-two, gathered his little herd of longhorns. With the help of two hired hands, he had embarked on a two-thousand-mile journey north. He found the land he was looking for in the valley and settled on a thousand acres which he enlarged to ten times its size over the years, eventually butting up against the boundaries of the Double-T spread. After several years of raising cows and fighting Indians, Bert took a Cheyenne Indian woman as his common law wife. In time she bore him two sons and a daughter, who combined the best genes of both races. Despite being called half breeds and red niggers behind their backs, they were widely respected as skilled cattlemen and many a white man came calling on Bert's attractive daughter.

Sanders had been in a towering rage ever since the rustlers had made off with his prized cows and it showed. Shortly after the old rancher's arrival, he, Savage and the marshal seated themselves around a small table in Savage's office. The morning sun was slanting through the open window and a mild breeze carried the sounds and earthy smells of the ranch into the room past the undulating curtains.

The old rancher sat stiffly in his chair, resting his arthritic hands on his thighs. "I guess the marshal told you that my Herefords were stolen. I hear you got a plan how to get our cattle back?"

"Yes, I do," Savage said. "First of all, I should tell you that we know where the rustling gang are stashing our cattle. One of my men and I rode up to a canyon northeast of here, about a two-day ride, and found about two hundred head stashed there. I have no doubt that the rustlers are busy adding to that number. They are–"

Listening to Savage, Sanders had been drumming his fingers impatiently. When he heard about the cattle, he raised his hand to stop Savage in mid-sentence. "You find my cows?" he asked.

"Bert, we couldn't make out any brands, even with the binoculars. The cattle were too far inside the canyon. That said, I wouldn't be surprised if your cows are among the ones we saw. Unless, of course, they are still being trailed up there," Savage replied. "My man is up there keeping an eye on the operation. I expect him back tomorrow to give me an update. So here's the plan. Even though we know where they are stashing our cattle, I intend to send out my hands on a deliberate goose chase to keep the rustlers thinking we aren't on to them. By that, I mean I will have my boys pretending to check out every part of the country north of here, except for that canyon."

Wait, wait." Sanders held up an incredulous hand to stop Savage. "Major, excuse me if I sound a little confused. You mean to tell me you're actually gonna allow those rustlers to steal your cows?" He looked confused and shook his white head. "No cowman in his right mind would stand by and knowingly let somebody rustle their stock."

Savage glanced at the marshal who was sitting quietly next to him before turning back to the old rancher. "I'll admit that all this sounds unusual, but I'm hoping that our plan will instill in the rustlers a false sense of security, make them careless and thus make it easier for us to close the barn door. No please, Bert." Savage waved his hand to ward off the older man's further protestations. "Please hear me out. Rather then trying to catch one or two of them in the act of stealing a few cows, we're hoping to nab them all at once. I may be wrong, but I believe that knowing that you and I are joining forces the rustlers will feel that they have to speed things up. They can only move so many cows and as soon as we feel that they are ready to move the rustled herd, we'll spring the trap."

Bert Sanders was not convinced. "What do you make of the plan, Marshal?" he said.

"I like it. Sounds like a good plan to me," the marshal said.

Sanders shook his head, still not convinced. "So, where do I come in?" he asked.

"There are a couple of ways in which you could be of great help." Savage said. "For one, we thought that it might be a good idea if one or both of your sons could join my scout up at the canyon. I know that both your boys are excellent trackers and four eyes are better than two."

Bert Sanders thought for a while, nodded, and ran an arthritic hand through his white hair. "Agreed. What's the other?"

"You could start a search for your cattle."

"I'm already doing that," the old rancher said irritably. "You didn't expect me to sit on my behind while some outlaws steal my cows, did you?"

"No, of course not," Savage hastened to reassure Sanders. "I didn't mean to imply that at all. I just wonder whether you'd be willing to play along by pretending to look for our cattle north of here while we keep an eye on the canyon. Once we know that they're ready to drive them to wherever they plan to drive them, we'll move in and take our cattle back." He looked expectantly at the old rancher, waiting for an answer.

Sanders took his time considering Savage's proposal. "Tell you frankly," he grumbled, "it basically goes against every fiber in my body not to go after these hoodlums and get my cows back. I had to fight for every head, every piece of land when I first settled here. The only way to stay alive was to hit back hard." He sighed and shrugged his massive shoulders. "I guess times have changed and I can see the benefit in what y'all are planning to do. So, yes, I'm willing to give your plan a try, especially if you think that it'll put a stop to rustling once and for all."

"Excellent." Savage slapped his thighs and got up. The others stood up also. "All we need to do now is set up some kind of system whereby we keep each other up to date on what's going on. I'd also like to introduce your sons to the man who's doing the scouting up at the rustler's Canyon." Ben paused and regarded the old rancher. "There's something I should tell you, though. My scout's Black. He's a retired Sergeant-Major. He's also the one who came up with the plan we just discussed. Do you think your sons would be willing to work alongside a Negro?"

"Why would my boys have a problem with that?" the old rancher scoffed. "Both James and his brother John have been called half breeds and red niggers all their lives. I'm sure your man and my boys will get along just fine."

"Good. That's settled then - oh yes, there's one more thing," Savage said. "We need to keep this plan to ourselves. My foreman knows about it but I don't think we should tell the hired hands what we're up to. If the word gets out, we'll lose the element of surprise and the whole plan won't be worth a damn."

Sanders nodded. "I won't tell anybody but my boys." The old rancher walked to the door and rested a gnarled hand on the doorknob. Savage asked him to stay for lunch but the old rancher declined. "I had best head on back. I can't spare both my sons but will send James over to your place as soon as I get back. You can fill him in on the rest."

Bert Sanders shook hands with the two men and left the room, closing the door behind him.

"I have to get back to town, Ben," Boudreaux said. "Keep me up to date on how this matter plays out." He picked up his hat. "Thanks for your hospitality. See you in town."

19

Amy had dismissed her pupils and sat behind her desk looking at a stack of essay papers which she needed to correct over the weekend. There was no hurry and she could not bring herself to read the mostly ink-stained papers on which her pupils had scribbled their assignments. Amy toyed with her pen and stared out of the small window with unseeing eyes, suddenly realizing that she was lonely. She wondered idly what it would feel like to be in love. The only interesting man in the valley was Ben Savage. The big rancher was clearly smitten with her but he was not someone she was willing to accept, let alone associate with. What nerve he had to come calling on her, catching her off guard. She shook her head angrily at the very thought of it. For all his wealth, good looks, manners and yes – she had to admit to herself – a certain charm, he was a callous, uncaring cowman. She smiled in grim satisfaction at the memory of having put him in his place.

Amy pulled the essay papers closer when she heard footsteps and a jingle of spurs. She looked up with a frown. For a brief moment she thought that Savage had returned only to find the grinning face of Seth Manson looming over her. The cowboy reeked of a mixture of sweat, liquor, and cow manure. His shirt was stained and covered with dust. When he saw her look up at him, he leaned forward on her desk with his hands, causing the young woman to shrink back into her chair.

"Sorry for the way I look, Miss Amy." He smiled apologetically. "I been ridin' all day and didn't have no time to get cleaned up. But I wanted to see you; I surely did." He remembered his hat and yanked it off, uncovering a shock of blond hair. "They's a dance tonight down at Murphy's Café and I'd be tickled pink if you'd accept my invitation. It's gonna be a lot of fun." He searched Amy's face. "You come with me and I'll make you have a good time, sure as shootin'." He gave her a beseeching look. "How about it, Miss Amy?"

The penetrating odor surrounding Seth Manson was so overpowering that Amy held her breath. His persistence in pursuing her annoyed her, and it showed in her face. Despite his engaging grin there was something menacing about Seth Manson, something that she felt but could not explain.

"I'm sorry I have to disappoint you again," Amy replied, trying to sound friendly. "Do you see all this homework?" She pointed to the pile of paper on her desk. "I need to work on this tonight." She forced a smile. "A teacher's work is never done."

Seth Manson's eyes narrowed and his grin tightened into something reminiscent of a grimace. "Aw, come on, Miss Amy. You can do that stuff some other time. Them kids won't mind a bit. You come dancin' with me tonight and I'll show you a real good time, I promise. How about it?"

"I'm sorry but I can't, Mr. Manson."

"It's Seth. If I didn't know no better, I'd think you're avoiding me. You got somebody else?"

"I don't think that that is any of your business, Mr. Manson," Amy said in a measured voice. "Now, if you'll excuse me," she reached for the stack of papers and pulled it close, "I have work to do."

Seth Manson's eyes went flat. "You think I ain't good enough for you because I ain't got much education. I don't need no book-learnin' to know how to make a woman happy." He leaned across the desk, causing Amy to shrink back further. "I don't like bein' turned down, hear? I'm gonna keep comin' after you till you give in." He leaned forward and the smile that made Amy so uncomfortable returned. "You'll learn to appreciate me yet."

Amy's eyes turned cold. "Don't trouble yourself, Mr. Manson. I have no interest in being courted by you. As a matter of fact I find it most annoying. You'd only be wasting your time. Now, if you'll excuse me, I have papers to correct."

The cowboys face turned red and his smile vanished. "You'll regret this, Missy. I don't take no fer an answer."

"Please go and leave me alone," Amy said.

Without a sound, but with a look that terrified Amy, Seth Manson stood up straight and looked at the homework on Amy's desk. With one swift motion, he grabbed the stack of papers and threw it across the room, scattering the pages. "There," he said with grim satisfaction. "Your homework's done. I'll be seeing you." Without pausing, he turned and strode out the door, slamming it shut, leaving nothing but the smell of his clothes and rank odor lingering in the room.

20

Sergeant Jefferson perched in his natural fortress surveying the canyon in front of him. Nothing new had happened since Savage's departure to arouse his interest. Most of the time the two rustlers guarding the herd lazed about in the sun. The shorter and skinnier of the two would mount up occasionally to round up strays and drive them away from the canyon's mouth. Munching on some hardtack, Jefferson watched the rustlers quarrel with each other, high-pitched voices growing louder, until the tall one drove his fist into the other man's face, knocking him off his feet. Jefferson cupped his ear straining to listen, but the rustlers were too far away for him to make out what the quarrel was about. After a while, the man who had been knocked down stirred, pushed himself off the ground, and disappeared in the dugout.

The sun had reached its zenith and its rays devoured the shadows filling his lookout, forcing Jefferson to move to a cooler spot. He flexed his shoulders and stretched his legs to relieve the strain in his back. Despite a small breeze, temperatures began to climb. The air in the canyon shimmered, transposing the grazing cattle into odd, undulating shapes. Insects buzzed among the flowers which sprouted from cracks in the rocks and the day settled into a slow rhythm. Jefferson's eyelids grew heavy, and his head began to nod.

He was torn out of his lethargy by three gun reports following in rapid succession. He grabbed his binoculars and scanned the terrain to his front. The man inside the dugout erupted from the door. The two rustlers jumped on their ponies and galloped toward the mouth of the canyon. Jefferson watched them rein in their horses. One of them waved his hat in a wide arc over his head. A short time later, he heard the lowing of cattle and a herd of Herefords moved slowly into view, urged on by four horsemen. When the herd came closer, Jefferson counted heads and arrived at a tally of approximately one-hundred-and-fifty cows. The horsemen drove the herd deeper into the canyon where they mingled contentedly with the earlier arrivals. Leaving the cattle to fend for themselves, the newcomers rode over to the dugout where they dismounted and slapped their horses' rumps hazing them into the corral. The short man unburdened the two pack mules the rustlers had brought along and carried the provisions into the dugout. The remaining five men squatted on the ground, smoking, talking, passing a bottle among them. There was occasional laughter, shouts, and more talking. It was obvious to Jefferson that the rustlers did not see the need to be vigilant and that they felt quite safe in their hideout.

The day passed without further developments; and when darkness set in, he left his post and returned to camp. He decided to spend another night and check on his prey in the morning before returning home. He felt satisfied, proud even, knowing that his theory had been correct. Now it became a matter of timing. How big a herd did the rustlers plan to put together, he wondered. Once they showed up in force it would be a sure sign that they were ready to remove the herd from its hiding place. That was the moment to spring the trap and get them all in one quick action. Timing was of the essence. He needed to get back to the ranch and share his findings with the Major.

Two days later, Savage stood on his porch, watching the tall Sergeant ride in.

"Any new developments?" he asked when Jefferson reigned up his Black in front of him.

"Yeah, just as I expected. The gang now has more than three hundred head stashed in the canyon at this point and it looks like they've gone back for more. There's still only two men guarding the herd."

"Did you by any chance recognize any of the men?"

Jefferson shook his head. "I counted six men. Didn't recognize any of them. Probably not from this neck of the woods." Jefferson took off his hat and wiped his forehead with his sleeve. "One thing I don't understand, Major. The rustlers didn't post any lookouts. They must really feel safe in that canyon." He picked up the reins of his horse. "I'm gonna get myself some shuteye. Been a long day."

"Thank you, Mr. Jefferson," Savage replied. "For your information, I'll be riding into town tomorrow to fill the marshal in on what you told me."

Jefferson nodded and turned his back.

"Sergeant-Major Jefferson," Savage called after him, causing the old soldier to pause, though he kept his back turned to the Major. "Just wanted to tell you that I appreciate what you've been doing to help me solve my rustling problem."

Without looking back Jefferson raised his hand in reply and rode off in the direction of the corral.

21

Billy Craig had been in the employ of the Double-T Ranch for the past two weeks. He was a seventeen year old bright-eyed, tow-headed kid of slender build who had learned cow on his Uncle Esau's small spread in New Mexico. His parents had died early; and his uncle, an embittered confederate survivor of the Civil War had taken him in and worked him hard. When Esau was thrown by a bronc and died, Billy decided to try his luck up north. His uncle's ranch had been all but worthless, but Billy had inherited a brand new fancy saddle which Esau had won in a riding competition and a rusty Colt which he carried with him but which he had never used. He and his friend Roberto had drifted north; and the Double-T ranch, desperate for hired hands, had been glad to take them on. Only two weeks later, the ranch foreman had sent him and his friend to look for strays that might be hiding in the many draws and coulees that dominated the north-eastern part of the ranch.

He and Roberto had split up this morning, each planning to make a wide sweep to search for strays and meet back at the eastern line shack in the evening. Billy was eager to prove himself in the eyes of both his employer and fellow cowboys and his search had taken him further than expected. Now he reined in his pony and looked around him. This new country with its lush vegetation and majestic snow-covered mountains, its streams and shimmering lakes was a source of endless fascination for him. He had heard that the winters were severe and long, but he was sure that he could adapt to the cold. Winters in New Mexico could be cold too. In his mind, the future opened up before him and he resolved to save his money, buy some cattle, and become a rancher himself. Maybe not as big as his new boss, the Major, but a prosperous rancher nevertheless. It was an exhilarating thought and he pictured the house and outbuildings which he would construct with his own hands. Maybe he would find himself a nice girl, willing to share her life with him. They'd have kids and ... Billy shook his head to clear his thoughts for the task at hand. He was eager to find some strays to please his foreman and show him that he was earning his wages.

The sun stood at its highest point when Billy thought he heard the lowing of cattle. He cupped his hand behind his ear and stood up in his stirrups to scan the terrain around him. There, he heard the unmistakable sound again. He touched his spurs to his horse's flanks and angled north to follow the sound. What a stroke of luck! This was great. He pictured the pleased look on the foreman's face when he and Roberto showed up at the ranch with a bunch of strays. That would show him that he was every bit as good as the more seasoned cowboys.

The bawling increased in volume and he was surprised at how many cattle could have strayed this far. He hurried his horse onto the crest of the ridge for a closer look. What he saw caused him to rein in his pony in surprise. He had found a bunch of cows alright, a big bunch, but they were being driven north by five cowhands.

"What the–" Billy began, but the zing of a bullet ricocheting off a rock on the ground next to him, followed by the report of a gun, cut him short. Consumed by a sudden fear for his life, he sawed his pony around. A rider was pounding toward him up the draw at full speed, his arms pumping in rhythm with his horse's gait. Billy dug in his spurs and bent low over the saddle to present as small a target as possible. As his pony raced over the uneven ground, he threw a glance back over his shoulder and saw the rider still in hot pursuit. He tried to outdistance the other rider frantically whipping his horse and applying his spurs, when he heard the report of a gun again.

"Oh God, please, no!" Billy prayed under his breath. He had never been shot at before and never had he been as afraid for his life as he was now. Coming up a small incline, his horse lost its footing and went down, spilling him out of the saddle. He scrambled to his feet and ran, trying to flee his pursuer. Another shot and this time the bullet caught the young cowboy in the back, breaking his spine and sending him sprawling face down. Billy tried to raise his head but then lay still in a spreading pool of blood.

Dan Hittle reined in his horse, stepped out of the saddle and walked over to the lifeless figure. He turned it over with the toe of his boot. "Shit," he said and took off his sombrero and used the back of his hand to wipe the sweat from his forehead. Shit! What in hell was the kid doing this far north? Billy's horse stood nearby, reins trailing and Dan approached it cautiously trying not to spook it. He grabbed the reins and examined the brand. "Dammit to hell." This was bad news. The kid had been riding for the Double-T spread. The young cowboy's compadres were bound to come looking for him before long. And when they did that, they were sure to stumble onto the canyon which would put their whole operation in jeopardy. He would have to devise a new plan and speed up getting the herd together. And it was time to post sentries, something he should have done from the outset. He had been too complacent. Well, that was about to change.

As he contemplated his next move, Dan fingered the saddle on the dead cowboy's horse. Where did such a scrawny kid with his threadbare duds and worn boots get such a fancy rig? *He must've stole it or won it playin' poker*, Dan thought. He looked at his well-used saddle and decided it was time for a trade.

He was changing saddles when two of his crew came riding up.

"I see you got him," one of them, a stocky man who went by the name of Conrad said approvingly. He stepped off his mount, knelt next to the dead boy and proceeded to go through his pockets. He came up with an envelope, examined it and tossed it aside. He pulled Jimmy's pistol out of its holster, shook his head in wonder and held it up to Dan. "Look at that thing," he said scornfully. "All rusty." He rotated the cylinder. "Hell, it ain't even loaded. That's the crappiest pistol I ever seen." He looked at the other man who was still astride his horse, "You want it?"

"Hell no, what would I want it for?"

Conrad shrugged and dropped the revolver next to Billy's body. He stood up and looked at Dan's horse. "Nice saddle you got yourself there, Dan," he said, a twinge of envy in his voice.

Dan ignored the remark. "Bury the kid and let's go. We got a lot of work to do, so don't take all day, hear?" He mounted up and rode off, trailing Billy's horse behind him.

"Get off that horse, dammit, and start digging." Conrad snapped at the other rider.

The other man took his time dismounting. "Shoot. Why bury him? Let's just throw him in the ravine here. I ain't gonna sweat up no storm digging no hole for some dead cowpuncher. C'mon. Help me pitch him over the side."

Conrad shrugged without replying. When the other rider had dismounted, they picked up the corpse by its arms and legs, swung it back and forth twice, and on the count of three pitched it in a high arc into the ravine. Bouncing down the steep grade, accompanied by a small avalanche of dirt and rocks, the body came to rest on the bottom. It looked small and insignificant lying on its side, discarded like a piece of trash. The men dusted off their hands and took one last look around, then climbed on their horses and followed Dan back to the herd.

Dan Hittle was talking to Cherokee Charley when Conrad rode up. "Didn't take you long to bury the kid." He growled. "What'd you do, just leave him layin' there?"

Conrad shrugged and offered no response. Hittle turned his attention back to the Indian. "Now, as I told you, that kid rode for the Double-T brand and his buddies are bound to start looking for him when he don't show up at the ranch. That means that we gotta hurry up and get more cows up here pronto, rebrand 'em, and get 'em the hell outta here." He rummaged in his saddle bag and pulled out a paper tablet and a stubby pencil. Bending over the pommel of his saddle, he licked the pencil and laboriously scribbled a note. He tore the paper off the tablet, folded it and handed it to the Indian. "Follow these directions and tell the boss and the others what happened. Tell 'em we need a change of plans. Tell 'em we need to round up a bigger herd, quicklike."

Charley took the note, tucked it into his vest pocket.

"Take the kid's buckskin, Charley. It looks like it's got bottom," Dan added.

The Indian nodded. He put his saddle on Billy's pony, mounted, and galloped off in the direction from which they had come.

"Hurry up and let's get these cows moving." Dan called to the remaining men. "We ain't far from the canyon."

22

The morning following Jefferson's return, Savage called to have his Bay saddled. Shortly thereafter, he rode out of the compound and turned south toward Riverside. His mind was on the rustling problem, and sitting astride his horse he reviewed his plan of attack, which he had promised to share with Ed Boudreaux. Having studied the layout of the rustlers' canyon, he and Sergeant-Major Jefferson had developed a strategy as to the deployment of his and Bert Sanders's men. Rather than ask Boudreaux to join him in the impending fight, Savage intended to recommend to the marshal to remain in town and keep an eye open for any unusual activities by strangers, such as the purchase of firearms or money transactions by strangers passing through town.

General Chamberlain was rested and eager to run, and Savage let him have his head. It promised to be a beautiful day and when the sun stood at the zenith, he stopped near a clear spring to rest his horse and to devour some of the biscuits which Trudy had wrapped for him.

It was getting dark when he approached the site of his line shack. Only the chimney remained. Nature had begun to invade the charred remains of the cabin, but his nostrils still perceived the faint but distinct odor of burned wood permeating the air.

Savage spent the night next to the burned shack wrapped in his bedroll. He was up again before dawn, stiff from sleeping on the ground. His fire was dead and he washed down a biscuit with water from the nearby spring, rolled up his bedroll, and saddled his Bay. *It was high time to build another shack, a better one*, he thought as he mounted up. But the rebuilding would have to wait. Right now he had more important things on his mind.

As Savage reached the outskirts of Riverside early in the afternoon, the smell of smoke caused him to sit up straight in his saddle. It was eerily similar to the odor of his line shack from the night before. Riding on, the acrid scent of burning wood and pitch increased. Savage raised his head sharply and looked about him. Further down the road, he spied a plume of black smoke rising from behind a stand of trees. Trees behind which stood Amy Cabbett's small school house. Filled with trepidation, he spurred on his horse and, bending low over the saddle raced toward the school. Over the rapid hoof beats of his Bay, he heard a cacophony of high-pitched screams and yells. As he raced past the stand of trees, what he spied filled him with a sense of dread. The small, wooden school house was nearly engulfed in flames. Smoke was pouring from the rafters; and through the shimmering waves of heat, he could see a corner of the roof collapse in a shower of sparks. Amy, covered in soot, lay on the ground, gasping for breath. She was surrounded by screaming children who looked at their schoolteacher in helpless confusion and terror.

"Don't just stand there," Savage shouted at them, jumping off his horse. "You boys go get help, fast. Go! Run as fast as you can." The boys, jolted into action dashed off in the direction of town. Savage pushed the children aside who had formed a ring around the prostrate figure on the ground, and kneeled down to feel Amy's pulse. A terrified scream from inside the burning building made his blood run cold. He jumped back to his feet.

A girl, tears streaming down her sooty face, tugged at his sleeve. "Mister, that's Joey. He and...and...Horace's still in there!" she wailed all the while pointing at the burning building. Savage tore the bandana off his neck, ran over to the pump and swung the handle to wet the cloth. He pressed it to his mouth and ran toward the building. The children stared in horror as he disappeared into a wall of dense, black smoke.

The inside of the school house was a scene of chaos and terror. Flames were licking across the wooden floor and engulfed a large part of the back wall. Thick, caustic smoke boiled around him, stinging his eyes and burning his throat. He could barely see the smoldering school desks immediately and front of him, much less the children.

"Joey, Horace, where are you?" Savage shouted, straining to hear. Off to his right, another portion of the roof collapsed in a shower of sparks. The smoke in the schoolroom thinned as it escaped through the hole in the ceiling. Breathing through his makeshift mask, Savage looked around frantically. Just as he thought he would have to give up, he spied movement out of the corner of his eye. One of the boys was crouching down, shaking another boy who lay motionless on the floor. A flaming bookshelf lay near the children, partially blocking their escape. But even as Savage saw them, the eddies of smoke closed in again like a curtain. The fire, fed by the extra oxygen from the collapsed roof, intensified; and the blistering heat ravaged the skin on his hands and face. Gasping for breath, he made toward the children just as another shower of sparks rained down on the three of them. He threw down his bandana and kicked aside the burning books. With his right arm, he scooped up the small prostrate body; and with his left, he grabbed the other boy, pulling him to his feet. "Let's go! This way." He turned back toward the door, took one step and stumbled. It was several moments before Savage realized he wasn't even moving. He still had a limp body half suspended under his right arm. The other boy lay whimpering on the ground to his left. All he could think of was the door, but in the infernal gloom his disorientation was total. Since he had stumbled, he had lost all sense of direction. God, where was that damned door?

Another wave of intense heat seared his lungs and prodded him back into action. Savage rose to his feet, picked up the limp body, and dragged the other boy towards what he hoped was the exit. He felt his strength escaping his body like air flowing out of a balloon. His foot caught on some unidentifiable object but Savage caught himself at the last moment. He knew that if he went down he would never get up again. He turned again, disoriented, searching for a way out. He saw nothing but patches of glowing orange masked by black smoke. His strength ebbed; and in a final act of desperation, he struck out in a random direction knowing that finding the exit were slim. Just then, another eddy revealed a hazy patch of light to his right. Summoning the very last of his strength, Savage pushed towards the opening. Outside, the children, still clustered around their schoolteacher, and a smattering of townspeople watched in horror as Savage staggered out of the blazing building. He was covered with soot. His clothes were smoldering and he was dragging Joey behind him and Horace under his arm.

Savage threw the limp body of the boy as far towards safety as he could, pushing the other boy forward. Completely spent, he sank to his knees.

"Watch *out*!" a chorus of voices screamed. Savage heard the flame-engulfed school house wall buckle; and, before he could move, felt the blazing logs crashing down on top of him.

23

It was a small, unfamiliar room that Savage awoke to. Sparsely furnished, it smelled of soap and chloroform. The morning sun sent its rays through the open window, past chintz curtains undulating gently in the light breeze. Outside the window he could hear the sounds of traffic and the muted shouts of drivers urging on their teams. His head hurt and he touched the bandage covering his scalp and forehead. His lungs were on fire and his entire body was aching. Something was wrong with his left leg. Savage snaked his hand under the covers and touched a cast which reached up to his thigh. He was thirsty. A carafe filled with water and a glass stood on the nightstand. But, lying on his back, Savage only managed to knock the glass off the nightstand when he reached for it.

The sound of the shattering glass caused someone to open the door behind his bed. "Who is it?" Savage croaked. "Where the hell am I?"

"There is no need to curse," a female voice gently admonished him. The door closed and a long gray skirt moved into his line of vision. He raised his eyes to see Amy Cabbett's unsmiling face bending over him. "How are you feeling?" she asked and busied herself arranging his blanket. "We have been waiting for you to wake up."

"I'm thirsty," Savage croaked. Her green eyes mustered him. "I'll get another glass," she said straightening up. "There's one in the cupboard." She collected the glass, filled it with water from the carafe, and held it for him while he drank greedily. "To answer your question, you're in the sick room of Dr. Wood's house."

"Thank you, Miss Cabbett." He coughed and gently pushed the glass away. He still remembered her cold dismissal the last time he had seen her and watched her with impassive eyes. "How long have I been here?"

"About a day and a half," Amy replied.

"A day and a *half*!" Savage tried to sit up but Amy pushed him gently back into the pillow. "You must lie still. You are in no condition to go anywhere. Doctors orders." She smiled for the first time.

Savage's heart skipped a beat but he maintained his guarded demeanor. Amy kneeled on the ground to pick up the pieces of the glass that Savage had broken. There was something different about the young schoolteacher.

"What did you do to your hair?" he asked.

"It's shorter. I cut off the singed ends." Amy stood up and dropped the remnants of the glass into the wastepaper basket.

Savage furrowed his brow, straining to piece together what had caused him to end up in Dr. Wood's clinic. He frowned at the young woman. "Miss Cabbett, I'm trying to recollect what happened back at the schoolhouse. I remember seeing it on fire, you lying on the grass and me trying to go after two boys who were trapped in the building." He coughed and it hurt. "Are the boys alright?" he said with difficulty.

Amy sat down at the edge of his bed. Her eyes were brimming with tears. "Joey is alright. Dr. Wood treated him for minor burns. He would never have made it if you hadn't..." she paused to collect herself.

Savage watched her in silence, fearing the worst. "And the other boy? Horace?"

"Horace did not make it, he... he died."

"Dead." Savage closed his eyes. A deep sense of sorrow engulfed him. "So I wasn't able to save the little boy." His voice betrayed his remorse.

Amy reached out and put her hand on his. "Please don't torture yourself," she said, fighting to regain her composure "You acted in a way few men would have, risking your life to rescue those boys. Everyone in town thinks of you as a hero. Dr. Wood says that poor little Horace," Amy paused again, "poor Horace was already dead when you picked him up and carried him out. There was no way you could have saved him."

Savage closed his eyes. If only he had been able to reach the little boy sooner.

"Miss Cabbett is right," a male voice said behind him. "You must not blame yourself for his death." Dr. Wood entered the room and bent over Savage. "I'm glad you're awake. Let me listen to your lungs. Take a deep breath." He placed the stethoscope on Savage's chest. "Sit up, please. Here, let me help you. Breathe deeply. And again. And again," he commanded as he moved the chest piece across Savage's back. "Does breathing hurt?"

Savage nodded.

"I don't think there's anything actually wrong with your lungs. The pain should go away in time," Dr. Wood said.

"Could I have some more water?" Savage asked. He reached for the glass that Amy held out to him.

Dr. Wood put his stethoscope aside. "You are a lucky man, Mr. Savage. Even though you must have inhaled a lot of smoke, your lungs seem to be none the worse for wear. Aside from singed hair and a couple of superficial burns on your face, arms and back, and, of course, a fractured leg, you have come through this ordeal comparatively unscathed. It could have been worse, much worse." He pulled up a chair, sat down and leaned forward to address his patient. "What you and Miss Cabbett did was nothing short of heroic and saved the lives of the children. The town will be eternally thankful to both of you."

"Please, I–"

"Well," Dr. Wood interrupted, "I can tell you that you have the town's eternal gratitude and Riverside will express this appreciation in an appropriate manner." He stood up and pushed the chair back against the wall.

"I would rather they didn't," Savage rasped. He fixed his gaze on Amy. "Miss Cabbett, would you do me a great favor? Would you please send a messenger to my ranch, telling my foreman that I'm alright but won't be back for a few days? They have enough work to do and I don't want them to send out a search party."

"Yes, of course. Now try and get some sleep." Amy said and stood up. She turned to Dr. Wood. "If you don't need me anymore, I think I'll go back to my house and get some rest."

"Of course, my dear," the physician said and patted the young woman's arm. "I will take good care of Mr. Savage."

"Will you come and see me tomorrow?" Savage asked as Amy walked toward the door.

She stopped and looked back at him before her eyes left his. Finally she nodded. "I'll try."

"Good," Savage mumbled, his eyes already closed.

24

James Sanders arrived at the ranch that very same night. Like his father, James was tall and powerfully built, but the supple way in which he moved belied his bulk. His long, black hair worn in ponytail fashion and his dark face contrasted vividly with his blue eyes. In place of a revolver, he wore a sawed-off shotgun in a special holster. A sheathed knife protruded from his left boot.

The next day, he and Jefferson rode side by side on their way to the rustlers' canyon. Like Jefferson, James was a man of few words. Except for an occasional brief comment, the two men were silent but alert, rifles laid across their saddles, eyes scanning the terrain around them. The night before, Jefferson had explained that he did not expect to run across any rustlers this far east; but that it always paid to be vigilant. He mentioned that the Double-T foreman had sent two hands to this neck of the woods to search for any stray cattle; but that their camp was well south of where they were headed, out of the way of any rustling operation.

Jefferson finally broke the silence. "How many cows did you lose?"

James' face darkened. "Every last Hereford that my dad bought from the Major. They didn't touch our Longhorns." He hooked his right leg around the swell of his saddle and pulled out his tobacco pouch and paper and rolled a smoke with deft fingers. He licked the paper and stuck the cigarette between his lips. "Smoke?" he asked and held up the makings to the other man who shook his head. James fished in his pocket for his matches and struck one against the sole of his boot and lit his cigarette.

"When did that happen?" Jefferson asked.

James thought for a moment. "Shortly before my dad talked to the marshal and the Major about it. When our cattle turned up missing, we tried to follow them but it rained for two days. There was no way we would have been able to track them."

"We were having the same problem," Jefferson admitted. "It helps to know where the bastards are holding our livestock. They're probably pretty busy by now, re-branding. I figure they'll steal about six hundred or so head and then drive them to wherever they plan to sell them."

James shook his head. "Our brand is pretty hard to change. We got the circle inside a square."

Jefferson nodded. "Yeah, the circle-box brand. I'm familiar with it. I don't know how they would change it either, but they'll come up with something at least as good for anyone who doesn't know much about brands. Or don't care." He shielded his eyes and looked at the sky. "Sun's going down." He motioned at the horizon. "Be another two hours before we make camp."

The next day they were up early. The morning fog was lifting, but still clung to the treetops when they saddled their horses and rode out. Following the cliff wall, they crossed over the chasm via the natural bridge and stopped for lunch – hardtack, flapjacks, and coffee - in a meadow guarded by whitebark pines.

"The cow thieves didn't post any sentries when the Major and I scouted the canyon," Jefferson said as he and James mounted up. "But I wouldn't be surprised if there was one now. So we need to exercise caution."

It was late afternoon when they approached the canyon. After quickly setting up camp, they stealthily made their way to the lookout post that Jefferson had used to monitor the goings on below.

The canyon was a beehive of activity. Several men were busy roping cows, dragging them over to the fires where others were altering the brands with their running irons. Men were shouting to each other and the bawling of the cattle reverberated off the canyon walls. The horned animals were milling about in confusion and the stench of burned hide drifted up to the two scouts' hideout.

"Holy shit," James breathed, "there must be at least three hundred, three hundred fifty head down there." He accepted the binoculars from Jefferson and scanned the scene below. "I count four–no there's another one back yonder–" he pointed, "–five men. Three of 'em roping and the other two at the fires. There must be more bringing another herd up here. Just how big is that gang anyway?"

"A small army, looks like and they'll all be wanting a piece of the pie." Jefferson scanned the canyon. "That's why I think that they'll have to bring up the herd to at least six hundred head to make it worth their while."

"Or they get greedy and rustle even more." James glanced at his companion. "I don't see any Longhorns, just Herefords."

"Better beef. Herefords bring a higher price and they're a lot easier to drive. These folks know what they're doing."

They spent another hour watching the activities in the canyon. Finally, James crawled back from the rim, stood up, and dusted himself off. "Well, I think we've seen enough for today, don't you think?"

"Yep, I guess you're right." Jefferson gave the scene below him another sweep with his binoculars and backed away from their observation post. They walked the five hundred yards to where their horses were tethered in the shade of a white bark tree. Leather creaked as they stepped into their saddles.

"Know what, Rufus? Just because we didn't see a lookout doesn't mean that there isn't one lurking somewhere. I think we should take a different route back to the camp. Also kind of get the lay of the land. What do you say?"

"Suits me. Lead the way." Jefferson said.

They rode single file. Before long, the land began to break up into coulees and draws. Occasionally, James bent low over the saddle, studying the ground. Suddenly he broke into a trot and Rufus put the spurs to his Black to follow him.

"Look." James pointed at a piece of paper and jumped out of the saddle. "Looks like a letter. He held the paper up to Jefferson.

"What's it say?"

"It's a letter addressed to a Billy Craig. Know anybody by that name?"

Jefferson unfolded the creased paper and turned it over in his hand. "Craig? I'm not sure. Could be one of the new hands the Major hired on. I wonder how the letter got here."

James squatted to examine the ground. "Look here. Four different hoof prints." He pointed. "And over there. Boot prints. Different sizes." He stood up and walked toward the embankment and Rufus followed him, his curiosity aroused. The embankment was scarred by hooves and it looked as if the rider had jumped off to save himself from being crushed under the weight of his horse. There were deep heel prints in the soft dirt.

Jefferson, still mounted, pointed. "What's that over there?"

James looked in the direction of his outstretched finger. He walked over and picked up an old, rusty gun. He rotated the cylinder. It was empty. "Some old six shooter. Ain't loaded. But here…" He squatted next to a dark brown blotch, touched it, rubbed his fingers together and smelled them. "Blood," he said and looked up at Rufus who was towering over him on his horse. "Looks like somebody got himself hurt. Let's have a look around."

James walked a few steps before dropping on his knee to study the ground. Jefferson, on a hunch, rode over to the edge of a nearby ravine. "Over here," he called out.

"What?" James straightened up, walked over to the embankment, and peered down. "Shit," he said. Billy's body lay on the bottom of the ravine, looking like a rag doll that had been tossed away by a careless child. "Sure looks like he's dead. But I'd best have a look." He dropped to his hands and knees and skidded down the steep slope, breaking his descent with the heels of his boots and the palms of his hands. Rocks and dirt cascaded down ahead of him, some coming to rest on the body. When he got to the bottom, James rubbed the dirt from his hands on his pants and kneeled next to the corpse. He examined it from all sides before looking back at Jefferson, who was staring down from above. He shook his head. "Some young kid. Couldn't have been more than sixteen or seventeen. Shot in the back," he called up, his voice tight. "The sons of bitches shot the kid in the back and tossed him aside like so much garbage."

"I'm going to find the bastard who did that," Jefferson said quietly, his eyes blazing.

James finished examining the body and stood up. "I imagine you will, if he's one of the rustlers." He looked back down at the boy at his feet. "We'd better bury the kid before the wolves get to him."

"What are you going to bury him with? We don't have any shovels," Jefferson called down.

James took off his hat and scratched his head. "The best I can do is pile rocks on top of him for now. We can't leave the poor kid just lying here. It ain't decent."

"You need a hand?"

James shook his head. "Naw. You stay up there and stand guard. I can take care of him." James gently laid Billy's body out and carefully covered him with rocks until he was sure that no animal short of a grizzly would be able to get to him. He took off his hat again and said a short prayer. He would like to have added a cross or headstone but that would have to wait. There was nothing more he could do. "Hey, Rufus," he called, "I'm done down here. Throw me a rope and pull me up?"

Jefferson shook out his lariat, and let it sail down to where James stood, waiting to loop it around his body. Rufus secured the other end to the pommel of his saddle and prodded his horse forward. As the powerful blaze-faced Black hauled him up the incline, James pushed with his hands and feet against the slope to maintain his equilibrium, sending another shower of dirt and rocks to the bottom of the ravine. When he reached the top, he crawled over the crest of the embankment, stood up, and slipped off Jefferson's rope. He brushed the dirt off his clothes and climbed onto his horse. His boots were badly scuffed and his face and hands showed the scratches incurred during the climb.

Jefferson waited until James was securely in the saddle. The young man's face was impassive as he stared back into the ravine he had just vacated.

"I think we ought to split up after we reach camp," Jefferson said looking to James for approval. "Given what we've seen so far," he paused, "and finding the murdered kid, I ought to ride back and alert the Major, provided he's back."

"Don't forget my dad and the marshal." James said, still staring into the ravine.

"I'll let the Major get in touch with your dad and the marshal." Jefferson responded. "You might want to stay behind and keep an eye on the rustlers. If there's any change, you–"

"I know what to do, Rufus. Let's not waste any more time yakking. I can take care of myself." He touched his horse's flanks with his spurs and loped off. Jefferson took one last look at the dark puddle where the young cowboy had lain, as if to engrave it in his memory. Then he turned and followed James to their camp.

25

"I only just took your cast off," Dr. Wood protested. "Are you sure you're well enough to ride?" He studied his patient, who was in the process of mounting his Bay. "You still look a mite peeked."

Savage swung his injured leg over the saddle and winced. He reached down to shake the hand of the lean, gray-haired physician. Ignoring the throbbing pain in his leg, he responded with a grim smile. "Don't worry, Dr. Wood. I feel fine. Thank you for taking such good care of me." He flicked the reins and turned his horse toward Main Street. Amy, despite her half promises, had not paid him any more visits. It had, after all, been profound foolishness on his part to believe that she would come to see him. His anger toward her had hardened, and he had resolved to put her out of his mind once and for all. His only visitor had been Ed Boudreaux and they had discussed Savage's rustling problem until Dr. Wood had ordered the marshal to leave.

"And I thank you for your most generous contribution toward my new hospital." Dr. Wood called after him. "With the money you and Miss Cabbett contributed, you fulfilled my biggest dream. We should be able to break ground in about a month."

"Miss Cabbett?" Savage reined in his Bay and turned back to where Dr. Wood was standing.

"Oh yes, Mr. Savage. Miss Cabbett made a sizeable contribution, nearly as big as yours. Our esteemed banker tells me that she is well heeled." Dr. Wood looked up at the rancher towering over him. "By the way, Miss Cabbett asked that you stop by her house on your way home, though I daresay neither of us thought it would have been so soon."

Savage heard the admonition but chose to ignore it. "She did? Did she tell you what she wanted?"

"All I know is that she asked to see you," Dr. Wood replied.

Savage nodded. "Thanks again, Doc." He touched his hat, reined General Chamberlain around and rode off in the direction of Amy's house.

Amy saw Ben Savage dismount stiffly from his horse as she looked from the parlor window. She was aware of her half promise to visit him but something had held her back. She watched as he wound the reins around a slat in the white picket fence and stood studying the house before stepping through the gate. He walked with a limp. She smoothed her skirt and waited for his knock before opening the door.

"Good day, Miss Cabbett." Savage removed his hat. "Dr. Wood told me you asked to see me?" His air was brisk and business-like, devoid of the charm and warmth that the young woman had unconsciously come to expect and – she found herself surprised to realize – look forward to.

"Yes." Amy stepped back, slightly unsure of herself and stiffly motioned for him to come in. "Have a seat, Mr. Savage. I hadn't expected you so soon. How is your leg? I'm surprised that Dr. Wood released you so early."

Savage gave her a wry smile. "I'm afraid that he had little choice in the matter, Miss Cabbett. I need to get back to the ranch as quickly as possible."

Amy sat down on a chair facing his. The big rancher's presence so close to her in her own house had a profound effect on her. However, his eyes, now cold and distant were most disconcerting. "Mr. Savage, I asked you to stop by to allow me to personally thank you again for saving those two boys, even though..." again her voice faltered and she stopped to collect herself. "Even though one of them did not make it. It was a heroic deed and I shall never forget it, nor will the town."

"Please, Miss Cabbett," Savage said quietly, his impassive gaze on the young woman. "You embarrass me. You've already thanked me. I only did what any other person would have done. Dr. Wood told me how you saved your pupils by risking your own life. I don't consider myself to be a hero. I did what I had to do."

"You are too modest, Mr. Savage. The reason I asked you here... well." She hesitated and looked down at her hands. "Do you remember Dr. Wood telling you that Riverside is planning to honor you–honor us–at a special ceremony? I–"

"No," Savage said simply and stood up in a manner that discouraged any further discussion on the subject. "I'll have none of that. It's very kind of the town to consider such a thing, but I abhor ceremonies of any kind. Besides, I need to get back to the ranch without delay. I've been away far too long." He turned to go.

"I'm glad to hear you say that," Amy said quickly and scrambled out of her chair to follow the rancher to the door. "I feel the same way but I wanted to hear from you how you feel about it. If you agree, I will seek an audience with the mayor to inform him of our decision."

"If you feel it necessary," Savage said formally. Without turning back to face her, he pulled out his pocket watch and glanced at it. "I had better get moving if I want to make it home on time," he said and re-pocketed his watch. He paused, then turned back to face her. "Is there anything else, Miss Cabbett?" He stood quietly, his eyes riveted on Amy's face.

"Anything else, Mr. Savage?" Her gaze was level but her voice trembled almost imperceptibly. "What would that be?"

The rancher regarded her silently, before turning back to the door "Nothing, Miss Cabbett. Nothing. Thank you. Goodbye."

"Goodbye, Mr. Savage," she answered quietly; but he had already left, closing the door behind him.

Standing at the window behind the curtains, Amy watched Savage ride away. The rancher's visit had disturbed her in a way she could not have anticipated. She had convinced herself that she disliked the man, but now her feelings were in a jumble. His demeanor towards her had changed. She was surprised by how much comfort she had taken in his warmth and by the emptiness she felt in its absence. Her mind turned back to the recent fire and nursing the rancher back to health.

Living in a frontier town, Amy had come to understand the code of the West which measured a person by his deeds and not his past. Watching over him that first night at Dr. Wood's clinic, she had had ample time to observe the man whose advances she had stubbornly shunned. She had to admit to herself that he was uncommonly, ruggedly handsome. And in his sleeping face, she thought she could see a man, who for all his wealth and stature in the Valley, appeared to be lonely at heart.

And she knew what it meant to feel lonely. Amy moved away from the window and gazed emptily around the parlor. What was it about Ben Savage that caused such confusion in her mind? She was beginning to understand that she had behaved like a petulant, self-righteous, and immature schoolgirl. She had allowed pride to get in the way of her true feelings and in so doing had deeply hurt this proud man. She had probably driven him away for good. Alone, she sank down onto the couch where moments ago Savage had been sitting and; despite the fire crackling in the fireplace across from her, she suddenly felt cold.

26

Josh stuck his head inside the kitchen door. "Trudy, tell the boss there's riders comin', two of 'em."

Savage heaved himself out of his easy chair, grabbed his cane, and hobbled out of the house. When he stepped onto the porch, Seth and Jonah Manson were riding through the gate. They trotted up to where the rancher stood and reined in their horses. Savage saw that they were armed and had their bedrolls tied behind their saddles.

"A good day to you, Major," Seth said in his cheerful voice. He took off his hat and wiped the sweat band with a dirty bandana. "Hot as blazes, ain't it?" He stared at Savage's bandaged head and bruised face. "Jesus, man, you look like you been through a meat grinder." He mustered Savage, his face suffused with sympathy. "I heard what you done. You're a real hero in town. Everybody's talkin' about you."

Seth, Jonah," Savage said in greeting and extended his hand. "Come in out of the sun. What brings you here on a hot day like this?"

The riders dismounted, looped the reins of their horses around the hitching rail and stepped onto the porch. "We heard that you was fixin' to go after them rustlers and we'd like to join up if'n you don't mind. Did the marshal tell you that them Herefords you sold us was stole?"

"Yes he did," Savage replied guardedly.

"Well," Seth said and took off his hat again to wipe the sweat off his brow with the back of his hand, "We sure as hell aim to get 'em back. We surely would like to tag along with your search party and pay our respects to them thieves. Would that be alright with you?"

Savage gave Seth a calculating look. After a pause he said, "Sure, I guess I can use some extra help. Come inside." He motioned the brothers to follow him into the house. "Trudy will get you something cold to drink and I'll fill you in on our plans."

"So, what's your take on this rustling business?" Savage asked the brothers when they were settled in his office sipping a glass of lemonade. He had declined a glass himself.

"This sure quenches your thirst," Seth said and put down his frosted glass. He would have preferred a shot of whiskey. "We have no idea who is stealing our cows, Major unless…" His voice trailed off.

"Unless?" Savage prompted him, his face impassive.

"Well, we don't want to point a finger at nobody, bein' that we ain't got no proof. But that Luther Eaton's been acting kinda strange lately. Luther don't give us the time of day. Last time we run into him in town he give us a mean stare and turned on his heels and walked the other way."

Savage frowned at Seth. "Are you implying that he is stealing our cattle?"

Seth shrugged. "Don't rightly know, Major. I just got my suspicions is all."

"So what are your plans, Major?" Jonah added.

"I'm getting a bunch of men together to scout up north where the rustlers hid their loot last time. If we don't find anything there, we'll search farther west. Bert Sanders is sending up a couple of his hands and if you two are willing to tag along, that'll give us two extra sets of eyes." Savage said. He made no mention of Jefferson's plan or his discovery of the rustlers' activities in the box canyon.

The brothers had listened attentively. "Sounds like a good plan," Seth said, nodding his head. "Maybe we'll catch them varmints red-handed. I'd sure like to get my hands on them what's stealing our cows. When do we start?"

Savage stood up. "We are planning to leave tomorrow morning. Why don't you boys stay the night? My housekeeper does some mighty fine cooking."

"Thanks for the hospitality, Major," Seth said. "Let's hope we find them rustlers." He looked at his brother. "C'mon Jonah. Let's put up our horses."

Savage stared intently at their backs as they led their horses across the compound before turning around and going back inside.

27

Before crossing the small creek on his way back, Jefferson stopped and let his Black drink. There was little doubt in his mind that Billy had been killed by the rustlers. He also knew that those rustlers were astute enough to figure out that, sooner or later, someone would come looking for the missing ranch hand. That meant they would have to speed up their operations. They were keeping their running irons busy even now and could always re-brand the rest once they were well out of range. And oddly, there had been no sign of a sentry.

It was high time to hightail it back to inform the Major of the latest developments. Jefferson applied his spurs and the Black pulled its dripping muzzle out of the creek and climbed up the small embankment. The land around him was beginning to flatten. The rocks among the tall grass were gradually being replaced by lush meadows dotted with multi-colored wildflowers and the going was easy.

Jefferson rode along a trail which was winding through a narrow coulee when he heard the pounding of hooves coming in his direction. He pulled his rifle out of the saddle scabbard while yanking his Black to the left to seek cover behind a clump of bushes. But the rider was upon him in a flash. Jefferson saw the shock in the man's eyes finding himself face to face with another horseman. With a hoarse yell, the rider pulled his gun and fired wildly. Jefferson jerked his rifle to his cheek, pulled the trigger and sent the other man sprawling off his mount. The downed man's horse ran another fifteen yards before slowing to a walk. It turned and wandered back to nuzzle its rider who lay on the ground, moaning and writhing in pain. Jefferson slid off his Black and walked over to his assailant, covering him with his rifle. The man looked like an Indian with long hair held in place by a filthy red head band. He picked up the man's revolver and stuck it in his belt. "What the hell did you shoot at me for?" he growled menacingly and booted his assailant for good measure. His bullet had hit the man high in his right buttock. When he bent down for a closer inspection of the wound, the Indian came out of his crouch, the knife in his hand aiming at Jefferson's belly. Jefferson jumped back and kicked the knife out of his attacker's hand. "Alright, you son-of-a-bitch, if that's the way it's gonna be." He grabbed the smaller man by his hair and savagely yanked him up on his feet. The Indian screamed with pain and slumped against him. He did not resist when his captor bound his hands. The bullet had torn right through the fleshy part of the buttock. Jefferson cut the wounded man's pants open and used a bandage which he had dug out of his saddle bag. "You were lucky, you good-for-nothing son-of-a-bitch. Getting shot in the ass." He uttered a harsh laugh. "I could have killed you, coming at me with your gun blazing. As a matter of fact I'm of a mind to leave you here to rot."

The man glared at him with a venomous look in his eyes.

"What's your name?" Jefferson asked. When his captive didn't answer, he grabbed his long hair again and shook him viciously. The Indian mumbled something intelligible under his breath.

Jefferson yanked his head back. "Speak up, man. I didn't hear you."

"Charley." He hissed with a sullen look on his face.

"Who do you work for?"

Charley shrugged his shoulders and did not answer.

"Okay Charley, never mind. It can wait. I think you're well enough to ride." He dragged the wincing man to the pony and lifted him into the saddle, reaching underneath the horse's belly to tie his feet together with a string of rawhide. "You can tell us all about it." Jefferson stopped short and whistled as he ran his hand over the pony's flank. "Well, would you look at that! That horse is the property of the Double-T spread." He climbed back onto his Black. "You shot the kid back yonder in the back and stole his horse, didn't you?"

Cherokee Charlie's eyes hooded and he spit at his captor. Enraged, Jefferson maneuvered his horse close and slapped him hard alongside the head. The blow would have knocked the man out of the saddle, had his legs not been bound together. Blood ran down Charley's nose as he slumped in the saddle. "Don't try that again," Jefferson cautioned Charley. "Next time I'll kill you." With that he turned his horse and continued his journey, trailing his captive behind him.

Later that afternoon Jefferson, his trussed-up prisoner in tow, ran across a young cowboy who was intently studying the ground from his saddle, oblivious to the riders approaching him. "Roberto, you looking for something?" he asked and stopped next to the young cowboy. "Your name is Roberto, right?"

Roberto's head jerked up when he heard his name called. "Yeah."

"Lookin' for Billy by any chance?"

Roberto nodded. Worry showed his face. His gaze flickered from Jefferson to the bound man straddling Billy's pony. "We was gonna meet back at camp night before last and when he didn't show I began to wonder whether he might have gotten hisself throwed or hurt or something."

"What are you doing up this far north?" Jefferson asked.

"Why, the foreman sent us up here to look for strays. We didn't find none where he thought they was supposed to be, so we ranged further. Maybe Billy might've got hisself lost. Though that ain't like him."

Jefferson edged closer to the young cowboy. "Roberto, I have to tell you something. We ran across Billy a ways back."

"You found him. Good," Roberto said and his face dissolved into a smile of relief.

"He was killed. Shot in the back."

Roberto sat on his horse, frozen in shock. He stared at Jefferson. Then a sly smile creased his face and he shook his head. "You're joshing me, right? Of course you are. I can tell. Why would anybody kill Billy? He couldn't hurt a fly. He–"

"Roberto," Jefferson said quietly, "no use kidding yourself. Your friend is dead. Billy was murdered. Somebody shot him in the back."

"You ain't funnin' me?"

Jefferson shook his head.

Roberto's eyes misted over. "Billy dead?" His turned his eyes on the sullen prisoner strapped to his horse. "This the bastard what killed Billy?" he asked in a voice suffused with fury.

"Don't know. He might've for all I know."

"Why, that's Billy's horse, you thieving murdering son-of-a-bitch!" Roberto cried in a strangled voice and went for his gun.

Jefferson reached over and quickly clamped the young cowboy's arm in an iron grip. "Listen, kid!" he bellowed to get through Roberto's red wall of rage. "Listen! As much as he may deserve killing, we need to bring him back alive if we want to find out more about Billy's murder. Besides," his voice was quiet now, "we're not in the business of shooting unarmed men."

Roberto shook his arm free and reluctantly slid his gun back into its holster. "That's what they done to Billy," he said hotly.

"Two wrongs don't make a right, son," Jefferson said and turned his Black. "Go back to camp, pick up your gear, and head back in. I got to keep moving. The Major's waiting."

28

Savage saw a commotion outside his window, grabbed his cane, and hobbled onto the porch for a closer look. Jefferson was riding up to the house with a trussed up man with long, black hair in tow. Several of the ranch hands followed Jefferson and looked up at him, asking questions. When Jefferson spied Savage, he guided his horse over to the rancher and stepped down.

"Brought you a prisoner," he said and used his gauntlets to slap the dust off his clothes. "He says his name is Cherokee Charley."

Savage took a step closer to look at the prisoner who sat crookedly on his pony, still trussed up and staring straight ahead, ignoring the men around him. "He's hurt. What happened?"

"I ran across the son-of-a-bitch and he started shooting. So I returned the compliment. Shot him in the ass."

The men standing around the prisoner's horse hooted.

Savage shot them a hard look. "Don't you boys have anything better to do except stand around here and gawk?"

The men drifted away.

"Is he one of the rustlers?" Savage asked.

"Don't know, might be," Jefferson said and hesitated. "I hate to tell you this, but one of your hands by the name of Billy Craig was shot in the back. And whoever did this, dumped his body into a ravine. James and me gave him a sort of burial."

Savage's face went dark and his jaw tightened. "I hired that Craig kid personally." He mustered Jefferson's captive with an icy stare. "Is he the murderer?"

"Can't say, Major. The greasy bastard won't talk, but he was riding Billy's horse. That ought to tell you something." He looked down at Savage whose rage was plain on his face. "What do you want me to do with him?"

"Lock him up in the room at the end of the bunkhouse. Keep him tied up so he won't be able to escape. Have Trudy get him something to eat, but don't let her take him food personally. Keep her out of harm's way."

"Don't worry. I'll take care of him." Jefferson replied.

"Okay. See me in my office when you're finished with him." Savage took one last look at the scowling prisoner and limped back into the house.

Later, in Savage's office, Jefferson filled the rancher in on what he and James Sanders had observed at the rustler's canyon. "After we buried the kid, I ran across the other, a man by the name of Roberto. I told him to collect his gear and come on in. Wanted to get him out of harm's way. He's pretty shook up. Billy was his friend."

"I'll have a talk with him," Savage said, looking grim. "This killing makes it even more imperative that we catch those murdering bastards."

"Yes," Jefferson agreed. "If it was the rustlers who killed him, which I don't doubt for a minute. If it was them and if they got any smarts, they'll move up their timetable. They've got to figure that someone will come lookin' for the Craig kid and that we'll stumble across their hiding place. If I was them, I'd make a final big push, steal a large bunch of cows all at once, and disappear. They can re-brand them anywhere."

"Which means that we should get ready to set the trap." Savage said.

Jefferson nodded. "James is still up at the canyon, keeping an eye on the rustlers. We ought to be ready to move out at a moment's notice."

Savage agreed. "I'll take Cherokee Charley into town and hand him over to the marshal. I'll fill him and Bert Sanders in on the new situation. We'll finalize the plans when I get back." He stood up. Jefferson stood also. "By the way, Seth and Jonah Manson joined our search party. I didn't tell them anything about the canyon where the stolen cattle are stashed.

"I'll do my best to stay out of the brothers' way," Jefferson said. "I'm liable to kick Seth Manson's teeth in if I see him."

Savage grinned and opened the door for Jefferson.

"I'd better get ready to go to town tomorrow and hand the prisoner over to the marshal. It'll be good to get this whole affair behind us," Savage said.

"Sure will." Jefferson replied.

29

When Savage delivered his captive to the marshal, Boudreaux immediately recognized him as one of the men who had been with Harvey on the day of the gunfight. Boudreaux was pleased. "I'll take good care of him, Ben," he promised his friend. "I think we may finally be getting somewhere." He sat down on his edge of the desk. "What's your next move?"

"I told my men to be ready to move out as soon as I get back. Bert Sanders is sending some of his men to join us. We have a good plan and if everything goes as planned, we'll make a quick job of it." He stood up and reached for his hat.

Boudreaux stood up also and held out his hand. "I hope you're right," he said.

Back in his room at the Majestic, Savage walked over to the open window and gazed down at the busy street. The noise of the freight wagons, the screeching sound from the distant sawmill, and the sawing and hammering of the construction site next to the Majestic hotel drifted up into the room. Riverside was prospering. It had recently added a tanning factory. A second newspaper, the *Riverside Sentinel*, had begun publishing in competition with the *Ledger*. There were now five law offices and two new saloons had opened their doors. It seemed that every day an old building, erected hastily when the town had first been established, was being torn down and replaced by a more substantial one. The townspeople seemed more stylishly dressed and a feeling of prosperity permeated the air. There was talk that the old silver mine west of town had been sold and would re-open in the near future, promising to give Riverside an additional economic boost.

As much as he tried, Savage could not get Amy Cabbett out of his mind. Here she was, not a five-minute walk from the hotel, and yet she might as well have been living on another planet. He looked irresolutely out of the window. Should he subject himself to another heart-sickening confrontation with the young woman or should he take the safe route and slip out of town the next morning? Savage looked at himself in the mirror and scratched his cheek. He needed a shave and a bath. "Better get a good night's sleep," he muttered to himself. He'd be on the trail first thing in the morning.

30

Dan sat on his pony at the mouth of the canyon, his right leg hooked around the horn of his saddle, fixing a smoke. His crew had finished re-branding the final batch of cattle and the men occupied themselves playing cards or working on their gear. The canyon was bathed in the late morning light, which transformed the small canyon lake into a pool of crystals reflecting the sunbeams with a brilliance that hurt the eye. Some of his boys had sought the shade of the cliff where they stretched out to catch up on their sleep. Dan studied the cattle which had spread out over the canyon. The herd collected in the canyon was worth twenty-five thousand dollars, or maybe more. He put the cigarette in his mouth, cupped his hands around the burning match, and took a drag, pulling the smoke deep into his lungs. It was a shame to have to split the money with his employer, particularly since he and his boys had done all the dirty work. It had crossed his mind more than once to simply spirit the cows out of the canyon, but he knew that he didn't have the contacts needed to unload the cattle. Even though he had supervised the changing of the brands, he was under no illusion about the quality of their work. It would be obvious to any honest buyer's trained eye that the new brand was a fake. And while changing the Double-T brand had not been easy, it had been nothing compared to the Sanders brand. No, he still needed his employer who claimed to have buyers willing to take the cows off their hands, no questions asked.

Dan took a last drag of his cigarette. He shredded the butt and dropped it on the ground. Every day that they remained in the canyon increased the likelihood that some Double-T cowpoke, looking for the kid he'd shot, would stumble across them. The sense of unease which had been nagging him for the past several days was growing. The rustling operation had gone too smoothly. The boys of the Double-T Ranch were out in force looking for their missing cattle in all the wrong places. And what about that old rancher, Bert Salters, or was it Sanders? Dan had heard that the old man had two grown boys, both half breeds, who were hot-headed and quick to take offense. They, along with their papa, clearly wouldn't take having their livestock stolen lying down. Talk was they were expert trackers. Stealing Sanders's cows had not been a smart move and had he been in charge, one that would have never even been attempted. But that was water under the bridge. No sense losing sleep over it. It was time to get the hell out of here.

Dan slipped off his horse and led it into the shade.

"Hey Dan, when are we gonna get a move on?" one of his boys asked him.

"In a couple of days. Why'nt you get some more shuteye. We got us some busy days ahead."

Dan ducked into the dugout, away from the others, and sat down. He settled into a more comfortable position and pulled his hat over his eyes. Buyers or no, if his employer did not show up within the next two days, he would push the cattle out of the canyon and trail them north without him.

31

"I figured you'd be back tonight, Boss." Josh said, watching Savage dismount. "That's why I waited up for you. I told everyone to be up and ready to move out at six-thirty." He grabbed General Chamberlain's reins. "Lemme take care of your horse."

Savage handed Josh the reins to his Bay. "How many men are we going to take along? Has Mr. Sanders sent some of his boys to join us?"

Josh patted General Chamberlain's neck. "There'll be twelve of our boys, fourteen including you and me. Eight of Sanders' boys will be joining us. Each man will carry a rifle and extra ammunition. I also rustled up enough grub and coffee to last us for about a week."

"Good work, Josh," Savage said and walked stiffly into the house. His leg ached. It had been a long two days and it would be a short night.

Pre-dawn the next morning he stepped onto the porch and looked up at the sky. Black clouds were billowing up in the west, presaging a major storm. The early morning breeze had died down and the air was heavy with a sense of foreboding. A rapid succession of sinister-looking lightning strikes illuminated the clouds from within.

The ranch compound resembled an armed camp. Men holding rifles, with pistols strapped to their waists, stood in groups next to their mounts, talking and smoking. A palpable sense of tension was in the air and they looked expectantly at Savage as he mounted up. When he stepped into the saddle, Bert Sanders rode up to him and they shook hands.

"Bert! It's good to see you. Where'd you come from?"

Sanders grinned. "I spent the night in one of your guest rooms and drank some of your whisky."

"Well, good for you. I didn't know that you were personally going to take an active part in this operation, but you're more than welcome." He gestured at the sky. "I wish the weather would play along."

"Looks like a bad one," Sanders said, following Savage's gaze. "What do you think?"

"No doubt about it. I'm afraid that we'll be in for a hell of a storm before long."

"You thinking of waiting it out?" Sanders asked, still looking at the towering clouds. Savage shook his head and urged his Bay on. "This has got to end, now."

Savage's small army reached the foothills in the afternoon. Earlier, around noon, a sudden flash of lightning had split the sky, followed by an earsplitting clap of thunder which spooked the horses. Crossing his hands on his pommel, Savage had watched a curtain of water move towards them, preceded by fat, heavy raindrops, and followed by torrents of wind-driven rain. Soon man and beast alike were thoroughly soaked. Visibility had been cut to a minimum.

The rain did not let up for the rest of the afternoon. It had been a hard day's ride, the men were drenched under their slickers and fatigue showed in their faces. The hides of their horses were slick with rain. The downpour had just slowed to a steady drizzle when Savage raised his hand cavalry fashion and told the men to dismount and rest their horses.

"Josh, Bert, over here." Savage beckoned. "Join us, Mr. Jefferson? We need to plan our next move." The four men walked their horses down to the small creek which, swollen by the rain, came tumbling down between the rocks and boulders.

"Okay, Sergeant-Major, how far is it to the canyon and what do you think our next move ought to be?" Savage asked over the roar of the rushing creek. He lowered his head and a small rivulet of water cascaded down from the brim of his hat.

"There's a rock formation about two, two-and-a-half miles from here with a big overhang where we can camp and dry out. I ran across it on the way back. It's a couple of miles out of the way but I recommend we stop there for the night."

"Sounds like a good idea," Savage said. He looked at the men around him, their shoulders hunched, water dripping from hats pulled down low. "Well, let's get moving. The sooner we get there the better."

A short time later, Savage's party reached the rock formation. The overhang was wide and deep enough to harbor both men and horses. The men peeled off their slickers and after repeated attempts to ignite the damp wood, soon had several roaring fires going.

Jefferson pulled the map out of the leather pouch suspended from his belt and spread it on the ground. Savage, Josh and Old Man Sanders lowered themselves on their haunches and watched Jefferson's finger move across the parchment. "We're here. We could reach the southern rim of the canyon in another six to seven hours. Be a hard ride, but it can be done. The entrance to the canyon is at the southwestern end, northwest of here. It is pretty narrow and it's the only way in or out."

"A box canyon." Bert Sanders observed.

"Right. My recommendation is this. We continue on, this way," he used his finger to trace a route on the map, "and place ourselves along the south rim, here, with a small contingent manning the west rim." Another stab of the finger. "So we'll have interlocking fields of fire." Jefferson looked at the men crouching in front of the map. "Any questions so far?" He watched them shake their heads. "Okay. I suggest we move into position tomorrow night and surprise them at sun-up, while they're still asleep."

"What about lookouts? These boys must have somebody on the rim, watching the approaches to the canyon. How do we take them out?" Bert Sanders asked. He stood up to stretch his legs, which were beginning to cramp up.

"You'd think they would have all kinds of sentries out, but for some reason they haven't. I've been wondering about that myself." Jefferson said.

Savage stood up and watched the old soldier fold up his map. "Good plan, Mr. Jefferson. Bert? Josh? Any concerns?"

The men shook their heads.

Savage turned to his foreman who had listened quietly. "Josh, post a guard and tell everybody else to get some sleep. We'll be leaving at first light tomorrow morning."

The rain was coming down hard again and shrouded the outside of the cave in a blue-tinged curtain when Savage and his men broke camp. A rumble of thunder could be heard in the distance. The weather was uncommonly brisk and caused the men to shrink into their slickers, searching for warmth and trying to stay dry. The horses were skittish, their rain-slicked backs steaming in the morning air. After the blankets had been rolled up, the last coffee drunk, and the fires scattered, Savage's army mounted their horses and, guided by Jefferson, commenced their second day in the saddle.

After several hours' ride, they made contact with James Sanders who was waiting for them at the meadow where he had pitched his tent. The rain had let up, but clouds heavy with moisture moved rapidly east, barely clearing the tree and promising another downpour.

"Major. Rufus. Dad." He said.

The three men acknowledged his greetings. "So, what's going on James?" his father asked.

"Not much, Dad, to tell you the truth. They've been mostly hanging low, doing some more rebranding. Other than that it's been pretty quiet out here."

"James, do they have anyone patrolling the rim of the canyon? On horse-back, maybe?" Jefferson asked.

"As of yesterday, they still hadn't. If you ask me, they seem pretty confident that nobody could ever find them out here."

Jefferson was incredulous. "Even after they murdered Billy? They must know that somebody will come looking for him and run across their trail."

"Look, Rufus, I don't know what they're thinking," James said, sounding impatient. "They probably figure that their tracks were washed out by all the rain."

"Well," Jefferson replied. "Seems like our luck is holding, even if the weather ain't."

"James, did the rustlers bring in additional cattle since Mr. Jefferson left you?" Savage broke in.

"No. Like I said, they've been busy branding. I think they got what they came for. You got here just in time. I think they're are getting ready to move their... our cows. Could be anytime, maybe even as early as tomorrow morning."

"We're planning to move into position before daylight," Savage said. "Tell us what's been going on in the canyon."

While the men huddled under trees trying to stay dry, James invited Savage and his father into his tent and pulled out a scroll of paper. "While I was watching what was going on below and waiting for you, I took the time to draw a map of the canyon to give you a feel for what the place looks like." He unrolled the scroll and secured it to the ground with two small rocks. "There's only one exit to the canyon. The rustlers, to a man I might add, always congregate near the canyon mouth. There's a dugout, a corral, and shade at various times of the day."

"So they finished branding?" Savage asked. He took off his hat and slapped it against his chaps to shake off the waters clinging to its crown and brim, spraying a small shower of droplets on James' makeshift map.

"Yep, they sure did, Major. Yesterday. Don't know why they haven't driven the cattle out of there. They seem to waiting for something. Or somebody..."

"How many men are down there, James?" Savage asked.

"Twelve, maybe fifteen. Couldn't tell for sure."

"Do you think they'll fight?"

"They'll fight alright." James affirmed. "They're all hard cases and know what will happen to them if they get caught."

"I hope we won't shoot too many of our own cows," Bert Sanders said.

"Not much chance of that, Dad. Most of the livestock is at the far end of the canyon near the lake. Except for occasional strays, I don't think there'll be any cattle within five hundred yards of where the men are. Once we start shooting, they won't have time to collect the cattle and we'll have them where we want them."

"As long as we can get some men over to the far side of the canyon so we have them in a crossfire," Savage added. He clapped his damp hat back on his head. "Thanks, James. You and Mr. Jefferson have done a great job. Let's move into position while it's still dark, say around four o'clock? That'll give us all a few hours of sleep."

James rolled up his map. "Four o'clock it is."

"We need to post a guard. It may not be necessary, but let's not take a chance this late in the game," Savage said. "They may be too thick for such a precaution, but it doesn't mean we have to follow suit."

The old rancher nodded. "Probably a good idea."

"Just like the army, eh, Major?" James grinned and tossed the scroll into a corner of his tent. "I'll take the first watch. Have somebody relieve me in a couple of hours." He looked at Savage and his father. "You're welcome to my tent."

Though tempted, Savage felt he should brave the elements with his men. He ducked his head to step outside. The wind had picked up, driving rain squalls sideways against his face. He glanced up at the forbidding sky, thick with rain clouds, thunder rolling in the distance, and could not help thinking that it was a harbinger of the violence to come.

Savage and the other men were up before dawn. Flashes of lightning briefly illuminated the camp and claps of thunder following each other in rapid succession announced that another storm was about to descend on their party. There had been no time to start the fires again and the men missed their morning coffee. They stepped into their saddles to the jingle of spurs and subdued cursing when James materialized out of the dark.

"Listen up, boys," Savage said to the riders who crowded around him. "You all know James here. I'm putting him in charge. He knows the terrain and the situation. This is our chance to catch those thieves and we can't afford to mess up this late in the game. It appears that they are overconfident and haven't posted a sentry but we've still got to be cautious." He turned back to the young man. "James, you got anything you want to say to the men?"

"Yes, I do. Listen up, boys. It's less than two miles to the canyon. When we get close, we'll leave our horses and walk the rest of the way. One thing we got to watch out for most is noise. It may be raining but you all know how far sound carries in the night. Once we dismount, there'll be no talking. I want you all to take off your spurs. Be sure your weapons are loaded, particularly your rifles. I don't want anyone injecting cartridges into their guns once we're in position. When we reach the rim of the canyon, I'll show you to your positions. Half of you will make your way to the north rim while we move into position on this side. Make damn sure that you don't alert the rustlers to our presence. Once there, you'll be well hidden. You'll be behind and underneath boulders and out of the rain. You won't have any trouble seeing what goes on below."

He paused and looked at the sky. "Well, you wouldn't have had any trouble under normal circumstances. It's looking to be a hell of a storm. Dunno if we'll even be able to see our hands in front of our faces in this soup. So keep a close watch on your surroundings. On the other hand, I figure that those cow thieves have no stomach for moving about in this kind of weather, which will be our advantage. Any questions?" James looked at the men facing him and turned back to Savage. "Major, you got anything to add?"

"Yes. Don't start shooting before I give the word. They'll try and fight it out, but I want to give them a chance to surrender. And for God's sake, don't make any noise before everyone's in position. Alright, let's go and get the bastards."

32

When Dan woke up it was still dark. He sat up, yawned hugely, and crawled out of his bedroll. He felt for his boots, stepped into them and buckled on his gun belt. His Winchester was leaning against the wall next to his hat, which he had hung on a peg the night before. The dugout smelled of unwashed bodies and damp earth.

When he stepped outside, bedroll under his arm, it was drizzling. He instinctively hunched his shoulders against the chill that permeated the air. In the dim light, he sensed more than he saw the shapes of his men sleeping on the ground next to the dugout. Heads on their saddles, hats pulled over their faces, they huddled under their slickers and none stirred as he saddled his horse. He hoped that his bosses would arrive today despite the storm and decided to ride outside to meet them. Before he mounted up, he peered up the canyon walls and examined the rim which towered above him, ominously black and silent. He saw the rocky outcroppings silhouetted by a flash of lightning from the west and noted the clouds which were headed this way, portending more rain. *What a hell of a time to move cattle*, he thought.

Dan reached for his makings but thought the better of it. He gripped the pommel with his left hand, put his foot into the stirrup, and pulled himself into the saddle. His pony tossed its head when he tickled its rump with his spurs and broke into a trot toward the mouth of the canyon.

Lying on his cot during the night, he had decided that he would round up the cattle and start moving them north if his employer did not show up come morning. Dan was nervous and knew their luck had been too good for too long. If they didn't move the cattle soon, some damn posse was bound to catch up with them. Moving cattle during a major thunderstorm would be perilous enough in itself. Herefords were more docile than Longhorns, but they would stampede for sure as soon as the storm broke. It would have been easier to contain them within the canyon until the weather cleared. But he was sure they couldn't linger for another day.

So far the whole scheme had worked as planned, which was all the more reason not to dawdle. He and his boys had been sitting on their hands for the past two days. For all its advantages, grass, water, and forming a natural corral, the canyon had only one exit. Once that exit was blocked, there was no escape. The thought of Savage's men finding them had been haunting him for days. And up until last night he hadn't been able to convince his boys of the need for a lookout. The threatening storm had them all on edge. It was a testament to the skittishness of the whole camp that the others had finally agreed to posting sentries. As he rode out of the canyon, Dan felt better knowing that they now would have advance knowledge of anyone coming within a mile of the camp.

33

At James's signal, Savage stepped off his horse along with the rest of the men. He staked the Bay to the ground, removed his spurs, and draped them over the pommel of his saddle. At another signal from James, the men moved forward in a ragged line toward the canyon rim.

Savage, carrying his Winchester inside his slicker, had taken the left flank. The terrain was soaked and he concentrated on keeping his balance. It was the hour when the night turned to gray, slowly bringing the surrounding countryside into a ghostly focus, but still dark enough to hide the man fifty yards to his right. The steady rain muffled the sounds of the men climbing laboriously to the rim of the canyon. Savage was walking stealthily, feeling his way along in the dark, when the toe of his left boot hooked into a soft object, causing him to lose his balance and pitch forward. Instinctively letting go of his rifle, he thrust his hands out in front of him to break his fall and landed hard on top of a man hiding in a body-sized depression in the ground. The concealed man gave a start and twisted under Savage. He tried to bring up his gun but the suddenness with which Savage had fallen on him had taken him by surprise. His timing was off by the critical fraction of a second that gave Savage the time he needed to act. Rolling to his left, Savage used his shoulder to pin the other man's weapon to the ground. If the sentry - and Savage was under no illusion that he was anything other than a sentry - succeeded in firing a shot or shouting a warning, the surprise upon which this operation depended would be jeopardized. The man had to be silenced immediately.

But the sentry was a powerful man. Savage used his right fist to strike out at the other man's throat, but the man partially deflected Savage's punch with his free arm. What should have been a throat-crushing blow turning into a glancing jab. Savage felt cartilage crush under his hand. The lookout gasped for breath, but he still managed to push Savage onto his back. Cold and mud seeped into Savage's clothes and he felt the rain beating on his face. A flash of lightning silhouetted his opponent's hulking form rising against the sky. Savage used the momentum of the roll and the sloping ground to scramble to his feet, scooping up a rock as he did. The sea of mud was slick and Savage struggled to maintain his footing. In the darkness, he could hear the other man's throat gurgling, as he tried in vain to shout a warning. Savage's blow may have missed the mark but at least he had succeeded in momentarily silencing the man. In a flash, the sentry brought his gun to bear; but Savage, acting out of instinct, smashed the rock down on the man's hand with all the force he could muster. The gun discharged. The report was swallowed by a booming crash of thunder on the heels of a flash of lightning and Savage felt a hot pain in his left shoulder. He struck the man's hand again and the gun dropped into the dark haze of rain and mud. Savage had flung back his slicker to free his own sidearm when the beefy sentry lunged at him, gripping his throat in an iron vise. Fighting for breath, his feet seeking purchase in the mud, Savage dropped the weapon and jabbed his thumbs into the sentry's eyes. The man's grip around his neck loosened and Savage used the moment to throw himself backward. He lost his footing and the two men came crashing down, knocking the wind out of Savage and eliciting a hoarse grunt from his opponent. The ground was slick as soap; and as the sentry tried to regain his footing, Savage slid downhill on his back. The cold rain and harsh mud seeping into his wound cut like a knife, and made it difficult to use his left arm. He rolled over and barely had time to push himself back to his feet before the other man rushed him again. This time the attacker's fist caught Savage alongside his head, spun him halfway around, and dropped him to one knee. A second blow to his jaw sent him sprawling back to the ground. Before he had time to recover, his opponent encircled his chest from behind, heaved him upright and tightened his arms in an iron grip, squeezing the air out of Savage's lungs. The pain from his wound made him feel dizzy and unable to breathe, he began to feel lightheaded. In desperation, Savage kicked out to free himself but his feet only met air. The black of the night was beginning to merge with the darkness of unconsciousness when the sentry's grip suddenly lessened. Savage heard him make choking sounds as if he were about to suffocate.

Unbeknownst to Savage, his initial blow had partially collapsed the other man's trachea. The crushing bear hug which had so nearly ended Savage had required the sentry to hold his head in a position which was hampering his own ability to breathe. Eventually the man's chest heaved and he dropped his arms and slumped to the ground. Savage slipped and dropped to his knees next to his opponent, struggling to regain his own breath. In the gray dawn he saw the sentry pick up his gun out of the mud. Savage lunged and reached for the weapon, trying to wrestle it out of the other man's hand. But he was too late. The weapon discharged. The bullet missed Savage by a wide margin but the shot reverberated loud and clear in the still morning air. The element of surprise, on which the success of this whole operation had been based, had been lost. His chest heaving painfully, Savage pried the gun from the sentry, who was attempting to rise to his feet. Swinging the gun in a wide arc, Savage laid the barrel alongside his opponent's head. The sentry slumped and Savage hit him again. A third blow made the sentry topple facedown into the mud and lie still.

Savage bent down to put his finger to the downed man's neck. There was no pulse. Exhausted from the fight, he dropped to the wet ground. His knuckles felt as if they were on fire. He gently probed the wound at his shoulder. In the darkness, he couldn't fully see the extent of the damage. But the cold rain running down his coat and into the raw opening stabbed him like a knife. Probing around the perimeter of the wound, his hand encountered a sticky wetness too thick to be water. If the wound wasn't life threatening, it was at least going to be a damn nuisance.

Savage clumsily got to his feet and slowly made his way to the canyon rim. His fear that the shot had alerted the outlaws' camp was confirmed when he dropped down on the edge overlooking the canyon. A brilliant flash of lightning revealed a beehive of activity. Men were running in every direction, some hurriedly saddling their horses while others sought the protection of the rocks.

"Shit," he swore. "Shit." Where was James? He looked around but in the haze and falling rain he couldn't make out much beyond the dark shapes of trees and scrub. Savage lay quietly, impatiently waiting for the darkness to lift. He assumed his and Sanders's men were positioned at short intervals along the rim with an eye towards an effective field of fire. Josh and his boys had been making their way to the far side of the canyon but Savage had no idea whether or not they had managed to make that journey before the camp below had been alerted. Every so often, one of the rustlers would make a move towards the mouth of the canyon, but a barrage of fire from the rim would send them running back for the cover of the rocks. The atmosphere was thick with a feeling of expectation and suspense. If the rustlers failed to surrender, they would be dealt with in whatever manner was appropriate. It was their choice.

Savage's head jerked up at the sound of branches moving nearby. Dammit, he hadn't meant to doze off. His shoulder throbbed and the pain and loss of blood were hampering his concentration. The black of the night had faded into gray but the rain still partly obscured the camp below. Savage heard the branches shift again and Bert Sanders emerged from the brush and dropped down beside him.

"Getting light," he mouthed and then started when he saw Savage's wound. "Your shoulder-" he began but Savage waved him off. The wound had stopped bleeding but in the morning light it was visible as a black mass of caked blood mixed with dirt.

"Where's James?" Savage asked.

"Was a man riding out of the canyon earlier this morning. James decided to follow him." He looked at Savage. "You look like hell. What happened to you?" He peered down at the frenzied activity below. "So much for the element of surprise," he added bitterly. "Was that you shooting back there?"

"No. The sentry I stumbled over. Nearly killed me." Savage looked around. "What's our status? Where's Jefferson?" he asked impatiently.

"Jefferson's around. Josh and his boys are pinned down on the west side of the canyon. That shot alerted the rustlers before they could get into position. Cover's pretty bad at that end and they're in a bad spot." He pointed at the opposite rim of the canyon. "Can't hardly make them out, but they can't move. Can't even raise their heads to get a shot off. A couple of rustlers tried to make a run for it, but they learned the hard way that we have this end covered. The rest of 'em are hunkered down wherever they could find cover. Major," Sanders looked at Savage, "as long as Josh is pinned down, we'll never get a clear shot at those bastards."

Savage felt the heat rise in his face. This was what he had feared. He strained his eyes, looking into the abyss below. Other than for the cattle in the distance, the canyon now appeared to be deserted, except for the tell-tale smoke emanating from the pipe protruding from the roof of the dugout.

Suddenly all the fury pent up in Savage burst forth. "This is your last chance. Give yourselves up, you thieving bastards, or we'll kill every last one of you!" he bellowed.

"Y'all come and get us, if you dare!" a defiant voice echoed from below. "See you in hell!"

The branches rustled again and Sanders touched Savage's arm. "It's Jefferson."

The old Sergeant dropped down next to Savage. "The rustlers aren't offering us much of a target," he said and looked up at the sky, "especially if the weather doesn't let up."

Savage was still seething. "Well, we can't just sit here in a stalemate."

"We could starve 'em out by bottling up the canyon," Jefferson offered.

"How could we starve them out?" Savage replied. "They've got plenty of meat down there and there's no shortage of water. Besides, Josh and his men don't have the luxury to wait them out. No. I need to get at these bastards now." He measured the distance from the canyon mouth to the dugout with his eyes.

"So what's your plan then, Major?" Jefferson asked.

Savage thought for a moment before answering. "I'm going to flush the bastards out, cavalry-style."

"That, Major, is a good way to get yourself killed. Remember Shiloh? We were almost cut to pieces. We were both lucky." Jefferson glanced at Savage and then to his wound. "You might not be so lucky this time."

"You don't have to remind me," Savage replied tersely. "This isn't Shiloh. I can't wait for Josh and his men to get to the far rim over there. They have a clearer view of the canyon from where they are pinned down but they can't get a shot off without exposing themselves. If we can take some of that pressure off by attacking from this side, they'll be able to provide covering fire and keep the rest pinned down while we mount a charge." Savage studied the far rim and then looked at Jefferson. "Well?"

Jefferson's eyes swept across the far rim and the canyon below. Then he shrugged. "It might work. On the other hand it might get you killed."

"Let's see what develops," Savage said.

34

Josh checked his Winchester as he lay behind a small clump of gravel and scrub brush. His back ached and the cold rain had permeated every seam in his clothing. To his left, he could see one of his men shift position ever so slightly, trying to restore circulation to sleeping limbs. They had been pinned down on the side of the canyon for the better part of two hours now. A shot had rung out earlier when he and his men had been making their way across a particularly exposed segment of the canyon's rim and within seconds the rustlers had spotted them. They had taken cover as best they could but the slope of the rim was such that the only protection came from hugging the ground. When any of them even as much as lifted their heads, they drew fire from below. Josh had managed to make it to the meager protection of his hiding place, but still couldn't get a decent shot off if he tired. They were sitting ducks and the rustlers weren't presenting much in the way of targets from this angle. If the Major could draw some of their fire, he knew that he could make it to cover and get a bead on those bastards below. Till that happened, though, he and his bunch would have to hang in there and wait.

In the early light, Savage was able to make out Josh and the others as they lay prone on the exposed side of the rock wall. He could hear the occasional shot fired in their direction and knew that the only option was to somehow draw those rustlers out so that Josh could finish his journey to the cover of the trees only a hundred yards away. The rain had abated somewhat but was still restricting visibility. *Damn this shoulder*, he thought. It was going to be more of a nuisance than he had hoped.

"Looks like they're pretty locked down over there," Jefferson said, gesturing in Josh's direction.

"Not much they can do on their own. Looks like we're going to have to make a move to break this stalemate."

"How many of them bastards you think are still down there?" Jefferson wondered, peering into the gray light of the valley.

"Dunno. Doesn't matter. We haven't got a choice." Savage slid back from the edge and rolled on his back, checking his rifle. I need to get down there and have a look. I want you, Jim and Andrew with me. We're going to try and flush them out." He clambered to his feet and looked at Andrew. "Go tell the others to keep up a steady barrage of fire to keep us covered and then join us back at the horses. I don't want to give them any chance to draw a bead on us before we get there. With any luck, once they're occupied with us, Josh and his boys can take them out from above."

Jefferson looked at Savage's blood-caked shoulder. "And what if they can't make it to cover?" he asked.

"Well, then this is going to be one short trip," Savage replied and started down the hill towards his horse.

Savage sat silently until Andrew rejoined them. "Major, I talked to the others as you told me and they will do everything they can to keep us covered." He mounted his horse. "Cattle's gettin' spooked. Can't say I'd welcome a stampede."

"Just be grateful they aren't Longhorns. They'd be running by now," Savage replied. "Let's get moving, then. From what I can tell, there's no window on this side of the dugout. That should give us some extra time before we're discovered. I wished we could smoke them out but there's nothing that'll burn in this rain." He looked at the others. "Ready? Alright, let's go."

From his perilous perch on the canyon rim, Josh watched the four riders round the mouth of the canyon. Except for the lowing of the milling cattle, the canyon was eerily silent. The intense shooting that had started as the Major slipped through the mouth of the canyon had stopped again as both sides had entrenched themselves under the best cover they could muster. Josh watched Savage and his men pick their way past the bodies of three rustlers who had been gunned down trying to break out of the camp earlier this morning. Rifles at the ready, Savage and the others dropped their reins, slipped off their horses and crept forward. From his vantage point, Josh could see the Major and Rufus move deeper into the canyon. The Major was approaching one of the spots where a rustler had hidden himself deep under the cover of brush and rocks. From a higher vantage point Josh might have been able to take the man out. But from where he was, pinned down behind some short scrub clinging to the edge of the canyon wall, there was nothing he could do but watch. He wanted to yell out to alert his boss, but that would only warn the rustlers of Savage's presence. He gritted his teeth and watched as the Major moved ever closer to the hidden menace. Josh took only seconds to make up his mind. Only one action to take. He scrambled to his feet and, his back to the danger below, sprinted up the short slope to higher ground. The slap of the bullets into the hill on either side of him was followed seconds later by the booming, echoing reports of the rustlers' guns. As he reached a small outcropping at the top of the incline, he swung around and in one fluid motion brought his rifle to his cheek. All he needed was one shot, and then he could drop down and find cover behind the brush at his feet. But as he drew a bead on the hidden rustler, he was rocked off his feet by a bullet that caught him just below his left collar bone. He went down on one knee and caught himself with his right hand. With his remaining strength, he brought the rifle back to bear. His vision closed in as though he was entering a long, dark tunnel and the end of his rifle swam in front of his eyes as he hunted for the man hidden in the bushes below. The sounds of the bullets ricocheting off the rocks around him sounded as though they were far away. With his ebbing strength, Josh pulled the trigger and fell face down in the brush and lay still. In the canyon below the hidden rustler was punched back into the bushes behind him, his eyes staring unseeing into the dark sky.

The exchange of shots caused Savage to seek cover behind a rock not twenty yards from the dugout. "Stay down," he mouthed towards Jefferson. He had seen Josh go down under the hail of bullets and understood the implication. Down on the floor of the canyon, it was impossible to see past the natural obstacles immediately around him. He knew the rustlers were hidden close by and Josh's sacrifice made plain the cost, should he chance onto one of them. "This isn't going to work at all," he muttered to himself. The outlaws were too well hidden and too spread out for him and his men to have any effect at all. "Sergeant-Major," he whispered and waved his hand, "over here."

Jefferson sidled along the ground and crouched down next to Savage.

"This isn't going to work," Savage said, checking his rifle. "I can't see a goddamned thing this low to the ground. Take a look about seventy to eighty yards to our left and tell me if you can see the big rock next to that large group of cows."

Jefferson slowly raised his head and popped back down. He nodded. "I see it. What about it?"

"Think you can hit that?"

Jefferson shrugged. "Sure, but it'll probably spook the cattle."

"That's the idea. I want them good and spooked. I want to get them moving. The only direction they can run is this way. I figure the shots ricocheting off the rock will do the trick. What do you think?"

"I think you're asking to be in the middle of a great big stampede."

"Don't see as we have a choice any other way," Savage responded. Jefferson just shrugged his shoulders. "Alright then, let's do it. Now!"

The two men stood up and started shooting at the rock as fast as the could pump their rifles. The culmination of the storm, lightning, and gunfire had the cattle at the end of their tether. Bumping into each other, their eyes white with panic, they crushed together near the edge of the canyon. Now the relentless rifle fire and the ricocheting bullets screaming overhead, accompanied by lightning and thunder following in rapid succession, increased their frenzy and caused them to break and run. Unlike Longhorns who bunched together when running, the more domesticated Herefords scattered, some stampeding toward the mouth of the canyon and others heading for the dugout and makeshift corral. As they moved, they overran the hiding places of the rustlers. In the ensuing bedlam, men were jumping out from the cover that had hidden them from the riflemen on the rim but offered no protection from the onslaught of hooves. Savage and Jefferson were engulfed in a sea of milling bodies and bobbing horned heads. Standing their ground amidst the rampaging beasts, they now concentrated their fire on the exposed cattle thieves. From the rim, Savage's men had witnessed the charge of the cattle and had immediately grasped its meaning. "Now boys!" one of them had screamed and they stood up, picking off the men who only minutes ago had kept them pinned down.

It was over in less than two minutes. The cattle had run the length of the canyon and some of them had escaped through the mouth before they began to settle down again. The rustlers, seventeen in all, lay dead where they had been felled by Savage's men or where the stampeding cows had trampled them. Savage stood, his smoking rifle cradled in his arm. The dugout had collapsed and the smoke that had been pouring from the pipe earlier was now seeping from between the fallen timbers. Rifle ready, Savage walked over to the jumble of logs and peered inside. Aside from a body lying underneath the branches which had covered the roof, the remains of the dugout were empty.

Suddenly Savage was very tired. Not a single outlaw had been taken alive. He gingerly ran his hand over the crust of dried blood on his shoulder. Was this the end, he wondered? Had they wiped out every last one of the rustlers? And who was the outlaw who had stolen out of the canyon before sunrise? Had he been the mastermind behind this rustling operation or was he reporting to someone else, someone who was established in the Valley?

Bert Sanders and the others joined him in the canyon. The rain had stopped but the low-hanging clouds prevented the rays of the sun from breaking through, adding to the gloom that pervaded the scene of destruction. Savage's men collected the corpses and laid them out in a row, throwing their weapons into a pile near the remains of the dugout, to be picked up later.

"Where's Josh? What happened to him? Is he okay?" Savage asked as Sanders rode up.

"He's hurt, but my man says he'll make it. He's a tough one. Insisted on riding back to town with the wounded instead of being carried." Sanders paused. "You know what he did for you, right?"

"I know," replied Savage, "and I won't forget."

"Recognize any of them?" Sanders asked as he looked down at the row of bodies.

"No, I wish we had been able to take at least one of them alive," Savage said. "We may never know who was behind this." He shrugged his shoulders. "Hopefully your boy had more luck."

It took Savage's and Sanders's men the better part of the morning to bury the corpses in the damp soil before rounding up the herd. Savage declined medical attention for his shoulder, preferring the dull throbbing pain of the clotted wound to a freshly opened one. He would have it attended to after he got back home. He and Sanders agreed to trail the cattle back to the Double-T Ranch where Bert's cowhands would cut the old rancher's cows out of the herd and drive them back to his spread. As the two ranchers watched, their men squeezed the cattle though the narrow mouth of the canyon as if they were being forced through a funnel, spreading out on the other side to follow the lead steer.

As the drive started, the two ranchers took it upon themselves to ride point and to look for a place to put up for the night. Moving along at a leisurely pace they talked about the events of the day and how the rustlers had outsmarted themselves by holing up in the canyon.

The old rancher shook his head in wonder. "I'm glad that we didn't get any of our boys killed. It was touch and go there for a while."

"I hate all that killing," Savage said. "But in this case I just hope that, when word gets around, it will be a warning to anybody who might have the notion to steal our cattle." He glanced back at the herd trailing along behind them. "I never expected them to give themselves up, did you?"

Sanders looked at Savage, "Naw, they knew what would happen to them if they was taken prisoner. It was better for them to go down fighting than being strung up later. Might have done the same thing if I had been in their shoes."

"I'm glad you're on our side, Bert," Savage said with a weariness in his voice. "I'd hate to have to fight you and your boys."

"Talking about my boys," Sanders said and pulled up, "look."

Savage followed Sanders's outstretched hand and saw James sitting on a rock two hundred yards ahead, his saddle at his feet. When he spied the two riders, he stood up and waved his hat back and forth.

"Where's his horse?" the old rancher said, puzzled. He broke into a trot. Savage followed close behind. When they reached the place where James was standing, they pulled up and stepped out of their saddles.

"What are you doing here, James? Where's your horse?"

"And a good afternoon to you too, Dad." He turned his head and pointed over his shoulder. "My horse is over there. Had to put it out of its misery."

"Shoot it?"

"Stepped into a gopher hole and broke its leg." James' grin was rueful. "Decided to wait here until you came along and hitch a ride."

"Damn, but that was a fine horse," Bert said wistfully.

"Look, I'm sorry about your horse." Savage tried not to show his impatience, "But what about the rider you were following? Did you catch up with him?"

"Sure did. I trailed him and watched him meet up with two riders headed in this direction. They had a pow-wow with a lot of pointing and arm-waiving, especially when the shooting started. They rode off together, all three, back down the trail where the other two had come from."

"Did you recognize the other two?" Savage asked.

"No. They were too far away."

"Did they look like the Mansons?"

"Maybe. I don't know those brothers all that well. As I said, they were too far away for me to identify."

Savage looked at James who met his gaze. "I wonder where they might be going."

"Seems to me they're headed for town." James pointed. "See that trail? It eventually runs into the trail that runs through your property, past that line shack of yours, the one that burned down," James said.

Savage put his hand on the pommel and pulled himself up into the saddle. He looked down at the old rancher. "Bert, would you mind taking over? I need to ride into town. No time to waste."

"Sure," Sanders said, puzzled. "What's in town?"

"Marshal Boudreaux and his prisoner. I want to fill him in on what happened this morning. Maybe this Charley can tell us who the mastermind is behind all this."

Savage turned his Bay in the direction of town and prodded it forward. "Tell Jefferson to meet me at the ranch, pronto," he called over his shoulder as he rode off.

Father and son watched Savage ride off. "You think the Mansons are involved?" Old man Sanders asked his son.

"Don't rightly know, Dad. Your guess is as good as mine." He heard the bawling of cattle and turned to look at the direction of the sound. "Good, here comes the herd. I sure hope the boys got an extra horse for me."

35

The Mansons and Dan Hittle rode side-by-side in moody silence. Dan had told them that he had heard heavy gunfire shortly after he had left the canyon. "Sounded like a whole army," he said. "They must of trapped our boys in the canyon. Probably gunned 'em down."

"What do you think the hell happened?" Jonah demanded.

"Don't know for sure but there's no doubt that the Major caught up with us." Dan fumed.

Seth beat his fist on the pommel of his saddle in a blind rage. "All that work gone to hell. How in the living hell did those bastards find us?"

"The marshal might of beat the truth out of Cherokee Charley or maybe they found the cowpoke Dan killed," Jonah suggested.

"Charley?" Dan pulled up his horse. "What do you mean the marshal beat the truth out of him?"

"Didn't I tell you? The Major's nigger caught Charley, and Savage turned him over to the marshal," Seth explained.

"Dammit to hell! They caught Charley?" Dan glared at Seth. "How'd you find out?"

"Whole town's talkin'," Seth replied in an aggrieved tone of voice, "and I figger Charley's been talking, too. How else would they've known where we stashed them cows?"

Dan was furious. "You shut your trap, dammit. Charley would never talk. Maybe it was the two of you what couldn't keep their traps shut."

"You're a fine one to talk, mister." Seth sawed his horse around to face Dan. "You come ridin' out of the canyon just before them other guys get shot all to hell. Good timing, I'd say. Maybe it was you who didn't keep his trap shut."

Dan felt the heat rise in his face. He yanked his horse around and confronted Seth, hand on the butt of his Colt. "If you got something on your mind, mister, spit it out or shut the hell up. Nobody talks to me that way, and that includes you."

Seth glared at him and reached for his pistol, only to find himself staring down the black muzzle of Dan's gun.

"Wanna try your luck, cowboy?" Dan's cold eyes bored into Seth's. Then his face creased into a malicious smirk.

Trembling inwardly, Seth dropped his gun back into his holster. His face registered barely suppressed fear, which did not escape Dan's notice. He gave Seth a look of contempt before returning his gun to its holster, as though wasting even a bullet on this coward was beneath him.

Jonah spat. He turned to Dan who sat on his horse, watching the brothers coldly. "What do we do next? Any ideas?"

"I know what *I'm* gonna do next," Dan said tersely. "I'm gonna spring Charley out of jail."

"Oh yeah? How do you plan to do *that?"* Jonah asked contemptuously. "That jail's probably got more people guarding it than a bank vault."

"I don't know how I'll do it yet, but I'll figure out a way." Dan answered with a stubborn look on his thin face.

"Well good luck, because that's what you'll need. Dumb luck" Jonah responded sarcastically.

They rode in silence, each of the men busy with his own thoughts. Suddenly, Seth gave his saddle horn a resounding slap with his flat hand. "Hey, I got an idea how you can get your boy out of jail." He looked expectantly at Dan who eyed him impassively.

"Yeah? How."

"Simple. We trade him."

"What in tarnation are you talking about?"

"Listen," Seth said excitedly. "It's a great plan. There's that schoolmarm in town by the name of Amy, right? Major Savage is crazy about her."

"So?" Dan was annoyed. "Where you going with this?"

"Just listen to me, will ya', for Chrissake? She lives with an old lady at the east end of town. I say we ride up to her place when it's good and dark, kick in the door, and pluck her out of bed. We take her to our ranch and leave behind a ransom note that says that we'll exchange her for Cherokee Charley. Well,

Charley and a nice little sum of money to boot, of course. What do you say? Does that sound like a good plan or what?"

Jonah rolled his eyes at his brother. "You're nuts," he said.

Dan raised a hand to stop Jonah. "No. Hold on a minute. Lemme think." He nodded his head and gave Jonah a thin smile. "Yeah. You know, I think your brother's using his brain for once. We grab that schoolmarm and if they want her back, they're gonna have to let Cherokee Charley go. Or we'll kill her."

Jonah rolled his eyes and shook his head, "Only one thing wrong with that hare-brained scheme of yours. Major Savage isn't holding Cherokee Charley, the marshal is. And he ain't in love with the schoolmarm. If you want to get to him, you'll have to find somebody who the marshal cares about."

"Dammit Jonah. If you're so smart, why ain't you rich?" Seth replied heatedly. "The marshal and Savage is close friends. If we get a hold of the teacher, the Major's gonna put a lot of pressure on the marshal to make the exchange. Besides, I hate that damn rich rancher and it'll be a great pleasure to make him sweat. We lost our cows and now we're gonna get that man to pay us a lot of money for his girl and spring Dan's friend to boot. It's like killing two birds with one stone."

"How far to town?" Dan asked.

"We could be there tomorrow after dark," Seth responded.

The men rode in silence, busy with their own thoughts.

Dan broke the silence. "Let's do it. I like the idea about collecting some money from that big rancher, but mostly I want to get Charley out of jail."

"You must really like that filthy Injun." Jonah said, with a sour look on his face.

Dan's hand flashed and before Jonah could react, he smashed the barrel of his gun against Jonah's temple.

"You ever talk about Charley that way again and I'll kill you, hear?" he threatened, leaning over the spot where Jonah had toppled from his horse, his face smeared with blood. "That Injun saved my life."

36

Savage was so tired when he reached the ranch at dusk that he barely had the strength to climb off his horse. His shoulder was sending waves of pain through his arm and upper back with each step General Chamberlain took. He was no stranger to this kind of fatigue. There had been many a time during the war when he had gone without sleep for days - moving, maneuvering, attacking and retreating. But this time he had an overpowering desire to sleep. Despite his fatigue, he allowed Trudy to clean and dress his wound before retiring. Even so, he was asleep by the time she had finished telling him how lucky he had been.

He was up again at dawn. Trudy served him a big breakfast and he drank her strong, black coffee to wash away the last cobwebs of fatigue. One of Savage's hands had saddled General Chamberlain and was waiting for him to come out of the house.

"Made you some lunch, Major." Trudy held out a bundle to him. "Might come in handy."

Savage hoisted himself into the saddle with his good arm. "Thanks, it might at that." He took the bundle and stuffed it into his saddlebag. "Trudy, Rufus should be riding in any minute now. Be sure to tell him to join me in town without delay," he said. "He can find me either at the Majestic or the marshal's office. I will be back as soon as I can." Trudy nodded and watched Savage ride off before returning to the house.

The morning was crisp and the big Bay moved along at a steady gait. He rode along the banks of Running Bear Creek, oblivious to the play of the waves and ripples of the crystal-clear water flowing swiftly between its high banks. Leaving his horse to find the way, his thoughts returned to the past few days. Despite the weather, the raid on the rustlers had gone well and he and Bert Sanders had retrieved almost all of their cattle. The Mansons would also be relieved to get their cows back. He remembered James telling him about the two men the lone rustler had rendezvoused with after leaving the canyon. Why would the Mansons have had their cattle stolen if they were part of the rustling gang? Why steal their own livestock unless… unless they had driven off their cattle to deflect any suspicion from them onto Luther Eaton, whose cows they had left alone? The more he thought about it, the more certain he became. Eaton might be an unpleasant person, but he was probably an honest man.

Consumed with the urge to contact the marshal, he angled away from the creek and struck out across the plain in the direction of town. The Bay sensed its rider's impatience and lengthened its stride. An hour later he entered a small forest of aspen and ponderosa pine. In its twilight, the air was cool and fragrant. Small animals scurried silently about on the ground, intent on escaping the Bay's deadly hoofs. The horse's footfalls were muffled. Trees swayed and whispered to each other in the mild breeze. For a moment Savage considered stopping for the day, but an uneasy sense of urgency caused him to press on and try to reach town before midnight.

37

Seth, Jonah and Dan crouched close together in the dark. It was an hour before midnight. The house across the street in which the schoolteacher lived stood black and silent. "I wonder whether she's in there," Seth whispered. "You think she's asleep?"

"Of course, she's in there, you dumb cowpoke," Dan said. "It's nigh on midnight on a weekday. Where the hell do you think she would be?"

"You sure we wanna do this?" Jonah whispered and gingerly fingered the welt on his temple. "We might get ourselves in a heap of trouble."

Dan snorted in response. "You steal cows for a living and you're worried about getting yourself in trouble nabbing some school teacher? Listen, she's my ticket to Charley and I aim to get him out of jail. You got any problem with that?"

Jonah shook his head. He realized that he was deathly afraid of the pinch-faced outlaw who had been known to kill without warning. He tried to convince himself that kidnapping the school teacher was not such a bad idea. After all, he and Seth were broke. They had spent all their money hiring a bunch of men to help them steal and sell a large herd which would have made them rich. That source of income had vanished under the guns of Savage's cowhands and ransoming the girl was the only other chance to recoup some of their losses. He knew that Seth had no compunctions about kidnapping the girl if only to get back at her. No, the best solution was to go along with Seth and Dan. "No, I got no problem with that, Dan," he answered. "Go do what you gotta do."

"Alright, you stay with the horses. Come on, Seth, let's do it." The two men stood up and walked up the front steps to the house and kicked in the front door. Seth flinched at the sound but rushed into the house after Dan, nearly tripping over a rocking chair.

"Damn, it's dark in here," Seth cursed and rubbed his chin. As if on cue, a door opened to the parlor and Mrs. Koslowsky appeared, holding a lighted candle and looking like an apparition in her white nightgown and wildly disheveled gray hair.

"What is going on? What are you doing in my house? HELP!" she screamed.

Dan backhanded the old woman, sending her sprawling. Mrs. Koslowsky tumbled backwards over a footstool, dropped the candle and fell, hitting her head on the ledge of the fireplace. She crumpled to the floor and lay still, blood oozing from her temple. Just then, another door opened and Amy appeared, illuminated by her own candle. She was dressed in a nightgown and a hastily donned robe which she held together with her right hand. Her terrified stare went from the intruders to the still figure of her landlady.

"Mrs. Koslowsky!" she cried and rushed to the landlady's motionless form. "What did they do to you? Can you hear me?" Tears streaming down her face, Amy cradled the old woman's body in her arms. Seth reached down, grabbed her by the arm and yanked her off the floor. Amy screamed and Seth slapped her across the face.

"Shut your mouth, bitch, if you know what's good for you," he snarled. When Seth dragged her out of the house, Amy fought like a hellcat, kicking and scratching. She screamed at him and when Seth put his calloused hand over her mouth to muzzle her, she sank her teeth into his fingers. Cursing with pain, Seth yanked his right hand away and cradled it underneath his armpit, while keeping a firm grip on her with his left. He was afraid that her screams would alert the neighbors and that they might have to leave her behind. Exasperated, Dan took two steps and swung his fist into Amy's stomach, causing her to double over, gasping for breath.

"Control her," he snarled.

The old woman came to and saw Amy struggling with the intruders. "Help!" she screamed at the top of her lungs.

Without a second thought, Dan drew his gun, pointed it at the old woman's head and pulled the trigger. By then Seth had Amy by the arm and half-dragged, half-carried her the rest of the way out of the house.

"Here, hold the bitch for a moment, will you?" Seth thrust the girl at Dan when he joined them, then darted back into the house, only to re-emerge moments later, grinning.

"Jesus Christ man, are you nuts? Firing your gun, waking up the neighborhood?" Jonah hissed at Dan when they returned to the horses. "Let's get the hell outta here before anyone sees us."

"I had to shoot the old bitch to keep her quiet," Dan said and holstered his gun. He was about to mount up when flames licked up the inside of Mrs. Koslowsky's house, igniting the curtains. Smoke poured out of the open door. He shook his head and fixed Seth with a look of utter contempt.

When Amy saw the flames, she screamed.

Seth hoisted the terrified girl onto the rump of his pony and climbed into the saddle. Straddling the horse, Amy's nightgown rode up high on her legs, exposing her thighs. Grinning, Seth reached behind him and stroked her bare skin. "Pretty legs, ain't they?" he said to nobody in particular. "See, missy, I told you I'd come callin' on you again."

Amy slapped his hand away and Seth grinned. "Just wait, you sweet thing. We'll go dancin' yet."

"You molest her, you son-of-a-bitch; and I'll castrate you." Dan hissed, mounting his horse.

"Well, lookie here, Dan, the defender of chastity," Seth scoffed. "What do you know."

"I don't give a damn about chastity." Dan's voice was flat. "That girl is Charley's ticket to freedom and I ain't gonna be stuck with no damaged goods. They might not want her back if they find out that she's been rutted by a misfit like you. So lay off her. Touch her all you want for all I care, but that's all. You hear me?"

Seth mumbled something under his breath. Dan crowded his mount against him and pushed his face close to Seth's. "I said you hear me?"

"Yeah, yeah, I hear you," Seth answered in an aggrieved voice.

"Alright." Dan gave him a warning look.

"Look!" Jonah exclaimed, pointing in the direction of town. They all turned their heads. Lights were coming on in the neighboring houses.

Seth shot Dan a venomous glance. "Jesus. Let's get outta here," he hissed. "We'll have the whole damn town down on us." They spurred their ponies into a dead run. Amy clung desperately to her abductor to avoid being thrown. She felt the horse's muscles expanding and contracting under her as they pounded out of town at breakneck speed. Behind them people streamed out of their houses staring at the raging fire which had engulfed Mrs. Koslowsky's house.

Amy heard the neighbors shouting for the marshal. Clinging to Seth, her mind went numb. This couldn't be happening to her. She had to be dreaming. But the pounding horse beneath her and the rank smell of her captor told her that it was all too real. "Ben!" she cried in a half whisper. Why her mind turned to him at a time like this didn't concern her. She only knew that suddenly and clearly she wanted to see him again more than anything else in the world right now.

Seth jabbed her in the ribs with his elbow. "Shut up, you uppity bitch. Your Ben ain't gonna help you." She heard him snicker. "I swear, he ain't never gonna find you. I'll make sure of that."

His voice sent her into another paroxysm of rage and fear. But fighting back her nausea, she steeled herself against the terror. If there was a way out of this… this hell, it would only come from her and her alone. She had to think! What had that ferret-like man meant when he told the Mansons that she was somebody's ticket to freedom? He had mentioned a name, something like Charley or another, she could not recall. What did he have to do with her?

Her abductors rode for over an hour at a hard canter. Amy's legs were on fire. Her whole body ached and she was beginning to feel sick. After what had seemed like eternity, the riders finally slowed. They turned off the path and rode north for a few miles before filing into a dense stand of pine trees. Seth slid off his mount, reached up, and pulled Amy off the horse. She dropped to the ground, wrapped her arms around her knees and stared defiantly at her captors. Dan jumped off his pony, strode over to Seth, and hit him squarely in the face with his fist. Seth staggered back against his horse, who snorted and stepped sideways, causing him to fall.

"What the hell was that for?" Seth yelled, aggrieved, and felt his swelling nose. His hand came away dripping with blood.

"You stupid son of a bitch," Dan snarled and gave him a vicious kick. "You just ruined my plans. While you two was gonna take the girl, I was-" he pulled out a piece of paper and waved it under Seth's nose, "I was gonna ride into town and push this ransom note under the marshal's door. You had to set that house on fire, didn't you," he aimed a savage kick at Seth. "You called the whole damn town down on us. All you got for brains is mush, you drunken slob."

"Was you shootin' the old woman what woke them up, you-"

"*Shut up!* Or I'll kill you right here!" Dan was in a blinding rage and he tugged at his Colt.

Seth was terrified. He scrambled to his feet and held out his hands in front of him as if to shield himself from Dan's bullet. "Don't! For God's sake, Dan, don't shoot! I didn't know what you was planning, honest, or I wouldn't have-"

"Aw shut up." Dan, still seething, dropped his gun back into its holster. "The damage's done." He turned his back to Seth, pulled his makings out of his shirt pocket and rolled a cigarette. "We'll rest here for an hour," he said when he had his voice back under control. "We got to settle on where we're gonna hole up."

"What about our ranch?" Seth offered timidly, examining his swollen nose with his clean hand.

Dan rolled his eyes and shook his head. "Jeez, use your head, you dumb bastard. You're so stupid you couldn't drive nails in a snow bank. You think the marshal ain't figured out by now who's behind the kidnapping? Your ranch is the first place they'll look. They're probably forming a posse right now to come after us." He searched his pocket for a match. "From now on, neither of you do nothing without asking me first. Nothing. You got that?"

The brothers nodded mutely but with a seething anger in their eyes. Amy was too numb with fatigue and fear to follow their conversation. Even the thought of Mrs. Koslowsky being shot to death caused her only momentary distress. She almost wished that she too had been killed. It would have been a horrible death - she trembled at the thought of it - but no worse than what was in store for her. Ransom or not, these fiendish men would never let her go. They knew that she would identify them and therefore they had to kill her after they were done with her.

The words spoken by the outlaw called Dan went round and round in her mind. *Ticket for somebody Charley's freedom.* What did he mean? Who was this Charley? Suddenly it dawned on her. The prisoner that Marshal Boudreaux had locked up in jail! Of course! That's what the ransom note was all about. They would offer her up for this Charley something to be released.

"Alright you two." Dan sounded like a drill sergeant. "Listen up. Here's what we're gonna do. You two take the girl. You ride west from here, then head north." He kneeled down and picked up a stick. "Someone light a match. Okay. You circle around here." He drew lines in the sand. "The canyon where we stashed the cows is here. About twenty miles west is a mountain that looks like a camel's hump. You'll be riding along a sheer wall till you get to a small woods. Make your way in there and look for an opening in the wall big enough to let a horse through. Ride through that opening and you'll be in another small canyon with a creek running through it. Me and Charley found that place by chance and I was probably the first white man to have ever been in there. Nobody's gonna find you there."

The match burned Jonah's fingers and he dropped it with an oath. Dan stood up and obliterated the scratchings with his boot. "That's where I'll meet you. You'd best get going."

"What are you gonna do?" Jonah asked suspiciously. It rankled him that Dan was giving the orders now. Dan was supposed to take orders from *them*, not the other way around.

"I'm gonna deliver the ransom note to the marshal."

"You're gonna *deliver* the note to the marshal?" Seth barked an incredulous laugh. His nose hurt like hell. "How you gonna pull that one off? Walk up to the marshal and say, 'Hey Marshal, here's my ransom note.'"

Dan glowered at Seth, murder in his eyes. "I don't quite know how I'm gonna pull it off, now that you screwed up things plenty. But I'll figure out a way." He turned to face Jonah, who looked back at him with a sullen look on his face. "If I was you, I'd take that nitwit brother of yours and start riding. Hide during the day. Don't forget you're on Double-T land. Whatever you do, don't let 'em catch you." Dan gathered up the reins and mounted his pony. He walked his horse over to Seth and looked down at him. "You keep away from that girl, you understand? If I find out that there's been any hanky-panky, I swear to God I'll kill you." Dan pulled out his gun and pointed it at Seth's head who shrank away. Then, touching his pony's flanks with his spurs, Dan holstered his gun and left the woods. He was instantly swallowed by the dark.

"Keep away from the girl. I'll kill you." Seth mimicked Dan's words, mocking him only after Dan was well out of hearing range. "Who the hell does he think he is?" he protested. "Where does he get off giving the orders? He works for us, don't he?"

"Worked is more like it," Jonah said and climbed into the saddle. "Past tense. I'm sure not gonna tangle with that guy. He's a mean hombre." He motioned to his brother. "C'mon, we'd better get going."

Seth cocked his head. "You afraid of him?"

"Yes. Aren't you?"

Now that Dan had left, Seth was full of bravado. "Hell, I ain't afraid of that no good son-of-a-bitch. He's all hat and no cattle."

"No cattle? You're right there." Jonah sounded bitter.

Seth dug into his saddle bag and came up with a bottle. He pulled out the cork with his teeth, took a healthy swig, and punched the cork back into the bottle with the flat of his hand.

Jonah heaved a sigh of disgust. "Let's get moving," he said.

Amy felt Seth's calloused hands on her and smelled the liquor on his breath before he leaned over in his saddle and yanked her to an upright position, causing her to cry out in distress.

Seth guffawed. "Okay your highness, let's go. Your steed awaits you." He grabbed the girl by the waist and hoisted her up behind his saddle. Mounting, he urged his horse into a lope and felt the pleasant sensation of the girl's arms around him. It was a good feeling. It had been a long time since he had been this close to a woman. Seth thought of Dan's warning to leave the captive unmolested. *One thing at a time*, he thought, *let's see how things turn out*.

Sitting behind the outlaw, Amy felt wretched, a feeling which quickly turned into rage overpowering her physical agony. The high cantle of her captor's saddle dug into her stomach, her bare thighs chafed against the horse's fur, and her legs began to cramp.

The ride seemed endless. It began to drizzle. The drizzle turned to a steady rain and the air turned cold, which only added to her misery. Her exhaustion, the cold, and her fear caused her to hallucinate. She saw Savage and the marshal ride towards her, deep in discussion, passing her and her captors without even a glance. She wanted to cry out to them to save her, but her voice would not obey. Amy felt abandoned. Nobody was coming to rescue her. Seth had boasted that Ben Savage would never find her, should he even bother to come looking. Despairing, she let go of her captor and would have fallen off the horse had Seth not caught her by the arm and eased her to the ground.

"We'll make camp here," He said.

38

"Miss Cabbett was kidnapped," Boudreaux repeated to a white-faced Savage and held the ransom letter out to him. Savage reached for it, blindly, and tried to focus on its scribbled rambling contents:

To Whom it May Concern, it began, in a strangely formal manner. *We got the girl and you can have her back if you give us back yor prisner the one called Cheruky Charlee we also want 10000 dollars in cash for the girl don't give the mony to Charlee don't follow Charlee when he is safe I will let you know where to leave the mony and where you can find the girl no durty tricks iffn you want her back alive.*

The letter was not signed. Amy kidnapped! Savage's feelings for the girl he thought he had been able to put out of his mind came crashing back over him like a giant wave, causing him to hold on to the marshal's desk for support. Any animosity he had harbored toward the young woman turned instantly into anguish and an overpowering need to find her. To save her. The thought of Amy in the hands of kidnappers was his worst nightmare come true.

"Goddamn those bastards," Savage's voice came out in a hoarse whisper. Ed heard the ice in his friend's voice and saw the fury in his eyes, causing him to take an involuntary step back. "Goddamn them to hell whoever they are."

Savage took a threatening step toward the marshal. "How the hell could you let this happen, Ed? This is your town, goddammit."

The marshal glowered at him. "Be fair, Ben. I can't blame you for being upset, but I don't have enough people to post a twenty-four hour guard in front of everybody's house. This kidnapping caught me surprise. I'm not saying this as an excuse. All I can say is that I truly wish I had been there to prevent it."

"I trusted you, goddammit. I depended on you, Ed. You let me down. You let those vicious bastards take her without a fight. You-"

"Stop it right there, Ben." The marshal's voice came out in a hoarse whisper.

Savage fought to get his rage and anguish under control and took a deep breath. "Do you have any idea who took Amy?"

Boudreaux nodded, still angry. "Some of the neighbors were awakened by the break-in, followed by a gunshot and the fire. And Ben," the marshal continued, "they killed Miss Cabbett's landlady."

"Jesus," Ben said softly.

"The neighbors are pretty sure that they identified the Mansons accompanied by a third person."

Savage stared at him. "The Mansons! Jesus, I should have known. I never trusted those bastards."

"Do you think the Mansons were the ones behind this rustling business?" the marshal asked.

Savage nodded. "I have no direct proof but I'm convinced that they did, especially now."

Boudreaux looked at the rancher. "You foiled their rustling plans and now they are holding Miss Cabbett for ransom." He watched Savage pace the room like a caged animal. "I'm getting a posse together at sunup. It's too dark to follow their tracks tonight and I don't have anyone who can read sign."

"Forget the posse, Ed." Savage's voice was flat with suppressed rage. "I've got Mr. Jefferson-"

"Ben, you can't-"

"Yes, I can. Don't tell me what to do, Ed. Jefferson's an expert tracker. As soon as he arrives in town I'll go after those sons-a-bitches, and when I find them…" He paused. "Here's what I want you to do," Savage said. "Let your prisoner go."

"Let my prisoner go? Why on earth would I…"

"Because he'll lead us to the others," Savage interrupted.

The marshal frowned at Savage. "I suppose I could do that but how the hell do we know for sure he's going to lead us to Miss Cabbett?"

Savage massaged his wounded shoulder. "We don't. But I expect that the brothers will be looking for him. They probably had a backup plan even before this Cherokee Charley got himself caught. Maybe they've got a place where they would meet if they were separated." He stopped to think. "I'll send for James Sanders, he's also an expert tracker. Now, if you'll excuse me, I'll go back to the Majestic and wait for my men." Without waiting for an answer, he shouldered his way past his friend and went out into the night.

Savage sat, drowsing in the armchair by the window of his hotel room, when a knock on the door brought him to his feet. He crossed the room in a few rapid strides and opened the door to find James Sanders standing in the hallway.

"Major," the young man said. "Sorry to wake you up, but the marshal sent me to fetch you. Your foreman and Rufus arrived at his office a few minutes ago. He wants to have a pow-wow, if you don't mind."

"Josh is here?"

"Yup. He was already in town being treated by the doc. Insists he's well enough to ride. Wouldn't let anyone tell him otherwise."

Without another word, Savage turned, grabbed his hat, and was out the door.

Minutes later, he and the others huddled in the marshal's office. Even though it was five o'clock in the morning, Anne Parker appeared with a basket of food before slipping quietly out the door to return to her room at the Majestic.

Savage swallowed the last piece of bread and took a swallow of his coffee. "Listen up, everybody. I don't have to tell you what this is all about. You all read the ransom note for Miss Amy's release. One of the conditions is to let his prisoner go and the marshal has agreed to release him. I believe that Cherokee Charley will lead us to the Mansons and their sidekick, whoever he is." He addressed James, "I want you to track the Indian. Take Josh with you, assuming you are still insisting on coming?" He looked at his foreman who simply nodded. "Okay. I'm going, too. Any questions? Suggestions?"

"Yes, I have a suggestion." James stood up and poured himself another cup of coffee, stirring in two spoons of sugar to mask the black brew's bitter taste. He blew on the cup, took a sip, and made a face before continuing. "I plan to go after Cherokee Charley, but not with Josh." He turned to address Savage's foreman. "No offense, Josh, but I think you, your boss, and Rufus ought to go after the Mansons and Miss Cabbett. We can't be sure that the marshal's prisoner will lead us to her. The rain probably washed out their tracks but if you keep searching north you're bound to come across their tracks eventually." James finished his coffee and set down his empty cup. "I'm taking my cousin Aenohe Nestoohe, Howling Hawk in English. He's Cheyenne and the best tracker in the whole valley."

"We don't have time to wait for any cousin of yours-" Savage began.

"He's waiting outside."

"Oh. Well, tell him to come in then," Savage said impatiently. "I want to talk to him."

"You may want to talk to him but he won't talk to you. Howling Hawk doesn't speak English and he doesn't talk to White men." James moved to the door, opened it, and stuck out his head, motioning his cousin to come in.

Howling Hawk followed James into the office. He was a big man and stood passively, thumbs hooked into his belt. His black eyes flicked from Savage to the Marshal and to Josh.

"Your cousin don't look friendly," Josh remarked, studying the Indian.

"The Cheyenne don't have much reason to be friendly toward you lot." James said.

"But is he willing to help us?" Savage asked.

James spoke briefly to Howling Hawk who nodded his head and responded in a short burst of guttural syllables. "He says yes," James translated.

Savage's impatience got the better of him. "Fine then. Let's get started. We're wasting time. Josh, Rufus, you come with me." He turned to James. "I expect our paths will cross within the next day or so."

James nodded. "I expect you're right."

39

The Manson Brothers were on the move again in the darkness with an exhausted and half delirious Amy in tow. The young woman was in total despair. Her hair was matted, her legs scratched by branches and underbrush. The soles of her feet were raw from walking barefoot on pine needles and rocks during their infrequent stops. Her nightgown and robe were torn and barely covered her. Amy had been yanked out of the safe, genteel environment of a comfortable home and a lawful society. She had been thrust into an outlaw's world where none of the rules which she had taken for granted applied, rules that had shaped her world until last night. She felt exposed, violated, and dreaded what her fate would be before they did away with her. Bouncing along painfully, holding on to the man in the saddle in front of her, she looked up at the sky, trying to determine which way the Mansons were headed. She knew that the North Star was among the most prominent in the firmament but she had trouble locating it among the hundreds of thousands of glittering lights in the night sky.

Amy was not at all certain that Ben Savage would track her captors and rescue her once he found out that she had been kidnapped. Not after the way she had rejected his advances. The rancher was a proud man and she knew that she had hurt him. Amy knew that tracking was an arduous, time-consuming task; and the rancher had a business to run. Besides, how would he know where to pick up her captors' tracks?

This country was so big, so remote, with so many hiding places. And yet he was her only hope. "*Oh Ben, I didn't mean what I said,*" she breathed to herself. "*I am sorry. Ben, you are my only hope. I swear I will make it up to you. I swear I will.*"

The Mansons made camp in a dense stand of timber at daybreak. Shivering with cold and exhaustion, Amy let herself be helped off the horse by Jonah. She wrapped herself into the blanket which he had tossed her and fell into a deep and troubled sleep. Hours later, she was awakened by the smell of coffee and bacon. She swallowed the hot and bitter black brew and ate what Jonah offered her on a dirty tin plate. Looking about her, Amy saw that they were closer to the mountains and realized that they were traveling north. The sleep had refreshed her and she knew that she would have to rely on herself if she planned to stay alive.

She thought of offering her captors money for her release, but it was a thin plan at best, with no guarantee that they would release her even if she did pay them. Still, it was the only viable plan she could come up with at the moment and, if nothing else, might buy her some time.

"Mr. Manson," she said.

Both men looked up from the fire and stared at the woman with the disheveled hair.

"Mr. Manson," she said again. "I can offer you money if you will let me go."

"Money." Seth scoffed and put down his empty plate. "Your schoolmarm's salary is what, maybe thirty dollars a month? I betcha' you're spending all that money on them fancy clothes I seen you struttin' around in." He looked at his brother and rolled his eyes at the ridiculous offer.

Jonah ignored him and addressed himself to the young woman. "How much are you willing to pay. What do you think your life is worth?"

"Ten thousand dollars."

"*Ten thousand dollars, hooweeh*," Seth mocked Amy. "That all you think you're worth?"

"Alright, fifteen thousand dollars."

Seth turned to his brother and shook his head. "The girl is loco. We got ourselves some nutty bitch here."

Jonah waved him off. He fixed Amy with his stare. "Where do you intend to get that kind of money?"

"I'm rich," Amy said.

"If you're so rich, what are you doing in teaching in a jerkwater town like Riverside?" Seth asked.

"I like to teach and I thought it was the right thing to do. I'm not doing it for the money."

"We've grabbed ourselves a goody-goody two-shoes." Seth smirked. "So, Highness," he stood up and executed a mocking bow, "where'd you get all that money from?"

She gave him a baleful look. "My father is one of the richest men in Boston. I came into my inheritance when I turned twenty-one," Amy replied. She sensed that Jonah Manson at least believed her and felt a glimmer of hope.

Jonah eyed the young woman. She sounded as if she were telling the truth. "How much money you got?"

Amy's gaze was level. "A lot," she answered.

"Where you keepin' the money? In Boston?" Seth demanded. Where the hell was Boston? All he knew was that it sounded far away.

"Yes, I keep most of it in a bank in Boston and the rest of it is deposited in the bank right here in Riverside."

"So, how do we get ahold of this fifteen thousand dollars?"

"I'll write a note to Mr. Hodges, the president of the bank in Riverside," Amy offered, "and ask him to hand the money over to you or whoever you send after you've let me go."

"Ask him?" Seth scoffed.

"Alright, tell him." Amy corrected herself.

Jonah nodded. "Good enough, me and my brother will think on it. But you'd better not be joshing us about the money or there'll be hell to pay, hear?"

Amy nodded, her fear returning. If nothing else, she hoped that she had bought herself some time. She only hoped that Banker Hodges would honor her note. Amy withdrew into the tentative safety of her blanket.

That evening, the ground became steeper and the night air was cool. Amy sat behind Jonah, whose horse sought its way over the soft, rain-soaked ground. Seth was riding behind as usual, his eyes glued to Amy's legs, which shimmered a ghostly white in the dark. He had just emptied his last bottle of whiskey. His head was pounding and he had trouble staying in the saddle. His stomach heaved. Without warning, bile rose in his throat and he bent over the side of his pony and retched.

Jonah pivoted in his saddle and looked disgustedly past Amy at his brother.

"Jonah, I'm sick to death," Seth croaked. "We gotta stop for a while. I feel like I'm gonna die."

"I hope to God you do!" Jonah shouted at his brother, incensed. "C'mon, we're wasting time."

In response, Seth slid off his horse and sat down on the wet ground, holding his stomach, rocking back and forth in agony. Mumbling curses under his breath, Jonah swung his right leg over his saddle and jumped down. "Stay where you are," he warned Amy. "No funny stuff if you know what's good for you."

Amy looked over her shoulder and watched the two brothers. Jonah was waving his hands, talking to his brother who continued to rock back and forth, shaking his head to what his brother had to say. After a few minutes, Jonah threw his hands in the air in a gesture of disgust and walked back to where Amy sat on his horse. He grabbed her roughly by the arm.

"Get down." He commanded. "We're gonna stay here for a while."

Pulling her arm free, Amy vaulted herself over the cantle into the saddle and pounded the horse's flanks with her heels, causing it to jump forward. Her legs were too short to reach the stirrups and she clung frantically to the pommel to keep from bouncing off the large animal who was now streaking down the incline at full speed. Jonah stood for a split-second, transfixed, staring after the horse which was carrying their hostage away. "Stop, goddammit!" he bellowed, before running to Seth's horse grazing nearby. He jumped into the saddle, forcing the animal into a dead run.

It did not take Jonah long to overtake Amy. Galloping alongside, he leaned over and grabbed the reins of her mount, bringing it to a halt. Without a word, Jonah turned his horse around and returned to camp, a frightened Amy in tow. "Don't ever try that again if you know what's good for you," he threatened in a quiet menacing voice. "Get down."

Amy obeyed. She was cold and wrapped herself in the blanket which Jonah handed her. Seth continued to sit where he had slipped from his horse, holding his stomach, too busy nursing his misery to notice that Amy had tried to escape.

Jonah seethed with rage. With Seth's boozing, there was a good chance that he would foul up their plans to get the ransom money. Jonah was glad that there was no liquor where they were headed.

He gathered some wood but it was wet and he had trouble starting a fire. When the branches caught after a good deal of huffing and puffing on Jonah's part, he built it up until the flames rose high. *Hell, if we can't move, we can at least be comfy*, he thought, moving close to catch the fire's warmth. Let Seth suffer. It served him right.

40

Shortly before sunup Ed walked into the prison, his elongated shadow sliding along the whitewashed wall behind him and set his lamp on the floor. Cherokee Charley sat up, squinted at his jailer and shielded his eyes from the light.

"Alright, Cherokee. On your feet. I'm letting you go." Ed inserted the key in the lock, turned it, and pulled the cell door open. It screeched in its hinges.

Cherokee Charley rose slowly from his bunk and shot the marshal a suspicious look. "You're letting me go? Just like that?" He frowned at Boudreaux, thinking. "What's the catch, Marshal?"

"There's no catch," Ed said. "Come on. Out! Your pony's outside, all saddled up, waiting for you. There's some food in your saddle bags."

Cherokee Charley stood rooted in his cell. "You're planning to kill me, ain't you? Shoot me in the back, claimin' I was trying to run away. Why set me free, suddenlike?"

"Alright, pipe down, I'll tell you," the marshal said and grabbed the prisoner by his arm to propel him out of the cell. "One of your fellow outlaws kidnapped our teacher with the intention of exchanging her for you. Since her life is worth a hundred times more than your miserable existence, I'm happy to let you go to get her back."

"That would be Dan," Cherokee Charlie said.

"Dan who?"

"Dan Hittle. He's a friend of mine."

Ed smiled. He felt vindicated. His guess as to the third man had been correct. During his imprisonment, Charley hadn't spoken more than a dozen words. Now that he was about to be freed he was becoming a fountain of information.

The marshal leaned casually against the open cell door and said, "That Dan can't be such a good friend, since he doesn't want me to give you the ransom money that he wants in addition to letting you go."

Cherokee Charlie focused his attention on the marshal. He leaned forward. "Ransom money? How much money we talkin' about?" he asked, his face conveying greed and excitement.

Boudreaux was enjoying himself. "Ten thousand dollars," he said. "I have a feeling that your buddy Dan wants to keep the money for himself and not share it with you or his other friends."

"His other friends? You talking about the Mansons? They ain't no friends of his."

"Did Dan have dealings with the Mansons?" Boudreaux asked innocently.

"Yeah, they worked together here and there. But like I said, them lame brains ain't Dan's friends," Cherokee said with heartfelt conviction.

"Worked together on what?" Ed asked and earned another suspicious look from the prisoner.

"You ask a lot of questions, Marshal." Cherokee Charley stepped away from the cell and gave the marshal a suspicious look. "You gonna let me go or what?"

"Yes, I told you. You're free to go. Use the back door. I guess I don't have to tell you that you might want to head out of town as quickly as you can. I don't want any of the good townsfolk to see you. They're liable to string you up without so much as by your leave."

Cherokee Charley started for the door but hesitated and turned back to face the marshal, "You gonna give me back my gun and my knife?"

Ed shook his head and flashed his prisoner a malicious grin. "Don't push your luck, Charley. I'm going to keep your gun and knife as a souvenir. Just get the hell out of here and make tracks before I change my mind."

Cherokee Charley shrugged, turned and walked out the door.

James and Howling Hawk crouched in the shadows in the alley between the jail and the adjacent boarding house. They came to attention when the back door to the prison opened and briefly illuminated the shape of a man. Howling Hawk asked a question.

"Yes," James responded, whispering in Cheyenne, "that's our man."

Cherokee Charley swung into the saddle and applied the spurs to his pony. Once his eyes adjusted to the dark, he put his horse into a lope and headed north. James and Howling Hawk followed him with their eyes until he was swallowed up by the dark.

"Let's see where he's headed," James said.

41

Amy was on the move again, sitting behind Seth, whose rank body odor once more threatened to overpower her. The brothers had argued viciously over who Amy would ride behind and Jonah had eventually given in. Seth, unshaven and filthy and reeking of vomit, had leered at Amy as he hoisted her up on his horse.

"Put them sweet arms around me, honey. You go on, hug me. Don't be shy." He stepped into the saddle, reaching back to pat her leg. "I'm so glad we finally got together."

Amy was too discouraged to swat away his hand. She held on to the cantle of Seth's saddle to avoid having to embrace her foul-smelling abductor. The brothers had given Amy paper to write out instructions to the bank to release fifteen thousand dollars and she caught snatches of their conversation which indicated that the money was on their minds. She was still overcome by fits of panic and hopelessness but resolved that she would come out of this situation alive. Would Mr. Savage come to her rescue after the way she had treated him? He had a small army of men at his beck and call and was familiar with the territory. Even if he did, Amy feared that he might be too late.

Seth was disappointed not to feel Amy's arms around his waist. He twisted around in the saddle and grinned at the girl. "Put your arms around me, sweet honeybunch, less'n you fall off my horse. We wouldn't want that to happen, do we?"

Amy ignored his entreaty.

"C'mon, put your sweet arms around me, honey," Seth urged her again, more insistently.

"Not till you take a bath. You smell awful," Amy said, keeping her voice level.

Seth laughed. "You sure do smell sweet to me, honey." He stroked her leg and faced forward again. "But bein' it's you, askin', I'll take a dip as soon as we hit some water."

The night turned to gray, accompanied by a warm breeze. Little by little, the dark shadows retreated before the early-morning light. Amy studied Seth's back. He was dressed in a stained checkered shirt which ended inside the broad leather belt holding up his cord pants. A second belt, cartridges filling its loops, slanted down to his left hip, ending in a holster carrying a large pistol. Amy leaned forward and surreptitiously touched the butt of the gun. Using her thumb and index finger, she tried to lift the weapon and found to her surprise that it seemed to be stuck. She had seen men draw their guns with lightning speed and was puzzled that Seth's pistol wouldn't budge. Leaning closer, she saw that the revolver was secured by a leather thong that its owner had slipped over the gun's hammer to prevent it from falling out of its holster.

Amy had only fired a handgun twice. She didn't like the sound of a gun and the way it jumped when she pulled the trigger. She had put the pistol away, resolving to never fire a weapon again. If she had access to a gun now, would she kill her captors? Yes, Amy thought. Yes she would, without hesitation. As if Seth had sensed her thoughts, he reached down to touch the butt of his revolver. Amy hastily withdrew her hand, but her eyes remained glued to Seth's holster. She would have to wait for the right time.

The rapidly rising sun bathed the looming mountains and surrounding countryside in daylight, devouring the last of the shadows clinging to the ground. To Amy's surprise, Jonah pushed on, pursued by Seth who kicked his mount to catch up with Jonah.

"Hey, brother. It's daylight, in case y'all hadn't noticed. Ain't it time to hole up in some thicket and wait out the day?"

Jonah pointed to the mountain range looming up in their immediate front. "See that yonder mountain, the one that's shaped like a camel's hump? Look, there's the wall Dan talked about. No sense wasting time. We can't be more than half an hour at the most from the canyon. Maybe less. The sooner we get there, the better."

"What if somebody sees us?"

"Somebody see us here?" Jonah scoffed. "Nobody's been up here in ages." He glanced at his brother. "Look, I'm tired and thirsty. Let's just get the hell to our hiding place and be done with it. Come on, we're almost there."

They rode single file along the rock formation heading west. Their mounts labored to keep their footing on the loose gravel. The rays of the sun bore down on them and reflected off the rock wall, which radiated waves of heat. Despite Jonah's estimate, it was almost an hour before they reached the base of the wall. Soon their canteens were empty and there was no lake or stream in sight. Amy felt weak with thirst and had to use all of her remaining strength not to tumble off the horse which stumbled along, urged on by its rider.

"Look." Jonah pointed at the woods a few hundred yards in front of them. His voice was hoarse and he swallowed painfully. "That's got to be the stand of timber Dan was talking about. We're close to our hiding place. Dan said there would be plenty of water."

It took them only a few minutes to reach the trees. They spent an indeterminable amount of time searching for the entrance to the canyon but could not find it. Jonah was about to give up and make camp when his horse raised its head, whinnied, and headed straight for the wall.

Jonah waved to his brother, "Hey, look, I found it." The entrance consisted of a slit in the wall hidden by dense underbrush. Bending low over the saddle Jonah preceded Seth and Amy through the opening. "Leave it to the horses to smell water!" he shouted over his shoulder.

Inside the canyon the horses tossed their heads and picked up their pace. High walls kept out the morning sun and the air in the canyon was cool. A brook ran down its northern wall, flanked on either side by dense, lusciously green grass. The canyon was small, approximately five hundred yards long and about two hundred and fifty yards wide at the entrance. The steep walls closed in toward the rear to form a cave, a rocky overhang providing protection from the elements. Dense brush lined the rock walls. The brothers nodded their heads approvingly and agreed that it was the perfect hide-out. Seth slid off the saddle, grabbed Amy by the waist, and pulled her off his pony. She twisted out of his grasp and ran over to the brook, threw herself down and drank greedily, not caring that her hair hung down into the water. The brothers squatted next to their horses, who had their muzzles in the creek, scooping up water with their cupped hands to quench their thirst.

A hand on her shoulder pulled Amy up. It was Seth. "Don't drink so much at once. It'll make you sick." He held her face between his hands and planted a kiss on her lips.

Amy broke free and slapped Seth, hard, causing him to step back. He glowered at her, hands on his hips, as if deciding what to do with her. Finally he made an about face and stalked off. Amy watched him go and slumped with relief only to be confronted by Jonah who had re-emerged from the cave.

"Go and make yourself useful. Make some coffee," Jonah said. "There's plenty of dead wood around. You do know how to make a fire, don't you?"

Amy walked over to the cave, acutely conscious how little her tattered nightgown and robe covered her. Her face was burning with the humiliation she had endured at the hands of her captor. She collected dry twigs and waited for Jonah to light the fire. She glanced at the gun belts which the brothers had unbuckled and left in the cave. Seth followed her eyes, grinned, and put them on a ledge out of her reach before walking toward the entrance of the canyon wall. There the stream widened enough to accommodate a single person. As Amy watched him out of the corner of her eyes, Seth pulled off his boots, shed his filthy shirt and trousers and dropped them on the ground in a pile. Standing about two hundred yards away in full view of the girl he pulled down his long underwear. Naked, he made a lewd gesture and waded into the stream where he stood for a moment, shivering, before lowering himself into a sitting position. Only his head was visible.

"Hey honey!" he yelled, sounding cheerful. "Get me some clean clothes out of my saddle bag, will ya? And bring it here!" When Amy hesitated, he called again. "C'mon, get me them clothes, darlin'! Hurry up, I'm freezing."

Jonah gave her a disgusted look, "Jesus, girl, get him his clothes, otherwise we'll have to listen to his caterwauling all afternoon."

Amy hesitated, looking at the fire.

"Yoo-hoo, honeybunch, how about my clothes?" Seth sang out.

"You can make the coffee later. For God's sakes, just get him his damn clothes before he drives me nuts," Jonah growled.

Amy approached Seth's pony. It raised its head to look at her and went back to cropping grass. She opened the saddle bag and was surprised to find pants and a shirt which were indeed clean and neatly folded. She closed the flap and carried the clothes to where Seth sat in the stream. She bent down to put the clothes on the ground. When she straightened up, Seth stood up and presented himself in all his nakedness, making Amy recoil in shame and disgust.

"You like that, don't you." Seth's face was contorted into the leer that she had come to know. She had never seen a naked man before. She ran back to the cave, legs flashing, her face scarlet, Seth's derisive laughter ringing in her ears.

42

"White men are stupid," Howling Hawk observed as he eyed the unmistakable tracks made by Cherokee Charley's horse. "No Cheyenne would ever leave sign like that."

"The man we're tracking is an Indian, a Cherokee, not a white man," James reminded him, which only earned him a dismissive wave by from cousin.

"Cherokees are as stupid as white men," Howling Hawk spat.

James reserved his judgment. The Cheyenne were an elitist people, who considered themselves superior to the other tribes and James knew better than to argue with his fierce relative. It was true that their prey had made no attempt to hide his tracks and seemed to be heading straight for his destination. This suited James just fine, since it made their job tracking him that much easier. He guessed that they were about three hours behind the fugitive Indian and passed his thoughts on to Howling Hawk who grunted a response which James decided to take for a yes. They were moving into the foothills and the trackers became more cautious to avoid being detected in the event that Charley doubled back to make sure he wasn't being followed.

Howling Hawk held up his hand and dismounted. He squatted on his heels, and checked the damp soil. James slid off his horse and squatted next to him.

"Look," the Indian said and pointed to a set of tracks which converged with the ones made by Cherokee Charley's horse. "Two horses. One carrying double."

James bent down and looked at the hoof prints that Howling Hawk was pointing to. The tracks ran parallel to each other and one of the horses had left deeper imprints which indicated to James and his cousin that it was carrying two riders.

"It looks like Cherokee Charley and the kidnappers met here and traveled on together." James said.

Howling Hawk shook his head. "The tracks made by the two horses are older, see?" He pointed to one of the prints. "The tracks are beginning to fill in. The ones made by the Cherokee's horse are still crisp."

"That means Savage and his men can't be far behind, unless they haven't come across the tracks yet," James said. He looked at the sky. "It's getting late. Let's make camp over there." He pointed at a stand of ponderosa pine a few hundred yards up the trail.

James and Howling Hawk walked their horses into the trees and dismounted. The Indian turned to look back in the direction they had come from and raised a warning hand. "Somebody coming," he said.

"Where? I don't… "

Howling Hawk gestured again, telling James to be silent. Rifles ready, they crouched at the edge of the timber and watched. It was getting dusk and the contours of the trees, the rocks, and the horizon began to wash into each other. James saw a movement and three riders emerged from the dusk.

"That's Savage, Rufus, and Josh. I'd recognize Rufus anywhere the way he forks his horse. Let's not startle them. The Major and Rufus are liable to drill us both."

Howling Hawk nodded in agreement. He and James watched the horsemen pass by. When they were at a distance of twenty yards, James stood up and stepped out of the trees.

"Major, Rufus, over here," he called in a low voice. "It's James. For godsakes, don't shoot." He held up his hands, watching the two men twist in his saddle, looking at him, guns in hand. The men stared at each other, frozen in their positions for several seconds before Savage and Jefferson returned their guns to their holsters. James exhaled. He lowered his hands and waited for the three men to approach him.

"What's the matter, James? You lost?" Josh called out.

"Keep your voice down, man," James shushed him. "We don't know how much of a lead Cherokee Charley has."

"What are you doing here, James?" Savage slid out of the saddle. James offered his hand and they shook.

"It's getting dark, but let me show you something." James led the way with Savage in his wake. Rufus and Josh, still on horseback, followed. After having walked twenty steps he squatted on his heels and pointed to the ground. "Look, three tracks. Here's the one made by Cherokee Charley and here," he pointed again, "are the tracks you're following."

Josh slid out of the saddle and studied the hoof prints. "The Mansons must be less than a day ahead of your man, looks like."

James nodded, "I think you're right. I think they angled west first and then headed north, while Cherokee Charley made a beeline for wherever he's headed. They had to cross paths sooner or later."

Josh stood up and fished in his pocket for a cigarette, which he had rolled on the way but had decided not to smoke till now.

"I wouldn't light up now, if I were you." James warned. "It's pretty near dark and you can see the light quite a ways off. We're planning on making a cold camp tonight."

The foreman gave his cigarette a longing look and put it back in his pocket. "That reminds me," he said, "where's that scary cousin of yours?"

"Around. If he wants to let you see him, he will."

Josh shuddered. "He gives me the creeps, lurking somewhere in the shadows."

James response was curt. "Give it a rest, mister. He's on our side."

Savage, Josh, and Jefferson picketed their horses, removed the saddles, and joined James for hard tack and biscuits. While they ate, Josh told James how they had spent all morning looking for tracks before Jefferson picked up the kidnappers' trail outside a thicket where they had holed up for the day. Once they had come across the tracks, the trail was easy to follow. They made good time and guessed, by examining the horses' droppings, that they were about a day behind them. The outlaws had made no attempt to hide their tracks, even though they must have figured that they would be followed. "I guess they probably thought they'd throw us off by heading west and hoping that the rain would wash out their tracks," Josh said. "From what I seen, I guess your man didn't bother to cover his tracks neither. None of these hombres seem too bright."

"How far do you think it is to where they're holed up?" Savage asked, staring intently into the distance as if to judge how far they had still to ride.

James shrugged, "We're in the foothills now. I figure half a day's ride, maybe more, I don't know."

Savage suppressed an oath. "Time's running out. We need to find Miss Cabbett before it's too late."

43

Amy, lying in the back of the cave, raised herself on her elbow and looked at her captors. Both were sound asleep. Seth lay on his back, mouth open, snoring loudly while his brother lay still, curled up in a fetal position. She pushed her blanket aside and got up quietly. She tiptoed past the men and walked the length of the canyon to the small entrance. Amy knew that she could not retrieve any of their guns without waking them up. The water in the small stream looked cool and inviting, its ripples catching the few rays of sunlight that penetrated the otherwise gloomy canyon. Amy had not been able to wash since she had been taken by force from Mrs. Koslowsky's house. But even with the brothers asleep in the cave, she was afraid to take off her tattered clothes. She had no desire to be even more vulnerable to the whims of those loathsome men. She eyed the small canyon entrance. If she slipped out of the canyon, she might be able to hide from the brothers until she was rescued. It never occurred to her that it might take days, even weeks before anyone would stumble onto her hiding place.

Suddenly, without warning, two arms encircled her waist and she felt herself being thrown on her back on the grass. Amy screamed. Seth towered over her, naked. He threw himself down on her, covering her, his hands groping. Amy screamed and fought her attacker with all her strength until he slapped her, hard, knocking the wind out of her.

"Shut up, bitch. Stop fighting," Seth snarled and hit her again. Amy's world went dark and she began to lose consciousness when she saw a second man looming over her.

Seth yelped in pain as he was yanked off the girl by his hair.

"Get up, you bastard," Dan hissed, eyes blazing. Seth's eyes bulged with fear when he felt the cold muzzle of Dan's gun press against his temple. "Didn't I tell you to leave that girl alone? I have a mind to put a bullet through that empty skull of yours, you worthless, mush-brained son of a bitch."

Seth cried out in pain. He grabbed Dan's hand to prevent him from tearing off his scalp. Dan gave him a vicious shove and Seth fell, face-down into the water. He came up, spluttering and coughing.

"Get up girl. Go and make some coffee," Dan said to Amy and held out his hand to help her up. Instead, she scrambled out of his way and made a dash for the anonymity of the dark cave.

Holding the gun by his side, Dan confronted Jonah, his ferret-like face contorted with fury. "Can't I leave you two bastards alone for a minute without your screwing up?" He swung around back to Seth and pointed his gun at him. "Don't even think of going into the cave. I don't want to see you go near the girl."

"I just wanna get my clothes," Seth said, shying away from the gun pointed at his head.

With a look of profound disgust, Dan lowered his gun. "Get his clothes," Dan commanded Jonah. Jonah turned to do as he was told; but Dan grabbed him by his shirt, spinning him back around. "I ever see that squirrel brained brother of yours lay a hand on the girl again, I'll kill you both. That's a promise." He released Jonah's shirt. "Now, get your brother's rags and have the girl make us some chow. I'm hungry."

While Amy cowered in the back of the cave, the three outlaws sat around the fire and talked. She heard Dan tell the Mansons that he had written another ransom note and had given it to a boy with instructions to hand the note to the marshal. "I gave the kid two bits and you shoulda seen his eyes light up," he said.

"How are you going to collect the money?" Jonah asked. "You can't just walk into the marshal's office and pick it up, can you?"

Dan responded with a disgusted look. "Of course not. I ain't stupid. I wrote in the note that the money is to be deposited inside the barn next to that Double-T line shack north of town. I think you know the one I mean. I gave instructions for the person delivering the money to come alone, drop the ransom, and ride off again. I'll be layin' in wait and pick it up when the coast is clear."

"Ain't no more shack," Jonah said. "Seth burned it down not too long ago."

Dan was incredulous. "What in hell is wrong with your brother? He try to burn down that ranch house of yours, too?" Dan asked.

"No," Jonah said.

"Yes," Seth replied which earned him curious looks from the other two men, "but Jonah don't know nothin' about it."

Dan frowned at him. "You burn it down to get a better price buyin' the ranch?"

"No, no!" Seth protested. "That was before we even thought of buying the spread."

"What was?"

"When I tried to burn down the ranch house."

Dan furrowed his brow. "Before you even thought of buying the ranch? What the hell did you do that for?"

Seth reached for his makings and busied himself rolling a cigarette. "Before my brother and me settled here, I visited Paradise Valley by my lonesome to scout out business opportunities, if you know what I mean." He looked at the other men to see whether they were in on his joke but they only scrutinized him with mildly incredulous looks. "Lookin' around, I come across the spread what belonged to the marshal, only he wasn't the marshal then, and saw this really good-looking woman. And I mean good looking. She was friendly, too and so I figured that she had taken a liking to me. There wasn't nobody else around. Her husband and all of his boys was somewheres, chasing cows I guess. I followed her into the house and put my arms around her. I guess she didn't like that one bit and so I got mad, what with her giving me the eye and then pretend that she didn't want nothing to do with me." Seth's face was set and he had a far-away look as if he was trying to relive that particular episode in his life.

"And?" Dan prompted.

"God, she was beautiful, every bit as pretty as our schoolmarm. When I was done with her and got off her, she grabbed the lamp on her nightstand and threw it at me. She missed. Well, I got mad and belted her one. I guess I hit her harder'n I intended cause I knocked her out. There was that oil on the floor and I had this pocket full of matches…" his voice trailed off.

"Jesus, Seth. The marshal lost both his wife and baby in the fire." Jonah said in an accusing tone.

"Aw, hell. I didn't know nothin' about no baby bein' in the house. Besides…" Seth shrugged his shoulders.

"You *are* one sick son of a bitch." Dan said. "Well, ain't my problem." He pushed himself off the floor. "I gotta go if I want to meet up with Charley and get to the barn ahead of whoever is delivering the ransom money." He took a few steps toward his horse and stopped. He turned around to face the brothers. "By the way, I upped the ransom amount to twenty thousand dollars. Easier to divide by four." He laughed. "I bet they's scrambling right now to come up with the extra money." He looked around the canyon. "You stay put until me and Charley get back and then we'll see what we wanna do with the woman. In the meantime if I find out that you've molested the girl I'll..." He aimed his index finger at Seth and made a popping sound. "Don't mess up if you know what's good for you."

"Ain't you going to take her with you and exchange her for the ransom money?" Jonah asked.

"Hell no. I said in my ransom note that I'd leave a clue at the barn where they can find her." Dan replied and climbed into the saddle. He took one last look around the canyon. The Mansons could not know that he had no intention of sharing the ransom money with them. They also did not know that Dan didn't care what happened to the girl. Once he was in possession of the money, he and Charley were leaving the territory and go back to Texas. With one final glance at the brothers looking up at him, he put the spurs to his horse and rode through the hole in the canyon wall.

Jonah watched him leave. "You think he's going to share the ransom money with us?" he asked his brother.

"Maybe he will and maybe he won't." Seth grinned. "Don't really matter. We're gonna collect for the girl one way or another. Fifteen thousand is a lot of money."

44

A gray dawn filtered through the branches of the trees, slowly bringing the terrain surrounding the woods into focus. Savage had slept fitfully all night, worrying about the young schoolteacher. Would they find her in time? Was she still alive? Had the brothers harmed her? A red blazing fury at the Mansons blossomed within him and he gave vent to his feelings of what he would do to them once they met face to face. He rolled out of his blanket and stretched the kinks out of his tall frame. The mountain air was fresh and cool with the promise of a pleasant day. A distinct feeling that Amy was close came over him and he was consumed by the urge to push on. He shook James awake with the toe of his boot.

"It's getting light. We should move on."

The horses, frisky and rested, snorted and sidestepped the approaching men before submitting to being saddled.

"Where's that Injun cousin of yours, James?" Josh asked, looking around furtively.

"Around." James said in a voice that discouraged further remarks about Howling Hawk. He pointed. "There he is."

The Indian stood at the edge of the timber scowling at the small group of men. He approached James and said a few words in Cheyenne. James nodded and faced Savage.

"Howling Hawk thinks he knows where they're holding Miss Amy."

Savage came alive. "Where?"

James conferred with the Indian. "He says he used to hunt in this neck of the woods with his father when he was a young warrior. About half a day's ride from here is a hole in the mountain which leads into a small box canyon. He used to make camp there. Just a minute." He tilted his head toward Howling Hawk and conferred with him again. "There's a small stream runs though the canyon. Plenty of grass for horses. A good place to hide out."

Savage couldn't contain his anxiety. "Is he sure?"

James spoke to Howling Hawk who gestured and spoke in a rapid-fire burst of words. He turned back to Savage. "He says there's no other place to go. The world sort of ends in a sheer wall which nobody can climb. If they're not hiding in the canyon, they're camping out in the woods in front of it."

Savage took the reins of his mount. "Can he show us the way?"

James spoke to Howling Hawk, who nodded. The tall Indian grabbed hold of his pony's mane and swung himself up on its bare back in one graceful motion. Without waiting for the others, he rode out of the woods. Savage and the others scrambled to catch up with him. They pulled back on their reins when Howling Hawk stopped his pony and turned back to them. He held up his hand, palm out, and uttered a few sentences in Cheyenne which sounded like a threat.

"Now what?" Josh was irritated. The Indian was making him nervous.

"All he said was for us to give him an hour's lead time. We're making way too much noise, me included," James answered and dismounted. "We might as well fix some breakfast while we wait."

Howling Hawk leaned over the side of his saddle, his coal-black eyes glued to the ground. He had identified four distinct hoof prints, all heading in the same direction at different times. The further he followed the sign into the mountains, the more convinced he was that the White woman was being held in the small canyon he remembered from his childhood. The entrance was well camouflaged and he felt a flicker of surprise that the men he was trailing would have discovered the hide-out. It must have been sheer luck. He also felt a deep resentment that those White men were despoiling the canyon, a Cheyenne sanctuary, by their presence.

When his cousin James had asked him to help him track a criminal, Howling Hawk, eager for the adventure, had agreed.

"Fine," James had answered, "under one condition, no war paint or breech cloths." He thought about what he had just said and laughed, "You'll scare the rest of the posse half to death."

In tribute to his warrior past, Howling Hawk wore an eagle feather in his hair. He was dressed in buckskin pants and a red and black checkered skirt, given him by James's mother, his aunt, who lived in the big ranch house. His wife Ayashe (Little One) had made his moccasins from deer hide. In the old tradition, she had fashioned the sole and sides from one piece which she stitched together on top with sinews. They fit snuggly as if they were part of his feet and he wore them proudly. Riding bareback, he carried the Henry rifle across his lap. His only other weapon was a large Bowie knife, which he had taken off a White scout whom he had killed many years ago. Howling Hawk knew how to handle both weapons and, being known for his short temper and his willingness to fight, was treated with respect by his peers and elders.

What rankled Howling Hawk most was the reversal of landownership. This land had been tribal property for untold generations until the White settlers crowded in. They brought with them their soldiers, who had eventually fought the native population to a standstill, subjugated them, taken their land, pushed them onto reservations and had destroyed their livelihood and way of life.

Fighting the White man had been heady times for a young warrior, making him feel alive, important, and giving his life a sense of purpose. Pursuing the kidnappers rekindled some of the exhilaration that he had felt as a young warrior and allowed him to use his innate skills. He savored the movement of his pony under him. He filled his lungs with the fresh mountain air and felt the presence of the ghosts of his ancestors looking down on him with approval.

Now Howling Hawk sat quietly on his pony, screened by a dense stand of Ponderosa pine and watched the two riders approach each other. He saw them shake hands and clap each other on the back in joyous greeting. After a short exchange of words which Howling Hawk couldn't hear, and which would have had no meaning for him in any case, the two riders turned their horses and rode south, heading back the way the Indian had come.

45

"Damn, it's good to see you Charley," Dan said. The planes of his ferret-like face re-arranged themselves into a grimace, the closest Dan could come to smiling. "I knew they was gonna trade you for that schoolmarm, and I figured I'd run into you about now. Did they cause you any problems?"

"Naw, wasn't no trouble. They let me out in the middle of the night. Gave me some grub but that son-of-a-bitch of a marshal wouldn't gimme back my gun."

"Anybody follow you?"

"No. Right after I rode out of town, I doubled back an' hid and watched, but nobody come after me." Charley scrutinized Dan. "So, you got the money?"

"The ransom money?" Dan shook his head. "That's where we're headed now. To pick up the ransom. Come tomorrow night, we're gonna be rich, you and me. Richer than we've ever been."

Cherokee Charley rode down the mountain alongside his friend. "Where's the girl, Dan? You gonna hand her back to the marshal?"

"No, nothing like that," Dan said with a malicious grin. "Those two idiot brothers are holding the girl. They think I'm gonna return and split the money with 'em." He laughed without humor. "They got a surprise coming."

"So, what's gonna happen to the girl?" Cherokee Charley asked.

Dan shrugged his shoulders. "That Seth's been trying to rut her and I pulled him off her. Jonah's been making eyes at her." He grimaced. "I seen her nearly naked. She got herself some pretty legs."

"You wasn't interested in her?"

"Naw," Dan waved the question aside and looked at the Indian riding next to him. "Too skinny for me. I like 'em with some meat on their bones."

They rode along in silence, each lost in his own thoughts. Cherokee felt indebted to Dan for springing him out of jail, but he wasn't sure he'd trust him where the money was concerned. He resolved to be extra vigilant.

"How much did you ask for, Dan?"

"Twenty thousand," Dan replied, "ten for me and ten for you. I'll never forget you for saving my life. It's fifty-fifty and that's the way it's gonna be."

They rode for a while without speaking. The only sound was the creaking of the saddle leather and the muted sounds of their horses' footfalls. Their descent was steep at times and their horses stepped carefully to keep their footing on the uneven ground. Cherokee Charley felt naked without his gun. He glanced at his partner. Dan wore a Schofield revolver on his hip, and the butt of his Henry rifle stuck out of the boot beneath his thigh. He also carried a thirty-eight caliber Navy Colt in his waistband.

"How about letting me have that Navy Colt of yours?" Charley asked and held out his hand. "We get in a scrape and I don't have no way to defend myself."

"Sure." Dan pulled the revolver out of his waistband and held it out, butt first. Cherokee closed his fingers around it, hefted the gun to get the feel of it, and dropped it into his empty holster.

"Thanks, now I feel like a man again," He said. "Tell me about your plan to pick up the ransom money."

46

"Riders coming." Howling Hawk had appeared at James elbow without warning. He pointed over his shoulder and dismounted. He and James talked while the others clustered around them expectantly.

Savage could not contain himself any longer. "What's he saying?" he insisted. But James just held up a restraining hand to silence Savage while he listened to his cousin.

When Howling Hawk had finished, James turned to Savage. "There's two riders headed this way. One of them is Cherokee Charley. Howling Hawk did not recognize the other, but I'm guessing it's the guy that I trailed out of the rustler's canyon a while back, the one who met up with the Mansons."

"His name is Dan Hittle. How far away are they?" Savage asked.

James consulted with the Indian. "Could be here any minute. They don't seem to be in a hurry, though."

"We'll waylay them right here," Savage decided. "This is as good a spot as any. They won't be expecting us." He turned to Josh. "You and Mr. Jefferson take up position behind that clump of trees over there. James, Howling Hawk and I will wait for them here. Let's try to take them alive."

Josh pulled his rifle out of the boot under his saddle and nodded to Jefferson. Savage watched the men trot over to the clump of trees he had pointed out to them. They disappeared inside the underbrush.

Good, Savage thought, satisfied. He turned to James who stood at his right elbow. "Lets…" he broke off, confused, and looked about him.

"Where's Howling Hawk? He was here just a minute ago."

James sighed. "It's not my job to keep track of him. He's probably up the trail, watching the riders."

"Will he let us know when they're close?"

"I would expect so," James said peering up the trail. "We'd best keep our eyes peeled." He stopped and pointed. "Well, speak of the devil. Here they come."

A breeze had sprung up. It made the tree branches sway and rustled the leaves as if to sound the alarm that there was trouble ahead. Savage and James watched the riders approach side by side, oblivious of the trap into which they were headed. Savage estimated that they would pass within thirty yards of them. Not only would they have to evade Savage and James, but they were also riding directly into Jefferson's and Josh's line of fire.

"Here goes," Savage muttered through gritted teeth. He emerged from his hiding place, rifle pointed at the riders. "Hold up and raise your arms!" he sang out. "Don't try anything-"

But at the sound of Savage's voice, Dan reflexively reined in his horse. Without a moment's hesitation, Cherokee Charley whipped out his gun, snapped off a shot at his challenger, and slammed his pony into Dan's mount. Grabbing the other horse's reins, he jerked them both down into the ravine to their right. Savage yanked the rifle stock to his shoulder and pulled the trigger. His report mingled with the blast from Rufus's rifle. Cherokee Charley's pony screamed, pawed the air with its forelegs, and toppled over the edge, spilling its rider as it went down.

"Damn." Savage swore. He lowered the smoking muzzle and looked over to James. "Now we'll have to pry them out of there. Could take hours."

He pumped his rifle over his head to attract Josh's attention and signaled him to come back.

"I don't think we'll be able to take them alive, unless they give up. What do you think?" Savage asked Josh after he had come trotting up.

Josh shaded his eyes with his hand and studied the terrain. He pointed to his left. "Looks like the ditch they're in kind of flattens out over there. Me and Rufus could circle around and get behind them."

Savage nodded his head, agreeing. "How long would it take you to circle around? An hour?"

"About that, if we want to avoid them seeing us."

Savage swore. "Damn it to hell! Another hour wasted, unless we split up." He stared in the direction from where the outlaws had come and then looked back at the ravine. "You and Josh keep those outlaws pinned down while James and I press on. Howling Hawk said he knows where there are keeping Am- uh, Miss Cabbett." Savage turned to James who had been standing quietly, his rifle cradled in his arms, listening to their conversation. "You agree?"

James nodded. "Sounds okay to me. We can ride on ahead and Rufus and Josh can follow us when they're done knocking off those bastards. Unless, of course, you want to capture them alive and tell you where they're hiding your woman."

"Damn, I hadn't thought of that. Do we need them? Didn't Howling Hawk say he knows where the Mansons are holed up?" Savage searched his surroundings. "Where the hell is that elusive cousin of yours?"

"I wouldn't worry about him. He'll catch up with us when he's good and ready."

"Look!" Jefferson shouted. Savage wheeled in time to see a fleeting movement in the brush that hugged the far edge of the ravine, followed by a muzzle flash. The gunshot report reverberated in the trees, mingling with a scream and a curse from the spot where the outlaws were hiding.

"Who in hell is doing the shooting?" Jefferson gave Savage a questioning look.

"Howling Hawk, most likely," James answered excitedly

Gunfire erupted from the ravine in rapid succession, five rounds in all. The firing had no sooner ceased when Howling Hawk burst out of the brush and leaped down, out of sight. The others rushed to the edge, guns drawn. Below them, the Indian raised the bloody knife triumphantly over his head and let out a blood-curdling war whoop. Dan lay crumpled, face up in an unnatural position, dead, with a circular hole in his forehead. Cherokee Charley lay face down, his shirt smeared with blood. The breeze drifting through the ravine ruffled his long hair.

"Well." James put away his gun. "So much for taking them alive."

Josh looked at his boss. "Say, Major, think we should bury them? Not that they deserve it but it's the Christian thing to do."

Savage sighed. "Yes, go ahead and do that. James and I will ride on ahead to find Miss Cabbett. We can't waste any more time. You and Mr. Jefferson can follow us when you're done here."

"Is the Injun going with you?" Josh asked.

Savage shrugged. "I would hope so, but Howling Hawk obviously has a mind of his own."

"I believe Howling Hawk will meet us up the road a ways to lead us to the hideout," James said.

"Your word in God's ear," Savage muttered and nudged his horse forward. "Let's move."

47

Amy sat in the darkest part of the cave, trying to keep out of Seth Manson's way as he squatted outside by the stream, stewing over the treatment he had received at the hands of that son-of-a-bitch Dan. He felt his scalp gingerly. It still hurt, as if some of the roots had been dislodged. "If I'd had my gun handy, I woulda put a hole in him so big you could drive a herd of elephants through," Seth mumbled to himself. He pictured himself standing over a prostrate Dan, holding a smoking gun in his hand. Dan would look up at him with dimming eyes and realize, as his life ebbed away, who had been boss all along. He would then reach into the dead man's pocket and retrieve his portion of the ransom money which he would split with Jonah – or maybe not – and take the girl and go to San Francisco. Once in the big city, living in one of those fancy hotels and showering her with gifts, she'd come around to liking him and give herself to him whenever he snapped his fingers.

The more he thought about his day dream, the more real it became. He'd wait for Dan to ride back in, shoot him, take the money and the girl. His brother had better not stand in his way. There was more than one bullet in his gun. Seth's thoughts returned to the girl who was hiding in the cave. Having mentally disposed of Dan, he was free to do with that little bitch whatever pleased him. Women always yelled rape as if that was the worst thing in the world that could happen to them. They screamed and hollered. But, hell, everybody knew that they liked to be treated rough. Once he'd had his way with her, she would beg for more. He remembered how she looked at his nakedness earlier today. She was fascinated. Probably wondering right now what it would have felt like if she had let him do her. The longer he thought about it, the more he was convinced that the schoolteacher was just sitting in there, waiting for him to come to her. It would be up to him to make the first move. That's the way it was done.

Seth heard Jonah talking to the girl, telling her to do something, heard the girl respond. A moment later Jonah stepped out of the cave and eyed his brother with disgust.

"Why don't you get off your butt and see if you can shoot us something to eat?" he spat.

Seth stood up and wiped his hands on the seat of his pants. "Who the hell do you think you are, ordering me around? Why the hell don't *you* go and hunt something? After all, you claim to be the better shot." His eyes fell on the girl who had come out of the cave and stood, both hands holding her shredded clothes together. She did not look at Seth as he leered at her, still convinced of the reality of his dream.

"Alright, I'll go." Jonah reached into the cave and picked up his rifle. He took his horse by the reins and walked toward the entrance to the canyon before turning back to face his brother. "You leave the girl be, hear?"

Seth did not answer. He watched Jonah step through the wall, leaving him alone with the schoolteacher. This was his chance. Putting on his most winning smile, he approached the scowling girl and took her by the shoulders. "How about a little kiss, Honey?" he asked pulling her close. Amy's body went limp as Seth's arms wrapped themselves around her. His breath was foul and she recoiled from the rank smell of his body. They stood like that for a moment, Seth's body pressed against Amy, whose arms hung loosely on either side of him. "Now that's not so bad now? Is it?" he whispered in her ear.

The girl's unresponsiveness angered him. Uttering an oath he grabbed her by the shoulders and held her at arms length. "Listen, bitch," he started when Amy kneed him in the groin with all the strength she could muster.

Seth cried out in pain and his eyes rolled up in his head. He bent over, his hands between his thighs. Cursing, he straightened up slowly, trying to steady himself. Amy stepped back quickly, brought her hands from the folds of her tattered garments to reveal Seth's revolver which she pointed directly at the center of the outlaw's chest. When Seth spied his gun in Amy's hand he stopped, unsure, frantically slapping his empty holster.

"Whoa, that's my gun. How'd you get it?" he asked stupidly, and took an involuntary step backwards.

Amy cocked the gun with both thumbs.

"Okay, now, give it here, woman, before somebody gets hurt," Seth replied nervously and held out his hand. "No need to get carried away, y' hear? I was just playin' with ya. I didn't mean no harm."

Amy aimed at the gun at Seth's head.

"Okay, okay." Seth backed up slowly, arms still outstretched.

"I'll kill you!" Amy screamed with all the pent-up hatred from the last few days. The gun kicked and roared. Seth stood rooted in his tracks. When he realized that she had missed, he lunged forward to grab the weapon; but he was too late. The girl had cocked the gun again and the impact of the next slug punched the outlaw backwards into the creek. He raised his head before falling back into the water, completely still.

Jonah, outside the canyon, heard the first shot that stopped him in his tracks. Hearing the second shot, he wheeled his horse around and pushed through the narrow entrance. Seth was lying half submerged in the small stream. The girl was standing over him with a smoking gun in her hand. He kneed his horse forward. Sensing movement behind her, Amy whirled, cocking the gun again. But Jonah had already reached for his holster and before she could bring her gun to bear, she saw him point his weapon and fire.

48

"There's the entrance, right there, behind that bush," Howling Hawk said to James and pointed.

"Is there any other way into the canyon?" Savage asked James, who translated the question. Howling Hawk shook his head.

"The first man who rides through that entrance is liable to get his head blown off." Savage said. "I'm sure they've got the entrance covered." He heard a woman scream and the report of a gunshot ricocheting off the canyon walls. Savage's blood ran cold. He kicked his horse towards the wall when a second shot rang out. As he made a dash for the entrance, he had a fleeting glimpse of Jonah who had been obscured in the shade of the trees. He was urging his horse through the gap just seconds before Savage, too preoccupied to notice his pursuer.

"Amy!" Savage shouted and forced his horse past the bushes, following Jonah through the opening in the wall.

"Major, don't!" he heard James call after him, but the rancher had already disappeared from sight. The canyon was colder and darker than the sun baked range outside and it took a moment for Savage's eyes to adjust to the subdued light. The sight that confronted him however brought a cry from his lips. Jonah was raising his gun and Savage saw him fire at Amy, who stumbled backward and slumped to the ground.

A red rage flooded Savage's brain. "Jonah!" he bellowed drawing his gun. Jonah jerked his horse around and fired at Savage, who ignored the round zinging inches past his head to flatten itself against the rocky wall behind him. Savage's own aim was true and his first shot penetrated the outlaw's heart, punching him off his horse.

Amy was lying on the ground in a small heap, near the prostate body of Seth Manson. Savage's throat constricted, making it hard for him to breathe. *They killed her*, he thought. *My God, I'm too late. They killed her.* Pushing his horse close to the still form of the young woman, he jumped off and knelt down next to her and touched her shoulder. She came alive with a gasp. Seth's gun was still in her hand and she whipped it around reflexively, pointing it at Savage.

"Don't shoot Amy, it's me. Ben Savage," he said, holding his arms out in front of him.

Amy stared at him with a vacant look in her eyes.

"Amy, it's me," he said again and gently reached out to take the gun away from her.

A deep shudder went through Amy's body and she started to cry as he took her gently in his arms.

Savage was aghast at the sight of the young woman. Her night clothes were in shreds, her arms and legs bruised. Her hair hung down around her face and over her eyes in a matted, tangled mass. Her face was smudged and there was an angry red welt across her temple where Jonah's bullet had grazed her. He patiently rocked her in his arms, making softly soothing noises. Suddenly she clung to him and shook, her tears wetting the front of Ben's shirt.

"Why did they do it? They had no right," she sobbed over and over. "Why me? I didn't do anything to them." She looked pleadingly at Savage and then at the men who had gathered behind him. "Are they…" she whispered. "Are they dead?"

Savage nodded. When she started to cry again, he picked her up and carried her to the back of the canyon. He sat down beside the sobbing girl, holding her hand. James had entered the canyon only moments behind the Major. He jumped off his horse and quickly untied the blanket from his saddle and covered the young woman who was shivering uncontrollably. Amy looked at Savage, clutching his hand as if afraid that he would leave her. As he watched, her breath came more evenly and her features softened. Her eyelids drooped and the grip of her hand on his loosened. Amy was asleep.

An hour later, Josh and the old Sergeant rode into the canyon, single-file. They looked at the bodies of the Manson brothers.

Josh swung out of the saddle. "How's the girl?" he asked, pointing his head at the cave. "She okay?"

"She's sleeping. She must have gone through hell, but she's pretty tough." Savage's laugh was harsh. "When I rode into the canyon, she had just killed Seth Manson." He pointed to the bodies and shook his head. "Amazing, I had heard she was afraid of guns."

"Killed Seth?" Josh marveled. "That girl's got sand." He looked at Jonah's body. "You kill that one?"

Savage nodded. "He was shooting at Miss Cabbett."

"I'm glad she's okay. So, what do we do next?"

"It's too late to start back today. We'll spend the night here and move out tomorrow morning."

"Sounds good to me," Josh said. His eyes searched the canyon. "Hey James, where's that Injun of yours? I ain't seen him anywhere."

James busied himself with making a fire. "He's probably on his way home. Killed himself two men. He figured his job was done here."

"Josh, let's bury the bodies before Miss Cabbett wakes up." Savage suggested.

Amy slept fitfully through the night. When she woke up the next morning, the small camp was abuzz with activity. James was tending to the fire and the smell of bacon and coffee permeated the fresh mountain air. Amy realized that she was starving. Savage, seeing that she was awake, brought her a tin plate heaped with bacon and biscuits. She smiled her thanks and ate ravenously, using her fingers, licking them when she was finished. Savage watched her wolf down her food with a mixture of amusement and relief.

"Would you like some more?" he asked and took the empty plate from Amy.

She shook her head. "Mr. Savage-"

"It's Ben, Amy," Savage corrected her gently.

She nodded. "Ben, uh... did you bring me some clothes?" she asked.

"Clothes?" Savage repeated, uncomprehending. "Oh Lord, of course! Clothes!" He slapped his forehead with the palm of his hand. "Why didn't I think of that?" he answered sheepishly. How stupid of him. How could he have forgotten about bringing clothes? Amy had been kidnapped in the middle of the night and would have been in her night gown. He had been so focused on the rescue operation that he had not given the matter any thought.

"I'm sorry, Amy," he said feeling genuinely contrite, "but clothes were the last thing on my mind. It was stupid of me."

"Seth Manson had a change of clothes with him. Perhaps there's a clean shirt and pants in one of their saddle bags." Amy said.

Savage found a clean shirt, pants and socks in Jonah's bag and took them over to Amy. Her kidnapper's garments were too large for her. She had to roll up the pants and the sleeves of the shirt, but for the first time in days she felt adequately covered. It was a feeling which gave her the confidence to be in the company of men who would not have to avert their eyes to avoid staring at her nakedness. While she dressed, the men broke camp, saddled up and mounted their horses. Savage helped Amy into the saddle of Jonah's mount and gave the signal to move out. "I'm taking you back to the ranch, Amy," he said. "You'll be safe there."

49

"Major, I'm truly worried about Miss Amy." Trudy's eyes were fixed on Savage, her young, pretty face showing her concern. "Ever since she's stayed with us here, she doesn't sleep, she doesn't eat. She just sits there and stares out the window. You got to do something."

Savage had returned from a long day in the saddle under a blazing sun and was grateful for the coolness of the house. "What would you have me do, Trudy?" he asked. His eyes showed the agony he felt about Amy. "Don't think that she's not on my mind all day long. I keep trying to cheer her up, tell her she's safe here. I try to spend as much time with her as I can. I tell her I love her more than anything." He made a despairing gesture. "I don't know what else to do."

"If you don't mind my saying so, Major, you gotta spend more time with her. That girl needs a lot of loving right now. She only feels safe when you're with her. You ought to marry Miss Amy. Marry her right now. This," Trudy swept her hand across the room, "would be her home then, a place where she belongs."

"Marry her! Lord, Trudy, if you only knew how often I have proposed to Miss Cabbett," He shrugged and decided not to finish the sentence. "If only she could be teaching school right now, give her a purpose and take hold of her life again."

"She didn't tell me much but I can imagine what that poor thing musta gone through." Trudy shook her head and made sympathetic clucking sounds. "Pure hell," she said, "*pure* hell."

"Where is Miss Cabbett?" Savage asked.

"She's in her bedroom, staring out the window."

"Thanks, Trudy." Savage walked down the hall and knocked on Amy's door. He listened, his ear close to the door.

"Come in," Amy said after a moment.

Savage stuck his head in the door and Amy greeted him with a wan smile.

"Hello Amy," he said with as much cheer as he could muster. He was appalled by what he saw. The young woman was a shadow of herself. Trudy had done everything in their power to make her look nice. Her hair was combed. She was wearing one of Trudy's dresses and yet she was pale. Her once sparkling green eyes, which Savage had found so alluring, had taken on a dull sheen, looking out at the world without interest but with fear. Fury at the Mansons welled up in him again for what they had done to this lovely girl.

When Savage took her in his arms she began to cry as she had so many times before. He had previously marveled at her bravery but was now deeply worried that she seemed to live in a constant state of terror. He was sure that the death of her tormentor at her own hand was on her mind.

"I'm sorry I was gone so long," Savage apologized and rocked her gently in his arms. She clung to him, her face buried in his chest and mumbled something which was muffled by his shirt.

"I'm sorry Darling, I didn't hear you. What did you say?" Savage asked and gently held her away from him.

Amy looked at him with tear-streaked eyes. "I want to go into town, Ben. I need to buy some clothes and other necessities. Will you take me there, please?"

"Of *course* I will, my darling, anytime you wish. We'll take the surrey and spend as much time in town as you like. We could leave tomorrow."

"Just the two of us?" Amy asked in a small voice.

Savage saw the fear in her eyes. He doubted with the rustlers gone that they would be in any danger. But to make the precious girl feel more secure, he was willing to call out the entire United States Cavalry.

"Would you feel better if we took some men along? Riding shotgun?" he asked.

The next morning the surrey carrying Amy and Savage, with Jefferson and half a dozen heavily armed men bringing up the rear, left the ranch and headed south. They made camp near the remains of the line shack and reached town the next afternoon. Amy averted her eyes when they drove past the scorched remains of Mrs. Koslowsky's house. After Savage had made sure that she was comfortable in her room at the Majestic, he drove over to the livery stable and walked across the street to tell Marshal Boudreaux that he was in town.

After three days in Riverside, Amy stunned Savage by telling him of her decision to return to Boston. His heart stopped. He was devastated. He pleaded with her, trying desperately to change her mind. But she remained firm, telling Ben that she was confronted with too many ghosts in Riverside, too many nightmarish memories which she could only forget away from this part of the country, as far away as possible.

"What about us?" he asked her. "Don't you love me?" She hung her head and replied that she wasn't sure, just as she wasn't sure of anything anymore. What she did know, she told Savage, was that she wanted to get away from here. She missed her family and it was time to go home.

Savage watched with a heavy heart as the lovely, pale girl entered the stage the following morning, which bore her away and out of his life.

50

Fall was particularly beautiful in the Valley but its brilliant colors were wasted on Savage. John Wilhelm had finished building a farmhouse on land which Savage had leased to him, and he and Trudy had left the Double-T spread to take up residence in their new home. Rufus Jefferson had asked for his pay and had moved on. Ed Boudreaux resigned as marshal of Riverside and retook possession of his old ranch, with Phil Garrett replacing him as the new marshal. After returning to his ranch, Boudreaux's first action was to raze and rebuild the ranch house which had been torched by Seth Manson.

Savage tried to devote himself to running his spread but his heart was not in his work. It became ever more difficult for him to dredge up the enthusiasm necessary for the day-to-day operation of the ranch. He lived for the days when mail arrived from Amy. Her letters varied little. They were cheerful and chatty. She wrote him about her life in Boston with her family but her letters lacked any clues as to her feelings toward him. "I miss you terribly. Do you miss me?" he asked in every one of his frequent letters to her, but Amy never answered this particular question to his satisfaction.

Spring arrived and with it a weighty dispatch from New York addressed to Major Ben Savage, Esq. Curious, he broke the seal and unfolded the letter. It read:

Dear Major

Now that Spring has arrived here in New York and, I presume, in your lovely valley as well, I am taking the occasion to renew contact with you regarding my proposition to acquire your ranch. My company has been active in purchasing other property in your general vicinity and your land holdings would fit well into our scheme of operation. We are prepared to pay you the price which I mentioned to you in my previous correspondence, which, I am quite certain, you will find adequate compensation for your property.

I am looking forward to your reply with great anticipation. Your letter will find me at the Astoria Hotel, a new establishment, which I highly recommend should your travels ever bring you to New York.

I am, your most humble servant,

John Brewster, Earl of Litchworth

Savage put the letter down and stared out of the window. The wildflowers were in full bloom, their radiant colors in stark contrast with the lush meadows and the young green leaves of the Aspen. He absently tapped the edge of the letter on the arm of his chair, lost in thought. The price offered by the earl was more than adequate. He thought of Amy and a plan began to form in his mind. Yes, by God, he would sell the ranch and return to Boston. If Amy would not come back to him, then he would go to her and woo her all over again before it was too late. Selling the ranch would be painful, he thought with more than a twinge of regret. He would miss the free life in the west, of that he was sure.

But he missed Amy more.

Buoyed by his decision he hurried into his office, sat down behind his desk and wrote to the Earl, accepting his offer.

Savage left the ranch at daybreak the following morning. The chilly air of the night dissipated with the early morning sun. He rode along Running Bear Creek, marveling at its clear water, teeming with fish. A hawk sailed silently overhead and Savage watched it drop from the sky like a rock and ascend seconds later with a small rodent in its talons. Meadowlarks perched on tree stumps and in tree tops and recorded his passing with their low, short whistles. His rifle across his lap, he rode past a large stand of timber and kept a wary lookout for the grizzly which he had encountered near these woods the year before, but the huge animal did not show itself.

Savage made camp next to the rebuilt line shack. He let General Chamberlain roll before he staked him close to the shack. He sat outside near the fire, late into the evening, smelling the fresh, clean air, listening to the sounds of the night. He thought about Amy, resolutely shoving aside any second thoughts about relinquishing ownership of the ranch to the Englishman. Lying under the blanket outside the line shack, his head resting on his saddle, Savage looked at the clear, endless western sky sparkling with stars which seemed near enough to touch before drifting off to sleep.

He rode into town early the following afternoon and stopped at the livery stable, handing Paxton his horse. Savage started to cross the street to mail his letter but stepped back quickly when the stage careened into the town, drawn by six lathered and blowing horses. They skidded to a dramatic stop in front of the Wells Fargo office, enveloping the coach in a cloud of dust which drifted lazily down the street, slowly dissipating in the still, spring air. A curious crowd had gathered across the street to watch the new arrivals, for many the highlight of the day. Savage joined them. The driver climbed down from the box and opened the door. A tall, well-dressed man stepped out first. He turned, smiling, to offer his hand to a slim young woman in a stylish gray dress alighting from the coach.

Savage's breath caught in his throat as the woman's emerald green eyes swept up to meet his.

"Amy?" he shouted. "Amy!" Savage dashed across the street, heedless of the heavy wagon traffic. Her polite demeanor, which she had reserved for her traveling companion, dissolved into a radiant smile when she saw Savage come running toward her. He skidded to a stop, swept her off her feet and twirled her round and round to the huge enjoyment of the onlookers.

Both were laughing ecstatically.

"Ben," she said breathlessly. "Oh Ben. Did you get my letter? I tried to like Boston again, but it was so big, so noisy, so dirty." The words tumbled out of her. "And I missed you so much. I want to be your wife, the mistress of your ranch. I want to be the mother of your children. Will you take me back? Did you miss me? Oh Ben, I love you so."

Ben's heart was about to burst. "I love you too, Amy." He smiled broadly and slowly set the lovely girl down, the letter in his pocket forgotten.

"You're just in time for Ed's wedding," he said.

FINIS

Made in the USA
Charleston, SC
13 July 2011